voice is as unique as the characters she has so skillfully
le Bird is sure to sing to readers long after the final page."

E WAGGONER, author of *Center Ring* and *The Act*

...ed being pulled into this mysterious world of love, loss, hope,
...hosts. *Gradle Bird* is a tale of self-discovery and redemption
...re world. It explores jealousy, fatherly love, the complexities
...uelty, and the consequences of guilt. Joy and tears mix in this
...e tale, which is beautifully rendered in Sasser's evocative prose."

N GOODWIN, Story Circle Book Reviews

...ird is edgy, thought-provoking, and anything but predictable."

NOVAN, Senior Reviewer, Midwest Book Review

...my Stamp of Pulpwood Queen Approval!" (*Gradle Bird* has
...a 2017 PQ Book Club read!)

L. MURPHY, aka The Pulpwood Queen

Praise for

GRadle BirD

"Anyone who doesn't fall in love with Gradle Bird, the character,
might want to stop by an Urgent Care facility for an EKG. Anyone not
totally mesmerized by the world depicted in *Gradle Bird*, the novel, might
as well forfeit his or her Human Being ID card. J.C. Sasser's invented
a complex, big-hearted, dirt-road-smart protagonist surrounded by
hilarious one-of-a-kind characters (and a ghost). Absurd, yet utterly
believable. Southern, yet universal. I'm jealous."

–**GEORGE SINGLETON**, author of *The Half-Mammals of Dixie*

"Think Flannery O'Connor riffing Elmore Leonard and you get
some sense of this wildly inventive, picaresque novel that stretches the
boundaries of what it means to be family and what it costs to love and
be loved. But don't get me wrong. J.C. Sasser writes in her own lyrical
style, weaving often tragicomic events into a mosaic of sometimes
hallucinogenic wonder. Her characters seemed swept up in an arc of
ever-pending disaster. And yet in the unforgettable presence of Gradle
Bird herself, the book's 16-year-old chief protagonist, you learn how
redemption can stumble into our lives at the unlikeliest of times from
the unlikeliest of places."

–**KEN WELLS**, author of *Meely LaBauve*

"I was caught in *Gradle Bird's* spell from the very first lines. J.C. Sasser
draws a magnificently weird cast of characters into a Gothic tale that
could only come out of the backwoods of the South. *Gradle Bird* is a
supreme mix of the gritty, the grotesque, and the haunted. Any fan of
Southern fiction will be transfixed, and any Southern writer should take
careful note."

–**JAMES MCTEER**, author of *Minnow*

"Lush, haunting and imaginative, *Gradle Bird* marks J.C. Sasser as America's new Southern Gothic darling, a name soon to be spoken alongside the likes of Harper Lee and Carson McCullers."

–BREN MCCLAIN, author of *One Good Mama Bone*

"J.C. Sasser takes us on a romp of an adventure through the life, eyes and heart of Gradle Bird's dark and twisted, but loving and hilarious world in rural Georgia. *Gradle Bird* reads like it was written, in collaboration, by the ghosts of Flannery O'Connor and Florence King, while finishing off a bottle of Battlefield Bourbon. And truth is, if it had been the fruit of the ghosts of two of the South's darkest and wittiest writers, we could only hope that they would continue the collaboration. But we're in luck as J.C. Sasser is alive and well and, hopefully, will be telling her stories for years to come. It's a wonderful story, a wonderful book."

–ROBERT HICKS, author of *The Widow of the South* and *The Orphan Mother*

"Any book that begins with the title character giving someone the bird on I-16 really speaks to my soul. *Gradle Bird* is like a good country song, and it features some of the finest cursing I've ever read. Christians are going to love this book!"

–HARRISON SCOTT KEY, author of The *World's Largest Man*

"*Gradle Bird* is a dark Southern Gothic teeming with bizarre characters lovingly drawn and perverse plot twists wrought by a master storyteller. This book—or perhaps J.C. Sasser's brilliantly imaginative mind—should come with caution tape around it. Stunned me again and again."

–NICOLE SEITZ, author of *The Cage-maker* and *Saving Cicadas*

"*Gradle Bird* is a dazzling debut dripping with detail and drenched with unforgettable characters. Heart-wrenched and rhythmic, Sasser's language breathes life to the page."

–DAVID JOY, author of *The Weight Of This World*

"J.C. Sasser can write a pretty s[...] in *Gradle Bird* is gorgeous and can h[...] William Gay or Barry Hannah and th[...] the real jewewl is Miss Bird herself a[...] that get in your head an become pa[...] that Sasser has been studying Elmor[...] Her characters are vivid and bold, an[...] There is magic in the South, and [...] Sasser has with *Gradle Bird*. The wor[...] Southern literature died with Larry [...] handing them a copy of *Gradle Bir[...] more to say. The world of Southern [...]

-BRIAN PANOWICH, author o[...]

"Sasser has written a vivid and [...] people are both flawed and wounde[...] times you want to turn away...but y[...] where there is as much to fear as t[...] secrets to make Faulkner blush, *Gr[...] classic Southern Gothic, taking the [...] with an unforgettable cast of chara[...]

–MICHELE MOORE, author [...]

"Reminiscent of Faulkner, *Gra[...] writing."

–MARY ARNO, author of *Than[...]

"*Gradle Bird* gifts the reader wit[...] one woven with prose that is no[...] Southern colors and characters yo[...] alongside the classics of Southern [...]

-JJ FLOWERS, author of *Juan [...]

"Sass[...]
crafted. [...]

**–NIC[...]

"...[...]
magic, an[...]
set in a b[...]
of human[...]
coming of [...]

**–B. L[...]

"*Grad[...]

**–D. D[...]

"Here [...]
been name[...]

**–KAT[...]

Gradle Bird
by J.C. Sasser

ISBN 978-1-63393-263-0

Published by

 köehlerbooks™

210 60th Street
Virginia Beach, VA 23451
800-435-4811
www.koehlerbooks.com

GrAdlE BiRD

J.C. Sasser

VIRGINIA BEACH
CAPE CHARLES

For my mama, Rubye Janette Trapnell, who taught me to love all creatures great and small. And for The Lone Singer, a creature both great and small.

But God hath chosen the foolish things of the world to confound the wise; and God hath chosen the weak things of the world to confound the things which are mighty.

1 Corinthians 1: 27

CHAPTER ONE

GRADLE BIRD SUCKED on a piece of penny candy and carried a sack of SpaghettiOs and an expired loaf of Wonder Bread she'd gotten on discount from the Timesaver up the road. A summertime growler stalked her back, and a pair of yellow butterflies quivered around her knees as she walked a stretch of Georgia's I-16 that wasn't good for much except semi-traffic, flying rocks, and the Fireside Motel. Her arm was about to give out, and the plastic flip-flops had burned blisters on the insides of both big toes. She laid down the sack to get a break, pushed her cat-eye glasses up her nose, and pulled the photograph from her bra that had been sweating against her heart on the six-mile walk there and back.

She blew on the photograph to keep it from melting and studied her grandpa and her mother, barefoot on the sugar-white banks of a black river. Gradle had worn the picture raw from handling it so much, and its caption, *Leonard and Veela 1972*, had bled a faint blue tattoo into her skin. Her mother wore a ponytail with thick raven bangs chopped crooked and too short, a pair of cat-eye glasses, and a green chiffon tank dress with a wildflower corsage. She held up a stringer of fish, and by the light in Grandpa's half-dimpled smile, there was no doubt Veela was his pride and joy.

A trickle of sweat ran down the inside of Gradle's thigh. She hiked her green chiffon tank dress to her knees and knotted it below her hips to get relief from the heat. Thunder clappers surrounded the entire globe now, and were cause for the line of semis with sighing brakes waiting their turn to park in the Fireside's pea gravel lot. People who drove this stretch knew the Fireside was the only place to lay your head between Macon and Savannah. It advertised air-conditioned rooms, cable TV, and negotiable rates, and it was where Gradle and her grandpa, Leonard, had been living in room 42, a standard double, since she could remember.

A Peterbilt she didn't recognize snatched her eyes from the photo when it tooted its horn, pulling out of the lot. The trucker looked down on Gradle, made a V with his fingers, and brought it to his tongue. Gradle blew him a kiss, shot him the bird, and stared him down until his dumb, silly smile left his face and she could no longer smell the tar from the pulpwood he was hauling.

She blew on the photograph again and lifted up her bra strap that had fallen off her shoulder. The bra didn't fit any better than it had when she found it two years ago, when the Fireside's pool still had water. It was left dangling on a lounge chair by a woman with Florida tags who sped-read bodice rippers, sipped Shasta Grape from a straw, and French-inhaled Misty Menthol Lights. Gradle was skinny as straw, still hadn't gotten her period, and figured the delay had something to do with the birthmark she'd inherited from her mother, a grey streak of hair that grew from the top of her head. She turned sixteen today, and maybe she was destined to skip her period altogether and go straight to menopause. So for now, she used the bra primarily as a purse, like her one and only role model, Loretta the lot lizard, who stalked the truck lot in the night.

Gradle's underwear didn't fit either—a pair of Fruit of the Loom briefs that sagged in the rear. They came from room 30, left to dry on the shower rod by a twitchy serpent lover on his way to the Rattlesnake Roundup.

But the one thing that did fit was the earring she wore in her right ear. She found it in the tub drain of room 25 clutching on for dear life, and if it wasn't for the gold cross at the end of its chain it would have been flushed to hell. Gradle considered it lucky, meant for this world, and after she found it, she brought out the motel sewing kit and pierced her ear with a needle she'd sterilized with a flame.

She kicked off her flip-flops, hooked them on her pinkie, and hiked the grocery sack up her hip. In the distance, the Fireside's neon vacancy sign sizzled to life. Duck, the motel manager, plugged it in only at twilight in an effort to save on electricity. She passed through the neon glow and walked toward the Fireside's marquee Grandpa had beautified with a bed of daisies. He'd planted them on Duck's request, a marketing campaign with intentions of attracting a more respectable brand of clientele. But Gradle liked to think Grandpa had done it for her, to give her something pretty to look at, a yard to run around in. Grandpa was the Fireside's maintenance man and worked off their rent by fixing whatever Duck said needed fixing. Punched walls, kicked-in doors, busted windows, and clogged toilets were the high-runners, and on occasion there was a big job, like the one he was on now. He stood on the motel's roof, manning a corn broom and a bucket of liquid tar. She picked a daisy from the bed, tucked it behind her ear, and stared up at him while he worked. He looked like a lightning rod, a God or sky wizard of some sort, with his white T-shirt and painter pants, his long silver hair whipping in the wind, and a silver mustache she imagined he could peel off and throw like a boomerang.

A raindrop smacked the part in her bangs, and she sheltered the photograph inside her bra, protecting it from a sudden onslaught. Gravel punctured her feet as she ran lightfooted across the lot. The doorbell jingled, and she entered the Fireside's lobby, an icebox of dark paneled wood, stale cigarette smoke, and amateur wildlife art. The Magnavox perched on the wall televised a suited-up weatherman in front of a Doppler radar map of Georgia. Tornado warnings in six surrounding counties. It was July in South Georgia, and while afternoon thunderstorms were typical this time of year, their persistence and hostility this season were far from ordinary. It had rained every day since the summer solstice. The rivers were out of their banks. There were no pond edges or dams to keep the gators and water moccasins from spilling into backyards and swimming pools. In the past two weeks, WTOC news reported five dogs had gone missing and one small child. And with the rain came mosquitoes, heaps of them. There wasn't a cemetery urn or pig trough in the county that wasn't teeming with wrigglers, and down in the really damp places, in the low-lying swamps, mosquitoes met in masses so thick they formed gauzy drapes one had to pull back to walk through. But Gradle didn't mind all the mosquitoes and rain. In fact, she found the mosquitoes a source of entertainment and spent hours watching them fill their bodies with her blood. And the rain matched her melancholy mood. She found it hard to be sad in the sun.

"Does it make you feel good to steal from people?" Gradle asked Duck, who sat behind the counter popping Fruit Chill Nicorette and counting the quarters he'd collected from the rigged vending machine that lit the breezeway.

"Gotta pay for the cable somehow," Duck said, punching out a square of gum and offering it to Gradle between a pair of nicotine fingernails.

"Negotiate better rates," she said. She set the groceries and flip-flops on the counter, took the gum, and chewed it into the piece of candy she'd sucked down to half its original size.

"How'd you get the candy?"

"I stole it."

Duck popped his gum. "How'd that make you feel?"

"Like shit."

A toothless smile folded his face in a million tiny pleats. He lit a Winston Red, spun his chair around, and sifted through a stack of mail. "You'll wanna get the old man to open this one," he said, and threw a letter on the counter. "Looks important."

They rarely got mail and whatever mail they did get Grandpa trashed and never opened. She wondered how anyone in the world knew he existed much less knew his whereabouts. She opened the letter and read it. It was a notice of condemnation regarding property at 263 South Spivey Street, Janesboro, Georgia, stating it was unfit for human habitation and dangerous to life and health because of rats.

"It's a felony to open other people's mail," Duck said. He ashed his cigarette in a tray full of them.

"Call the cops," she said, shoving the letter under her armpit.

"I been hollering at him for the past hour to get off the roof," Duck said. "That tar won't set in the rain."

"You know how he is when he cocks his mind on something."

"Gonna get struck by lightning, stubborn bastard."

"A little shock therapy wouldn't hurt him," she said. She grabbed the sack of groceries. "Can I borrow a quarter?"

"What for?" Duck asked. He popped another piece of Nicorette in his mouth and followed it with a drag from his Winston red.

"Pay the Timesaver back for the candy I stole."

"Clean number nine and I'll think about it," Duck said. He dangled the room key over her nose. "It's Friday night and raining.

It'll be busy."

Gradle took the key and walked out of the cold lobby onto the breezeway where rain ran from the eaves in strings of liquid crystal. She pulled the photograph from her bra to make sure it wasn't hurt, and stared at it as she walked toward her room.

A man with a toothpick, tight black jeans, and a Hawaiian floral shirt unbuttoned to the navel stepped back from the vending machine and kicked it with a pointy black boot.

"That thing eats quarters," Gradle said as she walked by.

The man spun around on his boot heel and tracked her up and down with his eyes. "You got any change?"

"Duck'll help you at the front desk," she said, hiding behind the sack of groceries, hoping the brown bag would bore his eyes.

"What're you looking at?" he asked, switched his toothpick to the other side of his mouth, and snatched the photograph from her hand. "Is that your Daddy?" he asked.

"My grandpa," she said. She snatched the photograph back.

"You look lonely," he said, moving into her.

She could smell the smoke and artificial spice in his greased-back hair. She felt shaky, and her head buzzed from the Fruit Chill Nicorette.

"You feeling lonely?" he asked, nodding at the room key. He came closer, skimmed his teeth with his tongue, and clutched his groin. "Let me help you with that." He went for the groceries and backed her into a pole.

Rain puddled in the pockets of her collarbone, and he dipped his mouth in and took a drink.

"I'm not a lot lizard if that's what you're thinking," she said.

His finger fondled her earring's long gold chain and continued down her neck where it picked up sweat and kept gliding down her chest and found the dip of her bellybutton. He hiked her dress, palmed her hipblades, and held her still so she couldn't run.

"You look like a whore to me," he said with his spoiled milk breath.

She spat the candy and Nicorette in his face.

He slung the groceries out of her arms, spat out his toothpick, and slapped her mouth with the backside of his hand. She felt her lip split, tasted metal, and saw a screen of bursting black dots. Blood dripped on the daisy he slapped from her ear. She checked for her earring and tightened its back, picked up the flower, and put it back.

"You ain't got any titties, but you're gonna be fun," he said through his teeth.

Over the rain she heard his loafers coming fast, and saw Grandpa running toward them holding his bucket, with his tar-drenched corn broom cocked behind his shoulder. The broom whistled through the air and slapped the man's ear. Specks of tar splattered against her cheek.

Grandpa whipped the broom against the man's ribs and struck him until the flowers on his shirt were all shiny and black. The bucket fell over, spilling tar onto the walkway. Grandpa clipped the back of the man's knees. The man fell to the ground where he wormed and rolled and coated the cement in tar. Grandpa threw down the broom and kicked his kidneys. With each blow the man winced less and less.

"That's enough!" Gradle screamed, tearing Grandpa off.

"What'n the hell's going on out here?" Duck yelled as he trotted their way. "Jesus Christ, Leonard." He tiptoed around the beaten man, careful not to get tar on his shoes. "He breathing?"

Tar covered almost every inch of the man, yet his toothpick stuck to his temple unscathed. Whatever damage Grandpa had done would be impossible to assess.

"Pull down your dress," Grandpa told Gradle. He stared at the man like he wanted to kick him again. He ran his hand down his mustache and flicked the rain and sweat away.

Gradle unknotted her skirt and hurried to collect the photograph, her flip-flops, and the groceries that had scattered in the fight.

"Who's gonna clean this shit up?" Duck yelled.

She felt Grandpa's breath against her back, panting as he walked behind her toward their room.

†††

Gradle stared in the bathroom mirror at her swollen upper lip and squeezed out a bead of Super Glue Grandpa had left out for her on the counter. She pinched her lip together, dabbed the glue over the cut, and breathed through her mouth until the glue dried and the scent died down.

She held the photograph up to the mirror and mimicked her mother's smile. She tried to keep the tears from coming, but she couldn't hold back the hurt she felt, not because she'd been hit, but because her lip would scar and distort the expression she'd spent years trying to perfect.

Through the thin motel walls, she could hear the thunder traveling on and Grandpa clearing his throat. She wiped the tears from her face, punctured a can of SpaghettiOs three times with a church key, and poured half on Grandpa's plate and the other half on hers. She watered down what was left in the jelly jar and spread it and some peanut butter on two slices of bread. The grape jelly syrup would last only a couple more sandwiches, and they would have to go without until she could clean enough rooms, or until Grandpa left money on the table for her to go buy more.

She balanced both plates in the crook of her elbow and practiced her mother's smile once more. The glue's seal split. She licked the blood with her tongue, put the photograph inside her bra, and entered the room she and Grandpa had split into halves.

On her side, a bookshelf Grandpa had made of scrap wood and cinder blocks, kept her things: a SpaghettiOs can full of ink pens and pencils at various states of decline; a dingy white sock half-full of lost-and-found jewelry she never wore; a bottle of red gooey fingernail polish; a cracked compact of eye shadow she used as paint to paint pictures in her notebooks and sometimes, privately, on her face. Most everything she owned she'd found left in rooms over the years, including her lineup of books, all of which she had memorized. The only thing never lost was the mobile made of birds that hung over her bed. It had been hers from the beginning, and on her birthdays Grandpa would make her a new bird out of copper wire and coathangers and use the lost-and-found jewelry she never wore to give it feathers and an eye. Today, July 10, 1992, she expected him to add her sixteenth bird.

On Grandpa's side, a shotgun rested by the door and an artistic clutter of tools decorated his pegboarded walls.

Grandpa sat at the table in a wife-beater, facing the curtain-drawn window and twisting copper wire around a piece of her lost-and-found jewelry. His hair was slicked back wet, and his skin was red from scrubbing the tar off with gasoline from the tank of his weed-wacker. The tiny room still reeked from the fumes.

Grandpa pushed the wire and jewelry aside as Gradle set down the plates. He cleared his throat and stared at his SpaghettiOs swimming in a red pool of sauce.

She sat across from him, took a bite of sandwich, and stared at his bowed head. "You gonna say the blessing or you want me to say it?" she asked, as she took another bite.

His hand began to tremble, and his fork tapped against his plate, and one by one he looped his SpaghettiOs on the tines of his fork until there was no space left. He took a bite and started over again.

"I should've kicked that guy in the nuts," she said.

A lock of hair fell in Grandpa's face and got caught in his brow, which reminded her of the black caterpillar of the Giant Leopard Moth. His brows were the only patches of hair on his body that were immune to his old age and hadn't turned grey. If it weren't for these little miracles she would have given up on him long ago.

"Cat got your tongue?" she asked. She looped the SpaghettiOs on the tines of her fork, mimicking him for attention. "You gonna say the blessing?"

"Pardon our sins, Amen." He finally got his four words of the day out, but he kept his head down and focused on nothing but stacking his Os.

"I'm gonna go clean room nine before you run out of SpaghettiOs." She removed her plate from the table, washed it in the bathroom sink, and grabbed the vacuum and her bucket of cleaning supplies from the closet.

"This came in the mail today." She threw the letter by his plate. SpaghettiOs sauce bled over the corners. "You've got forty-five days to do something about it or they're gonna tear it down," she said, slamming the door behind her.

†††

The sweaty night hummed with locusts and idling trucks as Gradle rolled the vacuum down the breezeway. The lot was half full, and all the rigs were lit up like Christmas trees. In the back of the lot, Gradle watched Loretta climb down from a cab in hooker shorts and one high-heeled shoe. She clasped her bra in the back, shuffled through a few dollar bills, and limped off into the dark.

Gradle slid room number nine's key in the knob and had to jiggle it before the door would open. She switched on the light and was hit with the stench of stale beer and vomit. Cigarette butts and Budweiser cans littered the room. The bed's fern-patterned comforter was wadded up in the corner, and the lampshades were askew. She put her forearm to her nose, picked the cigarette butts up from the floor, and dumped all the ashtrays. She collected the Budweiser cans, found one that was unopened, and set it on top of the Magnavox for later. She flipped the pillow over to hide the lipstick stain and made the rest of the bed. In the bathroom, she flushed the toilet of vomit and sprayed down all of the surfaces with watered-down Clorox. She shoved the shower curtain aside and found the other one of Loretta's high-heeled shoes taking a bath in the tub. She fished it out, set it beside the Budweiser atop the TV, and ran the vacuum over the room.

After the room was reasonably clean, Gradle sat on the edge of the bed, popped open the warm Budweiser, and took a swig. She slipped Loretta's high-heel on her foot and stared in the mirror at how long it made her leg. She imagined what it must feel like to be a woman, wondered what kind she would grow up to be, and if she'd still be cleaning rooms rented out by the hour at the Fireside Motel ten years from now. She'd always dreamed about stealing an eighteen-wheeler and driving to California, visiting the Petrified Forest in Arizona on the way. She was driving age now and could get her license, and at least that would make her dream somewhat legal.

Footsteps and laughter magnified outside on the breezeway. A key slid into the knob, jiggled around, and the door opened. Loretta wobbled in, leaning on the man Grandpa had beat up earlier with his broom. A Band-Aid striped his forehead, and a purple bruise puddled underneath his eye. He stunk of tar, and when his eyes met Gradle they immediately hid on his boots.

"I see you like my shoe, Gradle Bird." Loretta's grin flashed a fleet of silver teeth. "I'll let you borrow it if you want, girl."

Gradle downed the rest of the beer and shot it at the trashcan. She removed Loretta's heel from her foot and dangled it on her finger for Loretta to take.

"It's too small," she said, grabbed her cleaning supplies and the vacuum, and pushed on past.

The vacuum's wheels squealed as they rolled down the breezeway toward her room and scared up a cockroach that skittered in her path and slipped through their cracked door. An orange extension cord snaked from the crack all the way out into the parking lot where Grandpa worked under the hood of the old Chrysler New Yorker Deluxe that lived most of its life under a tarp. Rain danced like little winged bugs around the hook lamp above his head, and a sheet covered with car guts sat on the ground beside him.

She walked in their room, put the vacuum and cleaning supplies in the closet, and plopped face up on the bed. Her mobile spun above her in the air conditioner's cool wind. The bird Grandpa was working with before supper hung on its end. She stood on the bed and touched its red rhinestone eye and its silver-chained feathers. Another tiny miracle.

She cut off the lights, sat at the table by the window, and parted the curtains wide enough to watch Grandpa working on the car. She didn't know why he was the way he was, where his smile had gone, what had dampened his light. She couldn't remember a specific moment or a particular event. She only knew that it had been gradual, like his growing old, gradually painful, gradually deficient.

She wondered how long he would be out there working, how waterlogged he would have to get, how many parts he would have to clean and fix before he could settle down and rest. He rarely slept, rarely stayed still. He was a work junkie. If he could snort it up his nose he would. She closed the curtains, crawled under the covers, and held tight the gold cross of her earring as she said her prayers. The rain picked up, drummed her to sleep, and held her down through morning.

Light seeped through the curtain's crack and warmed the skin on her lids. Doves that fed on the breezeway each morning sprung to flight, their wings a soft rattle, when a car engine turned over outside. Her eyes didn't want to open, but just as they did Grandpa nudged her with the butt of his shotgun.

She sat up in bed, rubbed the sting out of her eyes, and saw their room was vacant, cleaned out of all their things, even her mobile. She checked her ear for her earring and found comfort it was still there.

"Time to go," Grandpa said, and he nodded her out the door.

CHAPTER TWO

THEY CAME IN the rain, when the moonflowers were in bloom. When they arrived, Ms. Annalee Spivey was staring through the attic window at the pall that forever loomed about her house. She watched them wheel into the drive in a vintage New Yorker Deluxe. Black. A '54 perhaps. Annalee lifted her grey, decrepit finger and hooked the dingy lace curtains back. They disintegrated in her touch, falling like ash on the paint-cracked windowsill.

There were two of them. An old man and a girl. She didn't know who they were or who they were some of, and couldn't remember for the life of her if they had telephoned in advance. *A bad omen,* she thought, *company arriving in rain.*

Regardless, she didn't possess the spirit or know-how to go down to the kitchen and make sweet tea and cucumber sandwiches, nor was she inclined to run out and greet them as a good hostess should. The saccharin had long ago dissolved in the bottle, the cucumbers had shriveled to weeds, and it had been decades since Ms. Annalee Spivey had put on a smile.

They were foreigners, lost, she gathered, after striking the possibility they could be kin. She had no kin left, and besides, anybody brave enough to come to the old Spivey house would sleep with snakes and walk on graves. They must not know its history.

The house was built in 1910, and at the time, it was a big, beautiful two-story home. Forty-eight windows. Six pocket-doors. A porch that wrapped all the way around. Today, the house was still big, but all of its beauty had flaked and fallen to pieces. The wraparound porch was water-warped. The windows were broken and their shutters were either missing or dangled like snagged teeth. There were no red geraniums to brighten the place, no wandering purple Jew or yellow roses to grace the lattice. Only the moon vine thrived here. It climbed all over the front porch and spiraled up the columns, peeling the paint along its way. It invaded the cracks and breaks, tangled up the roof, and surrounded the chimney, trapping the home in a sweet-smelling web.

The grounds were no better off. Thorns and thistles and nettles that sting flourished with absolute rage. Plant a petunia here and watch it wither. Of all the stock planted years ago, the camellias had put up the best fight. Spaced along the iron fence, they grew with great aspiration, as if their view of the other side might change their lives. Yet, still, they were too leggy and too old to bloom. The birdbaths and garden statues, once full of whimsy and charm were now blanketed with the vine, and had morphed into strange-looking lumps, as had the courtyard fountain whose faint, delicate trickle anyone with the courage to come close enough could still hear.

But the place wasn't entirely hopeless. The attic had a window. The porch had a swing.

Annalee looked down on this strange pair still parked in her drive. They weren't like the rest of the people who swerved or slowly rode by the place like it was some unfortunate stray they were too scared to rescue. These people were different. They had courage. They had actually pulled into the drive as if this old decaying tomb was a destination they purposely sought.

But did they know? Or were they out there wondering why somebody could let a place so beautiful go to seed? A lack of money? A lack of care? Both sides of the family couldn't come to terms? The superstitious crowd, which included the entire town, believed it was Ms. Annalee Spivey herself who had accelerated the home's fatal decline. She was born inside and had died inside, rotted away in the attic.

It was the postman who finally found her. He had a hunch when the mail started piling by the door but didn't investigate even after it started spilling down the front porch steps. It was a well-known fact Annalee shied from society. The maggoty stench of dead animal gave him the clue. He kicked in the door and followed the scent to the attic. When he pulled the attic flap down, the entrance was blocked with furniture, but after muscling through it, he found her stiff on the fainting couch shoved against the wall. Her arms were crossed over her heart as if she had hoped to die, and in her sparrowlike claws was a portrait that captured the beauty she once was. Her eyes were hard as marbles, her mouth was frozen agape, and sitting on her dried-out tongue was a sparkling diamond ring.

It had shocked him so that he fainted to the floor and woke ten minutes later in the split-pea soup he had for lunch. Once he collected his wits, he fetched the sheriff and didn't deliver the rest of the day's mail. When they came back to the house, the corpse was still there, her jaw still agape, but the portrait and the diamond ring were gone.

In small Southern towns such as this, the ghost stories are scarier than the ghost. Anybody who rots in the attic certainly has a ghost. When the gravediggers lowered her into the ground and the courthouse clock struck two, the Beasley house next door on the left caught fire and burned to the ground. The stove was off. The chimney was swept. The wiring was sound. Yet *poof!* Today a clan of wild cats lives in its lot, and the front porch steps are the only proof it was ever there.

The young Franklin couple who lived next door on the right packed up their belongings and walked out two days after the Beasley house burned. They claimed they smelled fire every day when their clock struck two and figured they could save a few of grandma's heirlooms if they got out now. That was decades ago, and the house had been vacant ever since. Its roof was sinking, and the FOR SALE sign had faded pink in the sun.

So why these people were still parked in her drive presented her with an impossible puzzle. They hadn't opened up a map or reversed to head in another direction. Through the gray and the rain and the dingy lace curtains, Annalee kept her eyes on the pair. The old man stared straight ahead through the windshield at nothing. His knuckles stretched white across the wheel, but his hold was not strong enough to hide the severe tremble in his arms. The girl was in the backseat. She stared at him, waiting and woebegone.

He put the car in park and turned off the engine. Annalee felt a sudden numbing dread. Should she change into her welcoming gown? Rush down and lock the doors?

Someone must have warned them. Surely, they feared catching fire. Surely, they were lost. Surely, they would leave.

But the girl got out of the car, and when she stood upright, Annalee swallowed a shot of cold breath, for it wasn't until then that her hard-as-marble eyes had seen the girl complete. She had a familiar and unusual pulchritude. She was beautiful like an insect, a green lacewing. Her appendages stretched long and balletic and had distinct segments, hinged with sharp balls and sockets. Her eyes were large and compound and possessed an infinite blue dimension that Annalee found startling she could see. If the girl had a pair of wings, surely, she would fly away.

Annalee kept studying the girl, tried to judge her age. She looked young as yolk, fifteen or sixteen, but had a patch of grey hair growing from the crown of her head. And there was something else delightfully strange about the girl. She appeared as if she wasn't from this age, as if she had been thrown back in time. She wore a ponytail with thick raven bangs chopped crooked and too short, a green vintage chiffon tank dress, and a pair of cat-eye glasses that gave her a dated, cockamamie look. She had no shoes to speak of, and she was missing an earring but wore the one she had as if wearing only one was by her design.

The girl slammed the car door and banged on the driver's side window, but the old man didn't move; he didn't turn to look the girl's way. Perhaps he was deaf. Perhaps blind. But Annalee never knew any blind man to drive.

Thunder rumbled and rattled the attic window, sifting flakes of paint to the heart-pine floor. Annalee, too intrigued with the girl, didn't mind getting wet from one of the ceiling's many leaks. The girl pounded on his window again. She placed both palms on the glass, tilted her head to the side, and drew her eyes on him as if he was the only thing in her world.

"Look at me!" she yelled.

The girl banged on the window again but stopped when a pack of shirtless little boys ran past. One of them tripped and fell face-first. The others kept running until they reached a safe distance. They turned around and hollered through the rain at the boy glued to the ground.

"Wallace! Get up! Get up! Ms. Spivey's gonna scratch your back!"

Annalee had heard the old proverbs a hundred times before. *Ms. Spivey's gonna scratch your back! Ms. Spivey's gonna snip your hair! Ms. Spivey's gonna snatch your tongue!* And a hundred times before she had witnessed panic in the child's eyes, the one wiggling on the cement, trying to get away from the fingernails that had long ago yellowed, turned hard, and curled off. Annalee usually left the window at this point. She didn't enjoy scared little boys and their fairytales. But the girl kept her there.

Little Wallace struggled until he finally got up. Head slung back and elbows jackhammering the air, he sprinted past where the other children stood and didn't stop to tell them goodbye and that he would meet them at the same time, same place tomorrow.

The other children stared in silence at the strange girl standing in the drive of the old Spivey house. The girl waved and spooked the children away.

She turned her attention back to the old man. "Grandpa!" she yelled, banging on his window.

The old man didn't budge. He sat still, faced forward, frozen. Annalee found it odd anyone could ignore a creature like that girl.

The girl swiped her forearm across the windshield. Raindrops scattered through the air like rounds of crystal shrapnel. She kicked the door, and as she drew back to kick the door again, it swung open and the old man got out. He stood tall as a tree. His hair grew to his shoulders and had the color and sheen of garlic skin. She squinted to get a closer look at the man, and when she did, he looked up at the attic window where she stood. Her bones rattled, and she could have sworn a beat pulsed through her shriveled up heart.

She backed away from the window, and for a long while all she heard was the sound of rain, but then came footsteps and the

creak of porch boards, the turn of the doorknob, and the break of
spiderwebs. When the front door opened, the hinges whined, and
Annalee felt the stale breath of her tomb release with a force so
strong it tugged her toward the attic flap.

†††

The door swung open, moaned until it hit the stop, and moaned
again as it stuttered back their way. Grandpa clutched his .22 as he
stepped over a mountain of brittle newspapers and yellowed mail
that had collected by the door.

Gradle followed close behind him and entered the stale, creepy
house. It smelled sweet on the inside, like flowers, and a bit like
death, the kind of death that had left skeletons of rats and snake
spines in open graves along the floors. Vines ran across the ceiling
like veins and rain trailed down the peeling plaster walls, making the
house seem as if it was weeping.

Grandpa went down the hallway and stood under the attic flap.
He tapped it with the barrel of his gun like he was trying to scare
something off. Dust fell from the ceiling and collected in the black
wires of his brows.

"Did you use to live here?" Gradle asked, knowing she wouldn't
get much of an answer. He didn't say a word about where they
were going the entire ride over, hadn't told her anything about it,
and probably never would. As with most things, it'd be up to her to
figure out.

Grandpa kept his eyes triggered on the attic flap, and when
his fingers coiled around the frayed string hanging down from it,
something from above tapped back.

"What was that?" Gradle asked.

He cocked his gun, and pointed it at the flap. "Rats."

"Since when are you afraid of rats?"

Gradle left a trail of wet footprints as she crept down the hall and went in and out of the neglected rooms, searching through the abandoned beauty for some clue as to why they had come here. There were no photographs or portraits hanging on the walls, no fingerprints to start a story. The only sign of the life that once lived here was in the mail that had collected at the front door. She went back there, sifted through the mound, and opened some of the envelopes. There were no invitations. No letters. Only unpaid balances for bills addressed to a Ms. Annalee Spivey, postmarked decades ago.

"Who's Annalee Spivey?" Gradle asked, as Grandpa's footsteps came near.

"It's a felony to open other people's mail," he said, and went down the porch steps to the car, opened the trunk, and unloaded two boxes and his work tools. On his way back to the porch, he kept his stare on top of the house. His eyes were hooded and suspicious, as if he was being watched by something from above.

"Pick out your room," he said, stepping over her and the mound of mail.

"We're staying here?" she asked.

She followed him down the hall to the room that had the most light and the most dead flowers on the floor, the one with the jewelry box and a vanity made for a girl. He put a box on the bed and left her alone in the room.

"I guess this is it," she whispered to herself and fell back onto the brass bed littered with dead flowers. She stared up at the vine-covered ceiling and imagined the possibilities of her very own room. This place was different. There wasn't a sign advertising rates. You didn't pay by the day. There was no front desk, no scent of smoke and diesel fuel. People didn't come and go. This place was a home, and as ruined and creepy as it was, it had a beauty, a permanence, and a hope the Fireside Motel could never possess.

Here, she could be a girl, or at least what she imagined a girl to be. She could play dress-up in front of a mirror. Keep her jewelry in a jewelry box. Reinvent herself. Maybe here she could make some real friends, have a sleepover, do what friends do. Maybe here she could meet a boy. Maybe here she'd have her first kiss.

She rose from the bed, opened the box, and began to unpack her things. She hung her bird mobile on the glass doorknob and put her sock of lost-and-found jewelry, checkerboard, ink pens, and pencils in the nook of the bedside table that kept an old hairbrush and a lamp with a torn taffeta shade tilted to one side. She righted the shade, sat at the vanity, and arranged her fingernail polish and eye shadow beside a perfume bottle on a moldy mirrored tray. She brought the bottle to her neck, squeezed its lavender bulb, and out came a dribble of concentrated stink.

Thunder boomed, shook the entire house, and made the chandelier in her room swing. She listened out for Grandpa and heard him stomping the floors as he unloaded the rest of his machinery and tools. She carried the box of leftover food and books into the kitchen, closed the stove's mouth that was parched and hanging ajar, and turned on one of its eyes. A flame lit, and before it sputtered to its death, it singed the silk of a spiderweb and sent its tiny sparks dazzling off into the air. Maybe here she could learn how to really cook, taste some variety for a change. And maybe over there, at the kitchen table, she and Grandpa could sit and converse and consume something warm for a change. She opened the pantry door and placed the Wonder Bread, grape jelly, and SpaghettiOs next to a sack of grits that worms had nibbled to dust.

With her books, the only thing left to unpack, she walked down the hallway toward the study. On her way, she passed Grandpa who stood under the attic flap, staring up at it, with his tool belt wrapped around his waist and his .22 shaking in his hand.

"Heard any more rats?" she asked.

He tapped the barrel on the flap again and flinched at the sound of skittering feet.

She stared at him and tried to get a read. "You spooked or something?"

He tapped the flap again, and his eyes roamed all over the ceiling, listening out for a sound that never came.

She went into the study, stepped over a couple of rat-shredded books, and on a shelf parted a row of rain-swollen books to make room for her own collection's spines: *Thumbelina, Strange Stories and Amazing Facts, The Big Book of Tell Me Why, A Guide to the National Parks, The Holy Bible, Webster's Dictionary,* and the bodice rippers left behind by the woman who drank Shasta Grape and smoked Misty Menthol Lights. She dusted off her hands. She was done, her life unpacked from a single cardboard box.

She followed the sound of Grandpa's drill back down the hall and into her new room. On top of her bed, bent-kneed and focused, he gripped her bird mobile between his teeth and balanced himself on the armrests of a tattered wingback chair. He wore his black-rimmed glasses he used for detailed work. She loved those glasses. They made him look softer, more approachable, and he talked more with them on, as if their glass shields made life easier to look at. She paused in the doorway, rested her cheek against the frame and watched him defy his age. She didn't know how old he was, just that he was old, but there were times like these that made her wonder if he had any age at all.

"What kind of flowers are these?" she asked, picking a dead flower from its vine.

He grabbed an eyehook from his tool belt. "Moonflower," he mumbled.

"Why are they all dead?"

He screwed the eyehook in the hole he'd started in the ceiling. "Sun kills 'em. They only bloom at night."

"Why do they only bloom at night?" she asked, picking some flaking paint from the doorjamb.

Grandpa took the mobile from his teeth and hung it on the hook. He blew hard and made it spin, lowered himself down, and put the chair back in its place.

"Look it up in your *Big Book of Tell Me Why*," he said, leaving the room.

"It's not in there," she said at his back. Most everything she wanted to know wasn't in that book. Like why wouldn't he tell her why? Like why wouldn't he tell her anything?

She plopped down on the bed and stared up at the mobile, as the rain came down steady outside. Her stomach growled, but she was too tired to pry open a can of SpaghettiOs. She pulled the photograph from her bra and stared at her Grandpa's half-dimpled smile until the rain lulled her to sleep.

Midnight, she woke to a powerful sweet smell and a dark figure moving across her room. She jerked up and watched it move toward the window, and as her eyes adjusted to the dark, she could see Grandpa's white hair glowing.

He opened the window as high as it would go, sat down on the edge of her bed, and lit a candle. In the warm amber light hundreds of flowers shown down like little moons from above.

"Watch," he whispered. He pointed at something that had flown in through the window. It fluttered past her ear, hovered above a flower, and tongued its long white throat.

"What is it?" she asked.

"A hawk moth."

After the moth drew in what it needed, it flew to another flower, while others came in through the window to feed. She lay back against the pillow and stared up at the ceiling at all the flowers above and their lovers, an entire hatch of them, fluttering at their mouths. There was magic all around. This place was different. She had to believe it was.

CHAPTER THREE

SONNY JOE STITCH rolled to a stop and idled low in the alley behind the old Spivey house in his souped-up Chevy. The truck was a '73 C-20 he'd bought off a yard, painted with two coats of silver spray paint, and tailed with a straight-piped muffler. He turned the volume down on the Panasonic jam box he kept in the rear window to compensate for the gutted-out radio.

"There she is man," he said, backslapping Ceif in the ribs. He leaned over Ceif who looked up from the joint he was rolling on the back of his threadbare Bible with a 70-millimeter Zig-Zag and some dirt-weed shake.

They stretched their necks and found an opening in the stand of camellias planted along the slanting iron fence. The girl sat on the back porch steps barefooted, with her knees catching the rain. She was staring at what looked to be a small square of paper and kept smiling at it, repeatedly, as if it was some form of exercise. They had been cruising by the old house off and on since they had spotted her yesterday standing in the front yard in the rain, staring into the passenger's window of a black vintage Chrysler. Sonny Joe regretted not stopping then, but he was late for a fish-fight, and used it as a good excuse to cover up his genuine apprehension.

"She's gotta be fucking crazy," he said. He took a slug from the half-pint of Southern Comfort he nested between his legs and chased it down with Mello Yello.

"She's beautiful," Ceif said.

"What the fuck is she doing at the old Spivey house?"

Keeping his eyes fastened on the girl, Ceif pulled a drag from the joint and passed it to Sonny Joe. "You say fuck a lot."

"Fuck you." Sonny Joe pulled on the joint. He dabbed his finger with a little bit of spit to stop the run.

"You gonna smoke the whole joint?" Ceif asked.

"You gonna stop staring?" He slapped Ceif on the back of the head and handed him a few puffs short of a roach.

"Don't you think she's pretty?" Ceif smoked the joint until it toasted the tips of his burnt-yellow fingernails. He flicked it in Sonny Joe's lap and laughed while Sonny Joe squirmed in his seat.

"Faggot," Sonny Joe said.

"Leprechaun."

"It's burning my pecker, man!" Sonny Joe fished the roach from between his legs and threw it out the window. He took another swig of hooch. "Let's go shoot the shit."

"I thought we're gonna go see Delvis," Ceif said.

"Let's invite her. She looks like she could use a couple of friends."

Ceif retrieved a pack of Midnight Specials he kept stocked in his left sock and started to roll a cigarette. "Don't mess with her, man."

"Why you gotta be a poof all the time, preacher boy?" he asked. He leaned out of the window and whistled wild and loud at the girl.

Her head jerked up, and her eyes found him in an instant. She put whatever she was staring at in her bra, walked down the porch steps, and glared at him through the rain.

He got out of the truck and hopped the fence while Ceif limped after him with the help of his whittled pinewood cane. The clouds parted as Sonny Joe approached the girl, and the momentary sunlight made it rain down gold. Steam rose from the colorful tattoo of a Siamese fighting fish that covered the right half of his back and bled from the frays of the T-shirt he'd cut into a tank top. He looked back to check on Ceif, who was still struggling to get over the fence.

"You lose your dog or something?" she asked.

Her words stopped his advance. His palms started to sweat, and his head grew dizzy. He swayed a bit, had to hold out his arms to keep from falling over, and couldn't tell if it was the weed kicking in or if it was the girl's aggression, her fearlessness and beauty that made him stagger. He took a swig of liquor and looked up into the raining, sunlit sky, wishing he had a cigarette.

"The devil's beating his wife," he said.

The girl cocked her head, confused.

"That's what it means when the sun shines while it's raining," he said.

"You learn that in church?" she asked.

"Church ain't my thing," Sonny Joe said. "People around here believe in shit like that."

"Shit like what?"

"Shit like the devil's got a wife."

"You from around here?" she asked, smoothing out her dated yet vibrant green dress.

"Yeah, I'm from here," he said. "But I ain't a believer like everybody else." He turned up the half-pint of Southern Comfort and winced after he was done. "You know this place is haunted."

"I thought you didn't believe in shit like that," she said.

He smiled and took another drink, unable to find a comeback line. "Me and my buddy back there are gonna go mess with this crazy man if you wanna come with us," he said, securing the bottle in the waist of his jeans.

She looked over Sonny Joe's shoulder at Ceif, who was making his way through the vine-tangled yard with one hand clutching his Bible and the other clutching his cane. She looked at him like most females did, first with shock, then pity, then with whatever it was that made women want to hold and cradle things in their arms. Whether Ceif knew it or not, his looks and his limp were to his advantage, and the kind of attention they demanded was always something with which Sonny Joe struggled to compete.

"Don't let his looks fool you," he said. He yelled back at Ceif, "Ain't that right, Tadpole?"

Sonny Joe called Ceif "Tadpole" for one good reason. He looked like one. He had a big head, not much neck, and everything below his runty shoulders tapered off to a point as if he was stuck in the middle of metamorphosis. His mouth was small, so small it seemed capable of only producing words like "shoo" or "sit" but nothing as big and round as "hello." He had sooty hair and a pair of shadowy eyes that made him appear severely malnourished and sleep deprived. He was both. He slept every night on an abandoned church pew and ate whatever Sonny Joe gave him or whatever he could steal. Ceif the preacher. Ceif the thief.

"Say something, Tadpole, so she knows you're for real."

Ceif hurried his pace. His bad leg tripped in the vine. He fell to his knees, and his Bible sailed through the air and landed at the girl's feet.

"I have this book," she said. She picked up the Bible and bent to Ceif's aide.

"He can get up on his own," Sonny Joe said, motioning her to step back. "Let the weak help themselves."

Ceif untangled the vine from his cane and pushed himself up. "My name is Ceif Walker." He removed his black and dirty tam hat and held out his hand. "He calls me Tadpole when he's feeling insecure."

"I'm Gradle Bird," she said.

"You gonna come with us?" Sonny Joe asked. He snatched the cigarette from behind Ceif's ear, lit it, and took a drag. "Give you a chance to work on your social skills." He wiped his mouth with the front of his shirt and flaunted some naked skin, hoping it would distract Gradle from the intensity of Ceif. "Come on, it'll be fun."

"I need to tell Grandpa where I'm going," she said.

A loud boom came from the side of the house. The porch light lit up, its bulb popped, and sprinkled smoky shards of glass on the floor.

"Piss!" a man's voice hollered out.

There was a shake and rattle of aluminum and then a thud, like a sack of potatoes had been thrown down from the roof.

Sonny Joe followed the girl around the side of the house and found an old giant with white shoulder-length hair and a mustache to match flat on his back. He had a pair of wire cutters in his hand that must have been the tool that had clipped the metal ring around the electric meter. The old man was trying to pull power, and it had gotten the best of him.

"Grandpa," Gradle said. She held her ear up to his mouth, shook his shoulders, and blew on his face. His eyes were still as stones, fixed on the thundercloud above.

"Is he dead?" Sonny Joe asked.

"No," she said. "He stares off like this all the time."

Ceif hobbled around the corner, knelt by the old man, and placed his palm on the man's forehead. "He looks like Moses," he said.

The old man cut his eyes into Ceif like a couple of switchblades. He got up to his feet and situated the ladder back under the electric meter. Sprigs of hair rose up all around his head like a globe of dandelion seed. He climbed the ladder, removed the meter's face, and performed some kind of surgery on it before he put the meter's face back on.

The electricity surged. Lights inside the house popped on, and a TV blasted the sound of a Franklin Chevrolet car commercial two windows down.

"These boys just invited me to go mess with a crazy man," she told her grandpa. "I'm gonna go with them."

Sonny Joe was surprised at her honesty and moreso her boldness. If it were him, he would have at least lied a little bit. He figured there wasn't a fat chance in hell that old man was going to let his granddaughter go off with a couple of strangers to go mess with a crazy man.

"He isn't that crazy," he said to the man in an attempt to help her chances.

But the old man just stood there still, staring at the electric dial spinning round and round. He'd frozen up at the sound of her voice, as if it had thrown out ice.

"Does he talk?" Sonny Joe asked, pulling on the cigarette.

"Yeah, but he doesn't have much of a vocabulary," Gradle said.

The old man came down from the ladder. He gave Sonny Joe the once over and spent a lot of time on his fish tattoo. The man's eyes were dark and mean, borderline badass. He gave Ceif the once over too, and spent most of his time on Ceif's cane and the ratty Bible in his hand. It was times like these Sonny Joe was fortunate Ceif's looks demanded a certain amount of pity.

The man held up the wire cutters and snapped them shut as if to say he'd have no problem cutting off their balls, crippled or not. He walked up to Sonny Joe, snatched his cigarette from his mouth, and took a drag. The cigarette cherried and burned into a long cylinder of ash. He handed what little was left back to Sonny Joe, grabbed his ladder, and walked past Gradle without looking at her even once.

"Was that a yes or a no?" Sonny Joe asked.

"I never ask for his permission," she said. "I just tell him what I'm gonna do."

The screen door snapped loud behind the old man, and he disappeared into the house. Sonny Joe shifted his pants, trying to harness his excitement.

†††

Gradle sat on the benchseat between the two boys, not quite sure how to act. She fiddled with her gold-cross earring while Sonny Joe reached behind her neck and pressed the play button on the Panasonic. The scent of his underarm, like overripe fruit, excited her, as did the aggressive drumbeat that stuttered out of the jam box's speakers. He cranked the truck, threw it in drive, and slung up mud as they fishtailed out of the alley and onto the wet asphalt street.

"What brings you to town, Gradle Bird?" Sonny Joe asked, turning down the volume a notch. He shook a Marlboro Red from a soft pack of cigarettes, and it sucked up to his lips like they were magnets.

"My grandpa," she said. "And that old house I guess. He's trying to save it from getting torn down." She liked to believe there was something more to it, that it wasn't just about the house, that maybe it also had something to do with her. That maybe he was trying to save her from getting torn down, too.

"Welcome to the neighborhood," Ceif said, as his sticky yellow fingers struggled to roll a cigarette.

"What happened to your lip?" Sonny Joe asked.

"It got busted," she said, rubbing her finger over the scab.

"And what's the story with this?" Sonny Joe asked, flicking his fingers through the grey streak in her bangs. "You stressed out or something?"

"It's a birthmark," she said.

"You know crazy people grey early," he said.

"I guess I'm crazy," she said. "You got any greys?" she asked, hunting through his peroxide blonde and rain-jeweled hair. The color was unnatural but natural on him, like the cigarette that hung precariously from his mouth as if it completely trusted his lips, like the fish tattoo swimming underneath his shirt that was thin as egg skin and a size too small. He was cool and unusual, beautiful actually.

"Would you leave her the hell alone?" Ceif said.

"Who gave you permission to talk?" He gave Ceif's ear a hard thump and pulled the truck into a drive-thru liquor store with a neon sign advertising LIQUOR and a smaller statement written on cardboard in black ink: WE DON'T SELL TO MINORS.

The tires ran over a hose and the air bell rang. A man with a lazy eye and a hammer-like head slid open the glass window and spat a shot of chewing tobacco juice from a pair of crooked lips.

"Hey Hammer," Sonny Joe said. "Two half-pints of Southern Comfort, a couple Mello Yellos, a sleeve of Black Cats, a pack of Marlboro Reds, and some Midnight Specials." He pulled out a wad of dollars thick as a brick from his jean's pocket and flipped through the bills.

"You got I.D.?" the man said real slow, as if he had a hard time lifting the words. "GBI's been up here."

"You know I ain't got I.D., Hammer."

The man surveyed his surroundings from the sides of his eyes. "She want anything?"

"What kind of fun do you want?" Sonny Joe asked. "Something fruity. Fuzzy Navel? Bottle of Hill?"

"I'll take a Budweiser," she said.

"Six pack, twelve pack, or a case?"

She lifted her skirt to air out the heat between her thighs. "You sell it by the can?" she asked the man.

The man nodded and slid the window shut.

"That's a pretty dress," Ceif said. "Green your favorite color?" His fingers shook and tore the paper while he struggled to roll the same cigarette he'd started a couple of miles back.

"How old are you?" she asked.

"Thirteen and a half."

"He's fast for his age," Sonny Joe said. "Don't treat him like a child."

The drive-thru window slid open. "Twenty even," Hammer said.

After Sonny Joe and Hammer made their exchange, he threw the pack of Midnight Specials at Ceif's head. It knocked the half-rolled cigarette out of his fingers and sent loose tobacco in a skid across his Bible.

"He's trying to impress you," Ceif said.

"Is it working?" Sonny Joe asked, turned up the half-pint of Southern Comfort, and chased it with Mello Yello. He threw the truck in drive and peeled out of the drive-thru leaving a trail of rubber and smoke.

She didn't know if it was working or not, all she knew is that she couldn't keep her eyes off him—how sweat lacquered his veiny arms and fish tattoo, how his upper lip flared like a flower petal, how the hole in his jeans looked rough. He was wild and dangerous and a little bit sad, like an animal separated from its mother too young. And there was this charge about him, a force that dominated everything in his vicinity. The music. The air. Ceif. Her.

"You might want to try harder," she finally said after Sonny Joe caught her staring. She turned up the can and gulped down half of the coldest Budweiser she'd ever had. She was thirsty, hadn't had much to drink since they got there except a little bit of rain water she'd collected in a bucket out in the yard.

They passed the Piggly Wiggly, Dixie Hardware, Main's Five-n-Dime, and the County Jail, and when they rode over the railroad tracks, Ceif lifted his feet, kissed his fingers, and made the cross.

"What's that for?" she asked. She took a swig of beer.

"When I get to know you better I'll tell you," he said, lighting his cigarette.

"He believes in ghosts," Sonny Joe said, as he made a turn down an empty highway bordered by two fields of silking green corn.

She smoothed the lap of her dress and looked down the highway's long tongue leading into the darkness of an oncoming storm. "Do you believe Annalee Spivey's got a ghost?" she asked.

Sonny Joe tossed the butt of his cigarette out of the window and turned down the music. "You in the mood to be creeped out?"

"Sure. What's her story?" Gradle asked.

"She died in that house," Sonny Joe said. "They found her in the attic. When they found her, she was holding on to a portrait of herself and had a diamond ring sitting on her tongue. Use your imagination." He ran his fingers through his hair and shook it in place. "They say when you go past there at night, you can see her looking out of the attic window."

"What's she looking for?" Gradle asked.

"Her long lost love," he said, his canine resting on his smile.

Gradle took another swig of beer. "How'd she die?"

"Suicide," Sonny Joe said. Smoke funneled out of his nose, and he gave the truck all it had.

As they approached the city limits sign, Sonny Joe snapped his fingers at Ceif. Ceif hunted the floorboard and handed an empty half-pint of Southern Comfort to Sonny Joe. With a flick of his wrist, Sonny Joe threw the bottle out of the window. It hit the sign with a loud bang and added to its collection of dents. Sonny Joe turned up the radio, and after Axl Rose screamed out all he had to sing, Sonny Joe made a turn on a dirt road pebbled with little orange rocks and flanked by tobacco fields.

They went on down the road for miles it seemed. The tobacco thinned out and turned to dirt striped with rusted barbed-wire fences. He slowed the truck and rolled to a stop in front of the county dump's plywood sign. A pack of mangy dogs nosed through the trash and tucked-tail in all directions when he revved his engine to a scream.

"If Delvis ain't here, he must be home," Ceif said, nodding Sonny Joe onward.

Ahead, a cowbird flew against the storm-dark sky. The tobacco came back higher and greener but got choked out by honeysuckle and shade as they traveled farther down the road. They came to a mailbox rusted and padlocked shut. Written on its side were the words:

NO TRespass-N. FoR FaNS aNd ReaLTrUe
FrieENds ONLY. ReTuRN to SENDer if NoT.
D-S Delvis MiLes The LoNe SiNger
Rural RoUTE I BoX 56-B

"Is that the crazy man's mailbox?" she asked.

"Yeah, but believe me, Delvis don't ever get mail." Sonny Joe slung his bottle out of Ceif's window and knocked the mailbox spinning off its head.

"That was mean," Ceif said, as Sonny Joe fishtailed and turned down a drive mohawked with weeds.

Gradle slid to the edge of the seat and pulled her glasses down. The man's shack sat on cement blocks and had a severe lean to the right, and it would have fallen over if it weren't for the enormous oak that had grown into its side. Boards covered up all of the windows, and resurrection ferns grew in cracks of the rusted tin roof. Nailed to the porch walls was a hand-drawing of the cross, flyswatters, aluminum pie pans, a badminton racket, four thermometers choking at different degrees of heat, and a homemade sign that read:

NO PichtER Tak-IN

Flytape hung from the porch's awning along with baskets of bright coral geraniums and a Coke can whirligig that caught the wind and spun like a flower on fire. Clawfoot tubs without the feet, refrigerators without handles, rolls of barbed wire, sheets of tin, birdbaths, washtubs, reflectors, animal traps, bicycle frames, stacks of bricks, pink plastic flamingos, water hoses, rooster teepees, and six gutted cars all with the hoods open and labeled UsED, littered the yard. A doghouse with a bowl at its door sat under the oak. The dog was nowhere in sight, but there were freshly dug holes around its house.

Gradle took a sip of beer and surveyed the man's garden that sat off to the side. Corn, tomatoes, peas, and several rows of sunflowers were ready to pop. Five scarecrows, each with a dead crow strung around their neck, held signs that warned:

SCARE! CRow!

"How crazy is this man?" she asked.

"He's off his rocker," Sonny Joe said. He put the truck in park and grabbed the packs of Black Cat firecrackers.

He and Ceif got out of the truck, and she stood by them and

looked over the crazy, junked-out yard.

"I bet he'll come out after five firecrackers," Sonny Joe said.

"I bet three," Ceif said. "Winner pays for the next game of pool at Frank's."

"Why don't you just go up and knock?" she asked.

"You'll see," Sonny Joe said, as he unraveled the firecracker's daisy chain.

Ceif limped toward the house and drew a line in the dirt with his cane. "Don't go past that line," he said, tilting his tam hat at her.

After the words came out of Ceif's mouth, Delvis's mongrel dog bolted out from under the shack with a mouth full of foam. Its brindled haunches rippled as the dog ran toward them, too focused to bark. Gradle started to run, but Sonny Joe grabbed her wrist and made her stay put. The dog kept coming, then suddenly, inches before crossing the line, the dog was yanked back by its chain. It got off its back, lunged forward, and barked as if it had gone mad.

Gradle broke free from Sonny Joe's hold. "Jesus Christ," she said.

The two boys laughed.

The dog snorted and crawled back underneath the shack where he continued to complain.

Sonny Joe handed her a firecracker and lit its fuse. "Throw it!" he yelled, and threw one of his own at the shack's front door.

She threw the firecracker and it exploded mid-air. She laughed and covered her mouth, startled by the sound it made. She couldn't remember the last time she had laughed out loud.

The front door flew open and Delvis bolted out of his shack like he'd been slung from a slingshot. He danced around a pack of Black Cats exploding at his feet, jumped off the porch, and landed crouched on the ground. He wore a dirty undershirt, powder-blue pants cinched with a silver-buckled belt, and a bright white cowboy hat. His feet were bare, but his knuckles were decorated with brass, and in one of his oversized hands he gripped a gun.

"I known it! I known it wasn't stars burstin' in the sky!" His eyes, chlorine blue, were frenzied, as if he couldn't quite manage what was going on in his head. "You outlaws! Outlaws tryin' to make my life a livin' hell!" He shot the gun in the air and placed it in a holster by his side.

The gun's crack startled the mongrel dog from under the shack. It bolted toward Gradle and the two boys, who were both frozen by the gunshot. The dog kept coming. Its chain snapped, and it crossed the line Ceif had made in the sand.

"Run Gradle!" Ceif yelled, as he limped toward the truck as fast as he could.

She couldn't move except to open her hand and let the firecrackers fall. She watched Delvis perform strange variations of kung-fu moves in his yard and didn't even flinch as the dog ran past her and attacked Ceif's bad leg.

The dog shook and wrestled Ceif to the ground. His cane flew through the air and landed on the dirt out of his reach, but its distance did not stop him from reaching for it, and when he did, the mutt bit into his outstretched arm and shook it like a dishrag.

Sonny Joe grabbed Ceif's cane and beat it against the dog's back. "Get up, Ceif!" he yelled, grabbed Ceif's arm, and tried to drag him away, but the dog kept fighting. He kicked the dog's ribs and used everything he had to try and keep it from killing Ceif.

A shot sounded. The dog let out a yelp, and an eerie silence absorbed the air as the gun's echo cracked through the dark grey sky. The dog had stopped fighting, but Sonny Joe kept on kicking and beating it with Ceif's cane.

Ceif grabbed his cane in a downswing and jerked Sonny Joe. He rolled the limp dog from his chest, threw his arm over Sonny

Joe's shoulder, and leaned on him while he helped him to the truck.

"Get in the truck!" Sonny Joe yelled at Gradle.

Her dress blew through her legs and her hair whipped, as she stood paralyzed and stared at the Coke can whirligig screaming and going ballistic in the wind. Sonny Joe grabbed her by the waist and yanked her out of the trance. He threw her into the cab, slammed the door, and gunned the truck down the long dirt drive.

Blood was everywhere. It smeared across the dashboard, fingerprinted the windows, and seeped through the seams of Ceif's grip as he tried to dam up the holes in his arm. Sonny Joe ripped off his shirt and threw it at Ceif. Ceif wrapped the shirt around his arm, closed his eyes, and pressed his head hard against the window.

Gradle turned around and stared through the cab at the crazy man who was on his knees, weeping over his dog. She crawled over Ceif's lap, pulled the door handle up, and paused for a second at the running road before she jumped from the truck. She rolled to a stop and felt the sky's imposing darkness pressing down upon her.

She brushed off her dress and picked up Delvis's mailbox that was banged up and laying on its side. She wiped the mud and liquor off with her hands and studied the address on the box's side. The writing was imperfect and crooked, yet there was something code-like and artistic hidden in the cursive manner in which only some of the letters were written.

Carefully, she situated the mailbox back on its base and walked up the drive until she could see Delvis again. He was still on his knees weeping. The sky broke, and large drops of rain fell from its blanket of grey. Delvis lifted his dog in his arms, rose from his knees, and carried it inside his shack.

For a long time thereafter Gradle stood in the storm, wondering if there could be any forgiveness for what she had done.

†††

Inside his shack, Delvis Miles laid Rain on his twin-size bed, put a match to an oil lamp, and with a pair of tweezers he dove for in a dumpster two months back, plucked the bullet from the dog's side and put it on the table next to the bed. The wind outside picked up and rattled the loose boards of his house.

He worked fast, pulling spiderwebs down from the ceiling and packing them in his dog's bleeding wound. He collected webs from the window casings, deer antlers, secondhand candelabras, and the cross made of Popsicle sticks nailed above his bed, and when there were no more cobwebs to collect, he packed what was left of the brown sugar in the hole of Rain's gut. Damn outlaws. Trying to make his life a living hell. Why them boys kept coming around his place, trying to burn down his house with fire-poppers was a big question mark in his head. Did they know who they were messing with? Everybody else around here left him alone, and they ought to know his house was stronger than the Fort Knox because he had built it himself and made sure of it. Maybe they didn't have no manners. Maybe they were trying to capture him for that bounty them crooks put on him several years back, or maybe they came by here today, trying to impress that pretty young girl they brung. He had to admit he tried to impress her, too. The minute he put his eyes on her, he pulled out his most dynamic kung-fu moves, the ones he had copyrighted in the Library of Congress up in Washington, D.C.

Rain whimpered and brought him back to the matter at hand. He knelt by the bed, rubbed him from head to tail, and bandaged his side with two strips of duct tape. He hugged his dog's head and pressed his lips against his hot, dried-out nose. It wouldn't be much longer before his breath went out.

A tear started in the corner of Rain's eye, rolled over his snout,

and warmed up Delvis's fingers. Delvis remembered the day he
found him beaten up and whining because some outlaw had left him
in the bottom of the county dumpster to die. He didn't know why
people wanted to throw life away like that. Them people belonged
in jail. He remembered standing on the rim of the dumpster and
looking down on him that day and how he learned right there and
then that the dog had the magical capacity to cry. Because of that
trait, Delvis named him Rain.

The first time he tried to lift Rain out of the trash, he was so
wild and scared he tore into his flesh. But that didn't matter because
Delvis Miles will accept any and all challenges. He tried and tried
again because he knew he was the only one in his right mind who
could save that dog from starving to death. It took him an entire
week, four jars of Jif peanut butter, and the sacrifice of a couple of
rain-damaged catcher's mitts, but eventually he gained Rain's trust.
He took him home, set his broken legs, and kept the maggots in his
wounds until they managed to clean them out real good.

Rain was his treasure, and although the dog despised every
other human being he ever encountered, he adored his master and
displayed his affections by fleaing Delvis's neck and dragging up
dead animals, mainly deer, when he heard the rumble of hunger
in Delvis's belly. They ran together. They hunted together, slept
and dreamed together, and when they swam in the creeks, Rain
would clamp onto Delvis's arm and lead him to shallow water
when he detected he had gone too deep. Rain was his protector, his
bodyguard, his one and only real true friend.

"I'm sorry, Rain," he said. "But I couldn't let you kill that boy."
Tears puddled in Delvis's eyes, and Rain cried along with him. "I
tried aimin' where you wouldn't die. But I'm only ninety-seven
percent accurate on target each and every time. I reckon I messed
up and hit you in the three-percent range."

He rose from the bed and stared at the bloody bullet on his bedside table. He picked it up and put it in his mouth to clean the blood off. The wind was coming in stronger and little slices of it blew through the cracks and cooled off his neck. He lifted his shirt, and with his switchblade, he slit his side, underneath the rib, in the same spot he had shot Rain. He pulled the bullet out of his mouth, clamped his jaw, and lodged it inside the slit.

"Forgive me," he said as blood seeped through his fingers.

He tore a strip of duct tape off with his teeth and patched up his side. He crawled in the bed, lay next to Rain, and stroked his cheek to the music of his Coke can whirligig spinning in the wind outside.

Rain pawed as close to Delvis as he could and licked the tears from his best friend's eyes until he had nothing left to lick with. Delvis felt the heat vanish from Rain's body, and when it was all gone, he stared at the ceiling and couldn't help but wonder if he would ever see that pretty girl again.

†††

Gradle followed the Chevy's tracks down the dirt road, through the tobacco, past the dump, and turned on the highway where she ran along the roadside into the mouth of a purple and violent storm. Wind bent the pines, and their needles fell to the ground and stabbed her path like pitchforks. A car sped by blowing its horn and flashing its lights, but she didn't heed its warning. Whatever wreckage the storm had in store for her, she deserved all of its punishment.

A vibration in the atmosphere raised the hair on her arms. It grew stronger, louder, and soon the sound of Sonny's Joe's tailpipe alarmed her ears like the sudden flutter of doves.

He crossed the Chevy over into the oncoming lane and pulled the truck in close. "Get in," he said.

She bundled her dress high above her knees and picked up her pace.

"Come on, Gradle Bird," he said. "Don't be hard-headed." His fingers called her his way.

"I'm not getting in your truck you asshole! Both of you are assholes!" she yelled.

"There's a bad storm coming," he said, nodding in the direction of her path.

She slowed and stared ahead at the circling mass of sky and saw what the speeding car had warned her of touch down in a distant tobacco field.

Sonny Joe reached through the window, looped his pinkie finger around hers, and reeled her back. "I ain't leaving until you get in," he said. His eyes dared her and the oncoming car that topped the hill.

She grabbed hold of his hand. There was something about his recklessness that made her feel safe. He opened his door, grabbed her waist, and lifted her across his lap next to Ceif, who was slouched against the window with his eyes closed. The side of his lip rose, acknowledging her.

Sonny Joe slammed the brakes and whipped the truck around. The tires smoked and squealed as they tried to catch hold. The oncoming car blew its horn. He shifted down a gear, the truck shot forward, and he sped down the highway, avoiding a crash and the twister sidewinding like a snake behind their backs.

"We made him shoot his dog," she said. The corners of her eyes grew hot with tears. "Why did we do that?"

Sonny Joe pressed play on his jam-box and turned the music up loud.

"We should go apologize," she said.

Ceif rolled his head in her direction. His face was pale but the purple under his eyes was getting darker, as if all of the color he was losing from his face was collecting there. "Your purity is astounding," he whispered, closing his eyes back shut, and rolling his head back against the window.

Sonny Joe made a turn down a dirt road and parked the truck in the woods. He laid Ceif's Bible on Ceif's lap and lifted him from the seat.

He nodded Gradle out of the truck, and they ran through the woods until they came upon a cemetery of an old abandoned A-frame church with its windows and door busted out.

She followed Sonny Joe through the cemetery with green crumbling tombstones that were all slanted back as if blown by a persistent wind. He led her into the church's dark and fish-smelling sanctuary the boys had made their home. Crosses were carved in two of the wooden pews where they slept, as if they needed extra help in warding off evil spirits. A can opener and two cans of Van Camps Pork and Beans sat on another pew. The other pews were empty except the one in the middle that shelved jar after jar of colorful fighting fish.

She walked down the right aisle and stood before the only unbroken window in the place, a stained glass window of Jesus washing his disciple's feet. He was on his knees and bowing in humble servitude in front of his dedicated flock.

"If I then, the Lord and the Teacher, have washed your feet, ye also ought to wash one another's feet," Ceif whispered, as he limped past her and toward the altar with Sonny Joe's help.

Ceif knelt at the altar, and Sonny Joe unwrapped the blood-soaked tank top from Ceif's arm. He doused Ceif's wound with Southern Comfort and heated a foldout knife with fire from his lighter. Ceif bowed his head until it touched the altar, and he began to pray in tongues. Sonny Joe placed the blade on Ceif's arm. It seared his skin and made his tongue scream and cry out its prayers. Sonny Joe palmed Ceif's head, parted his hair, and pressed his lips upon his crown, quelling the screams. Their devotion to each other was beautiful, like worship. It made her feel like she shouldn't be there, like she shouldn't watch, like she didn't belong.

She walked down the aisle to find her own altar, her own peace for the torment she felt inside. She climbed the pulpit steps and drew back a purple velvet curtain. Behind it was a small baptism pool of black water that reflected the ceiling's broken stained glass window where bats she scared up were rushing through. She entered the water, stirred up its shadows and its sweet smell of rot. She fell on her back. Her dress went abloom and scared a water snake through her long, splayed fingers.

"Forgive me," she whispered.

She begged the dark heavens traveling past. She begged them to get rid of her transgression, to do whatever it took to grant her refuge from the guilt of knowing she was the reason Delvis Miles killed his dog. There was a moment of brief relent, and a shaft of sunlight beamed through the window high above the pool. It made her body bright and made the raindrops shimmer like gemstones as they passed through the colorful and cracked stained glass. But soon the dark heavens came rushing back and shut out the light.

She didn't know how long it would take to be washed from her guilt, but she would beg until she filled up with water and sunk. When she swallowed that first drink of water, her mind went to Grandpa, and she began to thrash and kick. She snatched the photograph of Grandpa and Veela from her bra and cradled it in her hands as she carried it to the side of the pool. She blew her breath on them, trying to bring them back to life. A bit of her mother's green dress was missing, but Grandpa wasn't damaged at all. His half-dimpled smile was still there.

She rose from the pool, her dress glued to her bones, and found Sonny Joe shirtless sitting in a window, smoking a cigarette and watching the storm.

"I need to go back," she said. "My grandpa is probably worried."

Sonny Joe placed his finger to his lips, hushing her to protect the distant, delicate whispering of Ceif's mysterious altar prayers. His eyes were swollen, and there were tears and red in them that made his irises greener. She expected he might have been the type to hide his tears, but instead, he was the type to flaunt them.

The sound of Ceif's prayers came to an end, and Sonny Joe took a drag from his cigarette.

"Did you have fun?" he asked, as poems of pale blue smoke ribboned up from his sideways smile.

†††

Leonard sat in the dark in a rat-chewed chair staring at the TV and eating SpaghettiOs out of the can. On the screen, George "The Animal" Steele gnawed the padding out of the turnbuckle and rolled his green lizard tongue while "Macho Man" Randy Savage twirled around in his dark sunglasses and shimmering gold sequined cape.

A sound like someone tapping on the glass of the back door traveled up the hall. He stopped chewing the SpaghettiOs, turned the TV down, and cocked his ear. He turned still and silent. Ever since he'd come inside, the house had been making a lot of noise. He wondered if it was rats in the attic or Gradle coming home. He rose from the chair, grabbed his shotgun, and stared down the long dark hall at the backdoor's knob, halfway expecting it to turn.

He rattled his head, trying to shake off what could have been his imagination or the result of him being fried to the bone earlier today by a few hundred volts of electricity. He'd been on edge ever since he let Gradle go off with those two boys, which he shouldn't have allowed in the first place. But at the time, electricity was still boiling his blood, and he wasn't in his right mind. In fact, he was still addled by it, didn't feel quite right, felt like he was walking around with charge. Or maybe, he just might be a bit scared.

He walked back to the living room where the TV was caught in a spasm of scrolling horizontal lines. A shock traveled up his finger when he adjusted the antennae's tinfoil and gem clip rig.

"Damn it," he said, touched the tinfoil again, and got shocked again. He slapped the TV's ear, and Randy Savage appeared clear as day, sailing through the air well on his way to a body slam.

He sat in the chair, rested the gun across his lap, and turned the TV back up. He chewed the SpaghettiOs he'd squirreled away in his mouth and washed them down with a glass of rainwater he'd collected from the electrical storm that had violently rolled through. It had been a bad storm, but he'd worked through the whole thing, scraping paint from three sides of the house until he had a stinging blister the size of Jupiter's red spot on the inside of his thumb.

He took another bite of SpaghettiOs but his hand was shaking so bad the spoon missed his mouth, and little Os in red sauce dove off his spoon and swam in the wiry hair of his chest. He ate the Os off his chest while he watched George "The Animal Steele" waving his arms up and down like an ape.

He heard another sound, like a knock, and couldn't tell if it had come from overhead or from the backdoor again. He bolted up, knocked the can of SpaghettiOs over, and sent the spoon sliding across the floor. He gripped the gun and left Randy Savage flexing his chest and George dining on the ring ropes and turnbuckle foam.

"Who's there?" he yelled down the hall, as he pointed his gun into the dark.

He flipped a switch on the wall, and a light came on in the attic. Light pushed through the flap's seams and lit up the hall good enough for him to see. He crept down the hall, but no matter how careful and lightfooted he was, his loafers produced loud echoes that could be heard all throughout the house, even over the snarling and grunting George and the rowdy crowd egging him on. He toed off his shoes and continued down the hall, barefooted.

When he reached the back door, he flipped the porch light's switch, but no light came of it. He dropped his gun by his side, walked out on the porch, and crunched shards of broken light bulb under his feet. He picked a piece of glass out of his heel and surveyed the yard, looking out for Gradle, missing her, worrying, and wondering how much longer it would be before she came home. He sat in a rocker, rested the gun across his lap, and rocked while he watched twilight vanish.

A loud thud, like thunder, rattled the house and shook a piece of broken glass free from the windowpane. Leonard jumped to his feet, swung the porch door open, and readied his gun. His finger rested inside the trigger's curve, and he took aim at the attic's flickering light.

He walked toward the attic flap, and the whole way there he felt as if something was at his back, but he was too chicken to turn around. He stopped under the attic flap, and the light stabilized. The hair on his arms rose at the sound of feet sliding on sand. His hand fisted the flap's string and yanked it down. The ladder unfolded, and he ran up the rungs.

The attic smelled of sweetness and rot, and everything in it sparkled with dust. Moonflower carcasses littered the floor, and the new spawn bloomed with white abandon. Hawk moths darted through the air like tiny tornadoes, hundreds wormed out of pupas on the ground, while others swung trapped in webs, struggling to flee the rushing spiders. The attic was a hatchery of life and death, and it was all so damn frightening and beautiful he couldn't swear if any of it was real.

A shadow came and left the wall. He cocked his gun and shot at a rat scurrying across the floor. His ears rang, and among the ringing and echo of gunfire he heard laughter. He wiped the sweat from his mustache and shook his head, but the laughter grew louder and placed him back to the time when he and Annalee were young.

The attic light flickered. Leonard closed his eyes and counted out loud to twenty. He opened his eyes and shouted, "Ready or not, here I come!"

He heard the patter of feet race to the far corner near the slouching, vine-covered box labeled CHRISTMAS ORNAMENTS. It was the place he remembered her hiding the summer they were seven. He ripped through the spiderwebs and vines, broke open the box, and threw every ornament through the air until the box was empty.

He stumbled to the walnut hope chest, unhooked its latch, and threw the moth-nibbled quilts on the ground. He remembered finding her here the summer when they were eight. He remembered opening the chest back then and how she smiled at him before she gasped for air, as if smiling at him was more critical to her survival than her breath.

"*Pssst.*" He heard her hint near the wardrobe. He spun around, came at it quick, and pulled out the bottom drawer. That summer they were nine. That summer he found her quick, went straight to her like a hunting dog goes to doves.

He opened each of the drawers. His hands felt for her, and when he did not feel her, he slung the drawer against the wall. He lifted his nose high and snorted the air. He smelled death, SpaghettiOs in his mustache, and something reminiscent of her.

He followed his nose to the dollhouse, fingered away the spiderwebs, and peered in the windows of all of the rooms. He remembered when he found her here. They were ten by then, had grown too big to fold and curl, and could no longer fit in small and confined spaces. He had found her long before she knew he had, and when she caught him staring at her through the tiny bedroom window he did not try to hide his adoration.

Leonard flinched at the sound of tapping behind his back. He turned and pointed the gun at the gramophone. He remembered the summer they were fourteen. It was the summer he taught Annalee to dance. That summer he didn't bother seeking for her at all. He simply lured her out by playing the most beautiful music his ears had ever heard. He remembered her rising from behind the gramophone like steam from a rain-soaked road. He took her into his arms and taught her to follow with no instruction other than the strong gaze of his blue-gemmed eyes. They waltzed through the sonata, and long after the needle completed its voyage, long after the music stopped, they kept dancing.

Leonard threw his gun aside, rushed the gramophone, and put on a record. He cranked the handle and stood in the middle of the room while a piano sonata blared out. He waited for her to rise. He lifted his arms and waited for her to walk into them.

"Where are you?" Spit flew from his mouth and the hawk moths scattered. He spun round the room, shaking his fists in the air.

Annalee was dead. He had read her obituary decades ago, one simple sentence stapled to the documents willing him this home. But now he was standing alone in the attic wondering if he was fried in the head or if there could have been some sort of mistake, because inside the music he could feel her.

"Where are you?" he yelled.

The sonata crescendoed, and from the gramophone Annalee rose.

Leonard screamed and reeled against the wall. Her eyes had sunk into their sockets, but her lashes were still like spiders and her irises still like blue burning stars. Her skin had mummified, and yet still it glowed and accentuated her symmetrical bones. She had lost some hair, but the patches still rooted in her skull shimmered like gloss. Moonvine crawled through the holes in her black frock and the blooms floating around her neck gave her a sweet perfume. It was her. He could swear it was her. But she was so damn frightening and beautiful he couldn't swear if she was real.

"Annalee?" he whispered. He reached out, and after they touched they both jumped back from an electric spark.

Her jaw dropped. By the shock on her face and the rattle of her bones, it appeared as if she couldn't swear he was real either.

"You're alive," Leonard said. He stroked her cheek with his palm.

Her fingers fled to her lips, concealing her exhilarated smile and the unfortunate rot on her chin.

He took her fingers away, hooked his pinkie inside her mouth, and removed the diamond ring from under her cold, shriveled up tongue. He slipped it on her wedding bone, and when he did, he could have sworn a tiny bit of her finger had grown new skin. He raised her wrist up high, wrapped his arm around her back, and led her into a waltz of never-forgotten steps. As they glided around the attic, Annalee rested her cheek on his shoulder. Even though years had passed, and he was an old man, Leonard felt fourteen all over again.

Chapter Four

GRADLE OPENED THE truck door as Sonny Joe pulled into the old Spivey house yard and tried to get out before he put the Chevy in park. He flicked his cigarette out of the window and tugged her back by her dress.

"Do I scare you?" he asked, turning Metallica's "Nothing Else Matters" down a notch.

"I've dealt with scarier." She tugged her dress back and turned her attention toward the house.

Two of its windows were lit and all the rest were dark, except the ones reflecting the moon rising above the smoke of thunderclouds. The first floor window flashed with television color, and the one way up high in the attic shone the color of fire. Grandpa appeared at the window and passed by it as if he was floating. She pulled her glasses down her nose, and he passed by the attic window again. This time he looked like he was dancing.

Sonny Joe peered through the windshield up at the attic window. "What the fuck is he doing?"

"Dancing." Gradle smoothed her dress back and got out of the truck.

"You gonna let me walk you to the door?"

"Why?" she asked.

"So the boogeyman don't get you."

"I'm not scared of the boogeyman." She slammed the truck door and walked up the drive with her eyes locked on the attic window.

The moonflowers were in bloom and their smell was almost suffocating as she climbed the porch steps and felt their dead blossoms from the day before squish through her toes. She reached for the doorknob, and Sonny Joe spun her around.

He held her hands down, and her body tensed.

"When do I get to see you again?" he asked, as he released her hands.

"The next time you see me."

Sonny Joe smiled, ran his finger down the chain of her earring, and kissed its gold cross.

She pushed past him and turned the knob.

"Don't be scared of me," he said.

Gradle slammed the door in his face and walked down the hall into the living room where the TV blared a wrestling match between Hulk Hogan and Andre the Giant. A wingback chair sat a foot from the TV, and three empty cans of SpaghettiOs and an empty breadsack littered the floor. She sniffed one of the cans, scraped the sides with her finger, and ate what little bit Grandpa had left. She turned down the TV and heard the faint sound of music coming from above.

She followed the music into the hall and stared up the ladder leading to the attic. She climbed the ladder's rungs and poked her head through the hatchway into a flurry of flowers and moths. Music trickled out of the gramophone and Grandpa, covered in spiderwebs, waltzed with himself like an elegant madman across the attic floor.

Gradle froze. She wondered if he'd finally cracked and gone crazy. But the more she watched, the more she wondered if there was someone else there. As he traveled toward the dollhouse, he stared into the air as if it had eyes just for him, and when he lifted his hand to suggest a twirl, a bit of wind blew back his hair.

She crept up through the hatchway, sat on the floor, and tucked her knees inside her dress. He dipped and turned and stepped in threes. His feet fell so lightly that the pupas and moonflower he danced upon were miraculously left unharmed. He waltzed from one end to the other and back again, and as the music died, his movement slowed, and when the music ended he bowed and kissed an invisible hand.

"Where'd you learn to dance like that?" she asked.

Grandpa lowered the invisible hand, and his body stiffened. He turned around, looked at Gradle, and quickly turned back as if the sight of her seared his eyes. He stared at the wall as the gramophone's needle skipped and cracked. She wished she had never asked the question.

"Can you see her?" he asked in whisper.

"Who?" Gradle said.

"Annalee."

Gradle looked over the room. She listened, she smelled, she felt the air, stuck her tongue out and tasted it. But all she could see was Grandpa, all she could hear was him, all she could feel and taste was him.

"They say she committed suicide," she said.

Grandpa bowed his head, ran his fingers through his silver mane, and clasped them together behind his neck. He looked up toward the ceiling, drew in a deep breath, then stomped across the room and kicked the gramophone off its stand.

"Leave," he said.

"We're gonna run out of food tomorrow," she said, climbing down through the hatch.

She went into her moonlit room, lay down on her bed, and removed the photograph of her grandpa and mother from her bra. It was still wet from the holy dunking waters of Ceif's and Sonny Joe's church. She placed the photograph on the nightstand and stared at it in the blue moonlight, wondering if Grandpa had ever danced with her mother, and if she would ever be so lucky for him to one day dance with her.

✝✝✝

Gradle flinched awake and drew in her breath so fast she choked on it. She had been dreaming of Delvis Miles and his beautiful mongrel dog. She caught her breath and sunk back into the hot, sweaty pillow. In the nightmare, Delvis was hanging from a tree. A rope cinched around his waist and he swung back and forth, trying to swim through the air to reach his dog that struggled on the ground, bloody, writhing, and yelping in pain. Gradle was there watching. Thousands of crows squawked in the trees and firecrackers blew them up. When Gradle tried to run and help the dog, she realized she was buried halfway in the ground. All she could do was claw toward the dog while his black terrified eyes begged her to help.

She got out of bed and went straight to the study where she ransacked the desk, searching for a piece of paper to write Delvis a letter. She found a yellow legal pad bloated with moisture, grabbed an ink pen from her empty SphaghettiOs can, and aimed the pen at the paper.

Dear Mr. D-5 Delvis Miles The Lone Singer,

My name is Gradle Bird. I threw firecrackers at your house yesterday with Sonny Joe and Ceif. I'm not a bit proud about

*what I did. It was mean and cruel, and I'm honestly sorry.
I'm sorry about your dog. I wish I could have done something
but I didn't. I'd like very much to apologize in person if you
would allow. Please write back. My address is 263 South
Spivey Street, Janesboro GA 30431.*

Sincerely, a real true friend,

Gradle Bird

Gradle used her fingernail polish and eyeshadow to paint
hearts, birds, and flowers on the letter to make it special. After she
finished, she laid the letter on the bed to allow the polish to dry.
Her eyes rolled toward the dust-powdered nightstand where the
traffic of cockroaches crisscrossed under the damaged photograph,
its corners warped and curled from evaporation.

She picked up the photograph, stood in front of the vanity's
cloudy mirror, and smoothed her dress. She stared at her mother
and then stared at herself in the mirror. She brushed her hair into a
new ponytail, and fingered down her bangs just so. She slid the cat-
eye glasses up her nose, practiced her mother's smile, and shoved
the photograph in her bra before her grumbling stomach lured her
into the kitchen.

The kitchen gleamed and smelled of Comet and lemon. The
counters were wiped, the sink and stove were shined and spotless.
The floors were mopped, and the eating table was polished. On the
table sat a plate with a peanut butter sandwich made out of the two
end pieces of bread, a glass of water, and SpaghettiOs poured into
a bowl. Next to the plate was a small stack of one-dollar bills.

She scarfed down the food, folded the money inside her bra, and
went on a hunt for an envelope and a stamp to mail Delvis's letter.

She went through all the drawers in the kitchen, all the drawers in the study's desk, all the drawers in her vanity, and every drawer in every chest in the house, but she came up short. Out on the front porch she heard Grandpa's voice, and when she went to the door, she saw a sheriff's car pulling out of the drive. She opened the door and walked out on the porch where Grandpa was scraping paint from the house.

"Are we in trouble?" Gradle asked.

Grandpa stopped scraping and stared at the clapboards. "Not yet," he said.

Gradle wrapped her arms around one of the porch columns, rested her cheek against it, and watched the sheriff's car disappear down the street. "What'd he want?"

"Wanted to know who was living here." He secured a lock of hair behind his ear and went back to scraping.

"Do you have a stamp?" she asked.

The pace at which Grandpa scraped quickened, and flakes of white paint spewed all around him like snow. His head jerked with every jab, forcing his dirty hair to come unloose from his ear and fall into his eyes.

Gradle studied him as he went beserk with the scraper. His wifebeater was filthy and stained with armpit sweat. He looked haggard and old, like he hadn't slept in days. Sweat rolled down his temples and got lost in grey stubble that would soon remodel his mustache to beard.

She went to his side and stopped his jabbing hand. He flinched as if she'd stung him and dropped the scraper on the ground, its handle bloody from the blisters on his palm. She pulled his hair from his eyes, tucked his locks behind his ears, and tapped her finger on his forehead.

"Does anybody live here?" she asked, while he stared down at the scraper. "I'm gonna find us some food," she said. She ran out in the rain away from him so he wouldn't have to keep slaving so hard at running away from her.

†††

Leonard watched the sweat drip from his nose and dilute the blood on the scraper. Each drip of sweat jabbed like a pick into the storehouses of his mind. He recalled the pace at which the faucet dripped when he saw his wife, Dot, wasted in the tub. It was 1957, in the month of July, on a Saturday morning, the day a wild finch got trapped in the house. He had opened all of the windows and chased the wild bird in and out of the rooms with a broom. He chased the finch into the bathroom, heard the dripping faucet, and saw Dot's slick and skinny wrist dangling over the lip of the tub.

The water was cold. She must have been too hot, too tired to undress. The emerald satin nightgown she had worn on their honeymoon, the one that lit fire to her rose-red hair, clung to the round of her stomach. She was six months pregnant and passed out drunk.

He propped the broom in the corner and placed his palm over her belly's shallow button. It was the first time she had let him touch her since their honeymoon.

He pressed against her stomach walls and felt movement and then the pressure of his daughter's precious and scary little hand. It was a girl. He knew because she had stolen all of Dot's beauty. He wanted to cradle Veela then, but knew he couldn't, so he vowed over Dot's cold poisonous womb that if his baby girl made it out alive he would protect her with all his might.

Dot stirred and shoved his hand away. She leaned over the side of the tub and vomited on his feet. He drained the water, cleaned her mouth with his shirt, and put her to bed wet. He poured what was left in the pint of Maker's Mark down the kitchen sink as the finch winded his ear and flew out of the window on its own. He shattered the bottle in the backyard where he had shattered many before, so that if he ever failed at protecting Veela at least he could show her how much he had tried.

For the rest of Dot's life, he poured out her liquor and shattered her bottles until the day he found her cold in the tub with no life-blood left in her limp and dangling wrist. Yet the bottles still remained. He would find them hidden in Veela's closet, up under her bed, and as the years went by, his pile of glass grew from Veela's inherited addiction. After Veela was gone, he bought bottles himself, poured the liquor down the drain, and shattered them in the backyard. He had failed at protecting her, but still required continuous proof that at least he had tried.

Leonard wiped the sweat from his nose and picked up the scraper. He didn't know how much time had passed, and for a moment he didn't know exactly where he was. He looked around for Gradle, pulled his wallet from his pocket, and plucked out a stamp.

"Gradle?" he whispered, as he walked into her bedroom.

He sat on her bed and placed his palm on her recessed pillow. He hugged the pillow to his chest, closed his eyes, and breathed in. He could feel her warmth and could smell her smell, like feathers. He opened his eyes and saw the letter she needed to mail on the nightstand. He picked it up, smiled at her make-up art, and as he read what she had to say he wondered where on earth she got her good heart from.

He put the pillow back in its spot and placed a stamp in its middle, hoping she would be certain to find it among the deteriorating beauty of her room. He stared down at the dirty and dulled pennies in his loafers and listened to the rain pelt against the tin roof like flocks of suicidal birds. His ears started to throb, and they became sensitive to other sounds, like the one he'd imagined hearing all morning—a sad, weeping sound from above.

CHAPTER FIVE

GRADLE RAN DOWN the sidewalk in the rain, past the neighboring house with its sinking roof and faded FOR SALE sign, angry at Grandpa and his cold indifference. She wanted to cry, but she was too mad to cry, so she ran faster instead. She dreamed about running forever, to keep going until she hit the interstate, until she hit the Fireside Motel, until she could hijack a big rig, drive it out west to California and stop at the Petrified Forest along the way, but she was starving and needed to buy a stamp to mail the letter to Delvis.

She ran through the town's biggest intersection, and stopped to take a breath once she saw the Piggly Wiggly's bright red letters and the face of its happy little pig. Four cars sat in the Piggly Wiggly's lot, and a lovely steam left by the partly sunny thunderstorm that just came through rose from the asphalt. The Pig's automatic doors sucked open and her nipples grew hard when she met the cold conditioned air.

Although there were only four cars in the lot, the store was packed with more people than four cars could hold. She pulled a shopping buggy from the inventory and dodged huddles of people who had no business being there except to escape the heat. They asked the butcher questions that had nothing to do with meat and browsed the aisles with empty buggies while their barefooted children with black-bottomed feet cooled their faces and armpits with the produce sprinklers. When she passed these people they stopped what they were doing and stared. Whispers followed and mothers drew their children into their hips before she passed by. She was a stranger in this town, and by the way they acted she was the strangest stranger they'd ever seen.

She hurried down the aisles and threw seven cans of SpaghettiOs and a jar each of creamy Jif and Smuckers Concord Grape in her buggy. She grabbed a sleeve of Wonder White, broke into it, and shoved a slice of bread down her throat before she nested it in the buggy's baby seat. In the toiletries section she grabbed a value pack of Schick disposables and a bottle of White Rain that could double as shampoo and shaving cream to clean up all of Grandpa's hairs. She tossed them in the buggy, marched toward the first-aid section, and grabbed a box of Band-Aids for Grandpa's blisters. She did the math in her head and came up short. Twelve dollars wouldn't buy what they needed for the week, nor would there be any left for a stamp to mail her letter to Delvis Miles.

She looked around, but there were too many people staring. She mazed through the aisles until she found one that was empty and shoved the box of Band-Aids down her underwear.

Gradle waited wide-legged in line at the cash register while an old man, gaunt as a needle and dressed in a woman's blouse, stood at the counter buying a bag of rice, unable to decipher a nickel from a dime. As he handed the cashier his money, the butcher yanked Gradle by the arm.

"Shame on you," he said. His fingernails dug into her bones, and his cockroach-colored eyes turned skinny. "I saw you, so don't lie to me."

"I have money," she said, reached into her bra, and showed the butcher the bills. The photograph parachuted to the ground and landed atop the butcher's bloody shoe. She snatched up the photograph and put it back inside her bra.

The butcher got into her face. The overhead light shone on his bald head in a spot where she could see her reflection. "Exodus twenty-fourteen says thou shalt not steal." He shook her arm. "How should I punish you?"

"Let God decide her punishment." The voice was familiar and came from the next line over. Ceif limped toward Gradle with one hand clutching his cane and the other his Bible. A bandage stained with old blood wrapped around his forearm.

"Saint Matthew, chapter seven verse one says judge not, that ye be not judged," Ceif said. He paused and let the butcher take in the scripture. "In all due respect, butcher." He nodded at the man and nudged his tam hat forward.

The butcher looked down at Ceif's Bible and let go of Gradle's arm. He wiped his hands on his slaughter-stained apron. "Give me your money and what you stole, and don't ever step foot in here again."

She slapped her money into his palm, lifted up her skirt, and removed the Band-Aids from her underwear. "Here," she said. She threw the Band-Aids at his chest.

She pushed her buggy through the Pig's sucking doors into the heat and hid around the corner so nobody could stare at her anymore, and where she could cry in peace if she wanted.

A tapping sound that started off small grew closer and louder, and soon Ceif rounded the corner and stood beside her. He took off his hat and removed the two slices of bread sitting on his head. He pulled a package of bologna from inside his vest, made a sandwich, and as he took his first bite, he extended his good leg, shook his pants, and a shiny red apple fell to his toe.

"If you're gonna steal, you need to learn from a real thief," he said, kicking the apple toward Gradle. He crammed the sandwich in his mouth and chased it down with a bottle of milk he retrieved from the cinch of his belt.

"The trick is," he said, his dime-sized mouth covered in white, "steal what you can get by on. You steal more than that you become a glutton."

"It was only a pack of Band-Aids," Gradle said.

He pulled a cigarette from behind is ear. "God don't like greed," he said, lit his match one-handed, and blew a cylinder of smoke through his mouth.

"What does God think about throwing firecrackers at a crazy man's house and making him kill his dog on account of it?" she asked.

"He don't like it."

"How do you forgive yourself for all the stuff God doesn't like?"

"I pray a lot," Ceif said.

"Why do you do it in the first place?"

"For Sonny Joe's sake," he said. He took a puff of cigarette.

"Why do you worship him so much?"

"He saved my life. And I'm gonna save his."

"How'd he save your life?" she asked. She took a bite of the stolen red apple and listened as Ceif told her his history.

When Ceif was twelve, he left Cape Girardeau, Missouri for good, with nothing but a funeral preacher's Bible and a wad of graveyard dirt in his hands. Five minutes after they lowered his parents in the ground, Ceif asked the preacher if he could borrow his Bible and told the man that if what had just happened to his parents was because of *The Way*, *The Light*, and *The Truth*, he wanted to learn all there was to learn about it. After the preacher gave him his Bible, Ceif walked to the crossroad where a local work train had T-boned his parents' car, and he flipped into the next junker hauling scrap metal and lumber out of town. When a dirty-faced hobo with glowing white eyes sitting in a dark corner of the boxcar asked him where he was headed, he raised his Bible and told the man "Eden."

It took him a year on the rails to find his Eden, but eventually he arrived in the warm, fecund South he had read about in the various libraries he frequented to escape bad weather, but moreso to fulfill his honest desire to improve his mind. In the writings of Ralph Waldo Emerson, he learned the South was a place settled by those in search of religious hope who saw its alluring fertility as a garden where mankind could begin again. The South was the agrarian ideal, a place where a good American could thrive on a small little farm, where one could benefit from the purity of nature and escape the city's temptations. Since he was a man of the Bible, who wrote scripture on every wall in every boxcar in which he flopped, what he read all appealed to him. It was the place where he could find a church. It was the place where he could become a preacher, and it was the place where he jumped from a fast-moving train and broke his left leg. This was the place that crippled him for life, which only confirmed his belief the South was where he should be.

For three days, he crawled belly down with nothing to eat or drink until he finally gave out, his face buried in the white sand of a black river's bank, his dry and cracked lips a mere foot from the nourishment the river would provide. He lost grip of his Bible, and shriveled there for a couple of days until Sonny Joe came to the same river's bank, sent there by his voodoo-witch mother on a mission to find fresh water mollusk shells for a concoction that would bring her good fortune. He kicked Ceif a time or two and a couple of more times for good measure and one more time after that just for the hell of it. Sonny Joe took him for dead until he rolled Ceif over and saw white grains of sand fall from Ceif's lips when he attempted to mouth the word *angel*. Sonny Joe left the shells on the sand, flopped Ceif over his shoulder, and brought him to the abandoned church in the woods where he nursed him to health with one of his mama's potions that was known to steal away ills. It was Sonny Joe who splinted Ceif's leg. It was Sonny Joe who whittled his cane, and it was Sonny Joe who stayed by his side, cradled his head in his lap every night and loved him as if Ceif was now his mission.

"I owe him," Ceif said.

The sky shed soft drops of rain that soon became hard and wailing. Gradle and Ceif glued themselves against the building and rain dropped from the bill of Ceif's hat.

"Sonny Joe saved you from dying, but what does he need saving from?" Gradle asked.

"He's got a little bit of devil in him, don't you think," Ceif said. He looked in the direction from where a train's whistle blew, warning the car stopped at the crossing. He kissed his fingers and made the cross over his heart.

They stared at the train as it roared through town. Steel pressed upon steel. Hinges stretched and screamed as the boxcars sped by like a fast running rainbow, leaving everything in the train's wake more quiet and still than it was before.

"I'm sorry about your parents," she said.

"Ain't nothing to be sorry about. They deserved what was coming."

"Why do you say that?"

"They'd been planning a vacation," Ceif said. "We were supposed to go to the Gulf. I remember Mama and Daddy packing their suitcases with more than they would ever need for a week. But I really didn't think much of it until Mama made me go pay for the gas after we fueled up for the trip." He paused to take another rip from his cigarette. "I remember she had a nervous smile on her face, and I remember looking at Daddy, but he was too busy chain-smoking in the passenger's seat to look my way. I paid the attendant for five on number three, and when I walked out of the gas station I saw where they'd dumped my suitcase by the pump. They never let on they didn't want me, so I guess it took me by surprise. I heard screaming and saw their car at the train crossing stalled over the tracks, their windshield busted and bent from the railroad guards."

Ceif picked a piece of skin from the edge of his nailbed, put it in his mouth, and chewed on it for a bit. "I heard the train blowing its horn, screaming for them to get off the tracks. Everything was screaming. The train. My mama and my daddy. The gas station attendant. And all the screaming was louder than the explosion, and all that screaming stayed with me on every boxcar I ever rode. It stayed with me all way to Blackfoot, Idaho. To Evanston, Wyoming, Winnemucca, Lovelock, and Reno, Nevada. I heard it in Kansas, New Mexico, and Colorado." He paused and cocked his ear toward the train that just past through. "And if I listen real hard I still hear it. I'll hear it until the day I die."

Ceif took a drag from his cigarette and ashed it on the ground. "What's your story?"

"I don't have one," Gradle said.

"What about your parents? Where are they?"

"I don't know."

"You ever asked your grandpa?"

"He doesn't talk much."

Ceif clamped his cigarette between his teeth and unraveled the bandage from around his arm. "You don't want to know what happened to them?"

"Not really," she said. She would much rather know what happened to Grandpa instead.

"I like talking to you," he said. He licked the dog bites and rewrapped his arm.

"Sonny Joe saved your life twice," she said, wondering if maybe he could save hers, too.

†††

"Hey motherfucker," Sonny Joe yelled at Ceif from behind the Piggly Wiggly. "Hurry your ass up, everybody's waiting." He sprinted through the rain and huddled against the building between Gradle and Ceif. He lit a cigarette, pulled on it hard, and blew a chain of Os Gradle's way.

"You back for some more fun?" Sonny Joe asked, offering her a drag.

She put the cigarette between her lips and executed the smoothest French inhale he'd ever seen.

"I didn't know you smoked," he said.

"I don't." She handed the cigarette back.

"Wanna see some fish fight?" he asked, grabbed her delicate hand, and led her along with her shopping buggy in the alley behind the Piggly Wiggly.

There were men and little boys. Whiskey and Kool-Aid. Rednecks and preps. Charm and seed. Nested between two dumpsters full of soggy cardboard and stinking cabbage he had set up a table with a half-gallon Mason jar filled with water as its centerpiece. A plastic tarp supported by four lean-to sticks covered the table and protected it from the rain, but it wasn't large enough to cover the entire crowd that shoved for position around the jar.

He led Gradle through the mob. She held his arm tight, like she was scared, and he felt strong, vibrant, and in control. When the boys saw her, those who smoked froze and left their cigarettes dangling in their mouths. Those who drank lowered their bottles and didn't bother wiping away their whiskey or red-sugar mustaches. All the rednecks forgot about their crosses that hung around their necks on gold rope chains, and all the preps forgot about their slick watches. The youngest boy there tripped over a forty-ounce Cobra bottle full of rainwater and wrigglers that belonged to the oily bluish black man named Pierson, who propped himself against the wall drunk, and who opened his eyes only to watch her pass by.

"I know it's hard gentlemen, but try not to stare," Sonny Joe addressed the crowd, as he led Gradle to the best seat in the house, front and center.

He sat in a chair behind the table. "Y'all see Rhonda Sikes's tits when she walked out of the Pig a while ago?" he asked the crowd and received laughter. "Her nipples were hard as jellybeans," he said, motioning for Ceif to collect everyone's admission fee. "Gradle can watch for free."

He placed two clear plastic cups on the table. One held a Halfmoon with a blue head and flowing orange finnage, the other, a velvet red Apache. He held the cups high above the crowd. "Halfmoon against the Apache. Both have a gene pool mean as cat shit. You got two minutes to pick a fish."

The crowd lifted and shoved to get a better look at the fighters before placing their bets with Ceif, who recorded them with a knife-sharpened pencil in a spiralbound notebook. The butcher walked through the Pig's backdoor, lit a Parliament Light, and narrowed his eyes on Gradle as he inhaled a drag. He paid his admission fee, inspected the two fish, and placed his bet on the Apache. He propped his leg against the wall beside Pierson and enjoyed the rest of his smoke while he picked raw meat from beneath his fingernails.

Sonny Joe watched Gradle as she looked at the two fish like she had never seen anything like them in this world before. It was the same look she had given him the first time they met, a curious wonder.

"Why do they fight?" she asked.

"It's their nature," he said, turning the cups around in his hands. "They find it rewarding."

Sonny Joe had been studying Siamese fighting fish since the first time he had ever seen them battle. He was eight years old and his mama needed the ingredients of a potion that caused acute paralysis. A one-armed mechanic had broken her heart. She needed the tail finnage of a Blue Cambodian, bit off by a juvenile Doubletail Opaque known as the Holy Grail and thought to be extinct. On a mission to revenge her heart, she packed a bag with enough clothes to last six days, snatched Sonny Joe by the arm, cranked up the Pontiac, and drove down every dirt road and highway in the Southeast in hunt of two fish the size of a pinky finger. On the seventh day of searching, his mama had to wear her underwear inside out, but she found a thirty-year-old ex-beauty queen in Baton Rouge Louisiana who bred these fish in mud puddles in her backyard. She had shady ties with a breeder in Thailand and possessed a Blue Cambodian and one of the last doubletail opaques in existence, an aggressive juvenile.

His mama spent a week's worth of pay for these little fish and made him drive the Pontiac all the way back to Georgia while she sat in the passenger's seat and cuddled the fish in two plastic bags between her legs, in the naughty heat in which they thrived. She screamed at Sonny Joe every time he ran off the road or drove over a bump. She smacked him three good times, when too scared to swerve, he slaughtered an opossum that darted in front of their path.

His mama waited for a night with a blood-orange moon and a deep purple sky and placed the Blue Cambodian and the Holy Grail side by side in two separate cups. While she went to smoke a cigarette, he watched the fish communicate through their clear plastic homes. Once they saw each other their colors turned brilliant, and even the white seemed to glow. Their finnage extended, and their gills erected around their faces. At first he thought it was love, some way of one impressing the other, but soon he realized their beauty was disguised hate.

The Holy Grail jumped from its cup into the Blue Cambodian's and fought the blue fish until it was dead. Before his mama came back, he hid the Holy Grail in a cup of water under his bed. She figured the fish had jumped out of its cup through the open window and searched the ground for two hours with a flashlight, finally arriving at the conclusion the cat had got it. She ended up poisoning the cat because she had planned on reselling that fish to get her week's paycheck back. Yet, to her delight, three months later, the one-armed mechanic developed paralysis in his only hand, whether from the delusional success of her potion or from the inevitable result of nerve damage that existed years before.

After the capture of the Holy Grail, Sonny Joe spent most of his days in the library reading books on Siamese fighting fish. He learned everything written about the species and saved the money he stole weekly from his mama's wallet to buy the Holy Grail a female companion. He learned through careful observation Siamese fighting fish were socially intelligent and pursued wily strategies of manipulation, punishment, and reconciliation. He also learned through careful observation it was the male who protects the spawn. After laying eggs, the female tries desperately to eat them and is only prevented by the male from doing so.

He continued to steal money from his mama and continued

to spend it on fighting fish and everything that went with them. He bred different shapes with different colors. He bred Crowntails with Halfmoons, Veiltails with Spades. He bred blues with reds to get purples, greens with reds to get chocolates, chocolates with reds to get blacks. He conditioned some for victory and some for defeat so that when he organized a fight there was no surprising him who would win.

"How much money can you win if you bet on the winning fish?" Gradle asked.

"Depends on the day, who bets on who," Sonny Joe said. He took the wad of money from Ceif's hand. "If you bet on an unpopular fish and it wins, you can walk out of here rich." He held the cups of fish side by side. "Alright, gentlemen," he said, starting to pour the fish together in the jar.

"I want to bet," she said.

Sonny Joe halted his pour. "Put your money down."

"I don't have any."

"What you gonna bet with, Gradle Bird?"

"I'll show you my nipples," she said.

He leaned across the table and whispered in her ear. "I can already see them."

She looked down at her skinny breasts and acknowledged her nipples, hard beneath her green dress. "I'll show them to you naked," she said, steadying her gaze on him as if he didn't threaten her at all.

"Now, now, Gradle Bird. I don't want to give you a bad name."

"I've already got one."

"Alright. If I was you, I'd bet on the blue," he said.

Ceif limped over and stood by Gradle's side. "Bet on the red," he said under his breath.

"Which one's most popular?" she asked.

"The red," Ceif said.

"I'll bet on the blue."

"Naked nipples on the Halfmoon," he said, and he poured the two fish into the jar sitting in the middle of the table.

Gradle knelt eye-level to the fish, pushed her glasses up her nose, and watched with unwavering intensity as the blue and orange Halfmoon slowly swam toward the Apache. She didn't seem to mind the crowd of males shoving her chest hard into the table as they fought to get the best view.

The Halfmoon momentarily paused. The Apache glided its way, and they circled one another in a poetic ball of color. They broke apart, and their gills bloomed around their faces like the flowers of a pansy. Their fins erected. Dorsal. Ventral. Anal. Caudal. They were at their fullest, most colorful, most brilliant state. The Halfmoon deflated its gills, turned broadside, and beat its orange tail. From above they came together in the shape of a letter T. They exchanged positions, alternating from top to base, as they circled around the jar like lovers.

The Apache attacked. It bit the tail of the Halfmoon and spat out a shred of orange fin, which floated in the jar like a piece of confetti. The Halfmoon butted the Apache and nipped its ribs. The Apache fought back, taking bits of the Halfmoon's fin and making gashes in its side. The fish locked mouths, clenching each other's jaws. They twisted and tugged as they slowly sunk together to the bottom of the jar where they remained mouth locked for over a minute before they broke apart and swam up for air.

The fish repeated the sequences of threat and attack until suddenly the Halfmoon fled from the Apache who kept in close pursuit. The Halfmoon's fins became flaccid. Its colors bleached, and two dark horizontal bands appeared on its sides as it hid motionless in the far right corner.

Sonny Joe had been watching Gradle through the jar the entire time. Although the water distorted her image, he could see her magnified blue eyes spark as the fish began their sequence. He wondered if the fish could see them too and if their color had in any way stimulated their aggression, causing the Halfmoon to fight harder than expected. He could sense her intrigue. He could sense her understanding.

As Ceif paid out the winning bets, Gradle continued to stare at the two fish in the jar. The Halfmoon had swum to the surface and assumed a vertical head-up position while the red Apache continued to display behaviors of threat. He could have made it easy on her. He could have agreed with Ceif and convinced her the Apache would win, but where was the game in that?

"That was the most beautiful thing I've ever seen," she said, rising to her feet. Her eyes were wet and crystalline.

"Boys and gentlemen, leave us alone," he said. The crowd dispersed, all except the butcher who didn't leave until he finished his cigarette.

"I spared you an audience, but it's time for you to pay up, Gradle Bird," he said, plucked the slow dying Halfmoon from the jar, and tossed it to a white cat with serpent green eyes that was starved enough to leave the dumpster's shelter and sprint out in the rain to retrieve it.

She climbed across the table and moved into him, as if what she agreed to pay him with came easy. He could smell bread on her breath and the tangy, sweet stench of her armpits. A pain surged in his groin, and he swelled.

She crossed her arms at her knees and lifted the hem of her dress. It rose above her thighs, above the mouth of her Fruit of the Looms, above her tight stomach's button.

He grabbed her hands and stopped them from rising further. "I don't want to see your nipples."

She slid her fingers from his grip, brought her dress over her head, and laid it gently on the table as if she cared for it more than anything in the world. She unlatched her bra and paid no mind to the photograph that dropped to the ground. Her breastplate was rippled, her waist swerved fast and inward, and her hips were dangerously sharp, as if her body had been bred for violence. She was so stunning and so threatening he couldn't bear to look at her.

His eyes fled up and down the alley, looking for Ceif to save him, but Ceif was nowhere in sight. They were all alone, except for the white cat now hunched under the dumpster, teething the dead fish.

When he looked back at her again, she moved in closer, locked her mouth on his, and brought him down to the table on top of her. Her arms and legs wrapped around his back. Her hipbones stabbed.

Her eyes glassed up behind her goofy, rain-dropped glasses. He removed her glasses and stared deep into the marbly blue of her eyes.

"What do you want me to do?" he whispered.

"Save my life," she said, shutting her eyes.

He buried his face in the crook of her neck and held her tight. They lay still, feeling each other from the inside out. He had been with all kinds of girls before, but she was different. Either her starvation was contagious or else he had been unaware all this time he was starved himself. He unbuttoned his jeans and pulled her underwear aside. She was hot and wet and new. He closed his eyes and swam in her, but before he could find any rhythm, he felt her knees rise to push him off.

He opened his eyes and saw her with her arm stretched out, shaking as it reached toward the photograph on the ground. A drop of sweat fell from the tip of his nose and spanked her temple. She kneed him in the groin, rolled from beneath him, and dove to save the photograph from being beat up any more than it already had by the rain. She sheltered the photo with her pale, slick body and crawled underneath the table where she used her dress to dab the rain away from photo's film. She put on her bra, climbed into her dress, and placed the photograph against her heart.

She crawled from beneath the table and stared at him in his disheveled state as if she had forgotten she had made him that way.

"You look pale," she said, put on her glasses, and pushed the shopping buggy down the alley while Sonny Joe stared at the back of her brilliant green dress, feeling nothing but defeat.

††

Gradle pushed the rattling buggy down the sidewalk as the rain came down hard on her head. She tried to make sense of what happened in the alley with Sonny Joe. She felt like a fool thinking he could ever love her like she needed to be loved, that he could somehow save her, sustain her through what her life lacked. She had gone too far before realizing it was not his love she needed. She wondered why she didn't feel any different, why she didn't feel more like a woman. She would have expected a bit of weeping or lament, perhaps even a bit of blush or glow. But they didn't finish or really start. It didn't even hurt, and so she wondered if it counted, if technically she was still a virgin.

She ran the buggy up into the yard of the old Spivey house and unloaded the SpaghettiOs. The house looked sad in the rain. The porch frowned and the windows, like crying black eyes, shed tears that fell like waterfalls from the awnings. A can slipped from her grip and rolled down the walkway, stopping shy of the front steps, as if it was too spooked to go any further.

She bent to collect the can and saw a river of rainwater and blood splitting around her ankle. She checked her dress. There was blood on the skirt. She rubbed its fabric, but the rain was too weak to make the red go away. She grabbed the shampoo from the buggy, ran inside the house, and stripped to her underwear in the kitchen. She plunged her dress in the sink and squirted it with shampoo. She turned the faucet but nothing came out except a couple knocks of air.

She lifted the dress out of the sink, ran to the back porch, and held it under the awning where rain ran off in sheets. She scrubbed the fabric and rinsed, but the blood was still there. It looked as if it had already set. She shaked out more shampoo, scrubbed and rinsed, scrubbed and rinsed, and prayed the whole time for it not to be ruined. She kept scrubbing until the threads began to tear. She rinsed it one last time, squeezed the rain out, and laid it upon her bed to dry.

She lay on the bed next to the dress and spooned it as if someone she loved was inside it. She nuzzled the fabric with her nose, closed her eyes, and remembered the day she first put it on. It was four years ago, and she was alone in room 42 sitting on her bed, reading *The Holy Bible* that came standard with every room. The closet door was open and a shiny-backed cockroach froze mid-journey up the closet wall. She hopped off her bed, and as she chased the cockroach with the Bible, she saw a swatch of vivid green poking through a corner hole in a box sitting high on the closet shelf.

She let the cockroach have his life, brought the box down from the shelf, and swept off its dust. The masking tape came off with ease, its glue old and no longer good. She plunged her hands into the box and took hold of a bundle of green chiffon. As she lifted it from the box, the skirt unraveled to her shins and dropped a pair of cat-eye glasses, an old photograph captioned *Leonard and Veela 1972*, and a corsage of dried flowers that broke to dust when it hit the floor. On the dress's bodice above the heart was a piece of torn paper stabbed with a straight pin and signed with a dedication: *For Gradle, my little bird.*

She brought the box and everything it had in it into the bathroom and locked herself inside. She brought the photograph up to her nose and studied it and all of its detail. The photo was proof she had a mother and proof that at one point in his life Grandpa was happy.

Gradle put on the dress, stared in the bathroom mirror, and compared herself to her mother. She didn't need a mirror to see her reflection or a family tree to explain her lineage. She was an exact replica of her mother, down to the streak of grey hair growing from the top of her head.

She heard Grandpa come in the room and drop his tool bag to the floor. She smoothed the skirt of her dress and walked out of the bathroom door.

"How do I look?" Gradle asked, while Grandpa fiddled with the belt of his electric sander. When Grandpa turned to see, she spun around, and the dress's skirt bloomed out like a flower.

Grandpa stood, removed his glasses, and stared at her as if he was trying to figure out who in the world she was. He came toward her, cautious at first, but his pace soon quickened. He dropped to his knees, bundled the green dress in his hands, and sunk his entire face into it. He drew in a deep long breath as if that air was the most sacred thing he had ever put up his nose.

"Veela," he exhaled in a whisper.

He held Gradle's hands and pulled her down into him. He wrapped his arms around her, palmed her shoulder blades and kneaded the bitty bones of her back. She couldn't remember the last time he'd hugged her or the last time they'd touched. He'd never been one for affection, and she always thought it was because he didn't know how to handle a girl, but on that day on the floor of room 42, he handled her with the perfect amount of strength.

He cradled the back of her head, buried his forehead into her neck, and rested there long enough for what felt like warm tears to seep through the chiffon of her dress.

"You wanna go fishing?" she asked, and he let her go just as fast as he held onto her.

He got up from his knees and went back to fiddling with the belt of his sander.

She ran back to the bathroom and stared at the photograph of Grandpa and her mother. If her mother was dead, she knew she couldn't raise her from it. If her mother had just run off somewhere, she knew she couldn't call out her name and make her come home, but maybe, if she could look enough like that day in that photograph at least she could bring Grandpa's smile back from whatever dark place it had gone. If she could look enough like that day, maybe, just maybe, he would hug her again. She pulled her hair back into a ponytail, grabbed the blunt scissors from the motel's complimentary sewing kit, and cut her bangs crooked and too short. When she was finished, she put on the cat-eye glasses, and practiced her mother's smile.

Gradle took the dress away from her nose, opened her eyes, and rose from the bed. The rain drummed gently on the tin roof, and moonflower buds had started to bloom. She turned on her nightstand's lamp and sat in front of the vanity. Her face drew in close to the mirror, and she studied her first-kissed lips. She pressed her fingers into them, feeling to see if they had changed, and noticed a small square of paper stuck to her cheek. She pulled it away and cradled the stamp in her palm. A tear rolled down her cheek as she stared at the vine-covered ceiling and listened to the dwindling sound of music and the shuffling of Grandpa's feet upon the attic floor.

CHAPTER SIX

THE GRAMOPHONE'S NEEDLE skipped, and Leonard's steps slowed to almost nothing. Annalee welcomed the change in tempo, for she was worried about his heart's speed and the bleeding blisters he'd danced into his feet. He had come up to the attic as it had started to rain and had caught her staring out of the window as she so often did.

"Why are you crying?" he had asked.

She found it peculiar he could hear her cries when she had no tears to cry with. She hadn't shed a tear in years no matter how long and how hard she had mourned.

"Why find me now?" she had asked, but Leonard had not answered.

Instead he had cranked the gramophone so hard he broke off its handle and then had forced her to dance when she really hadn't felt like dancing.

They had been dancing for hours. It was getting dark, and he stunk of sweat. His feral hair hung in his face, hiding the sickles under his eyes that had turned purple from lack of sleep. His temple dropped to her shoulder, and she dipped from his slippery weight. She tried to gather him into her, but he was too much for her to hold. He sunk down her sternum and collapsed in a heap on the floor, drunk from exhaustion and perhaps a tinge of madness. He had always suffered from an addictive disorder but she had never seen him so belligerent. She had seen it in his eyes—a wild delirium as he spun her in what must have been over a thousand spins with a drive so intense, she honestly feared he would dance himself to death.

She knelt on the floor and laid his head on her lap. She combed her fingers through his hair, spreading his silver strands out to shine like rays of some dying sun. It had been decades since she had seen him, and while she would expect that amount of time would age a man, she never imagined it could be so cruel. His blonde and blues had tarnished. His lips had lost their pillows, and his wrinkles were so deep some of them needed stitches. The ones clawing at the corners of his eyes appeared as if they had been carved out by the constant rush of tears. In fact, his entire face clamped down in what appeared to be a permanent attempt to dam up grief.

She smoothed her fingertip over his lines, wondering what had caused them to become so deep, if his life had been anything akin to hers. For years she had drifted about this house, completely befuddled as to why she wasn't picking daisies somewhere in The Promised Land. At first, she thought this place was temporary, but after years and years of wandering about, she presumed she was here to stay, for what she took to her grave was unspeakable, even to the greatest, most holy ghost of all. There are things that can haunt you until your dying days, and there are some things that can haunt you even after death.

She palmed Leonard's cheek and remembered the last time she had seen it, tear-streaked and red from the mark of her mother's quick hand. All this time had passed, and only in the next world did she ever think she would see him again.

They were first cousins. Leonard was her father's brother's son. They were born only three days apart and would have arrived on the same day if her Aunt Missy hadn't labored for so long. Regardless, they both bore the Lee name, Annalee and Leonard Lee, after their great grandmother, Sarah Lee Spivey.

Leonard's family lived up north and visited for two months every summer. As infants, Annalee and Leonard shared a porch crib and tugged on each other's toes while their parents ate tomato sandwiches and got drunk on gin.

When they were old enough to crawl, they shared a playpen, and when they were old enough to walk and climb, they shared the attic. For as long as Annalee could remember, every second week of June she perched from the attic's window, the home's highest point, and watched for Uncle Reece's car to turn left on Spivey Street. She would wait for Leonard to bolt from the backseat, his eyes two streaks of blue, and his dirty blonde hair rushing back on the tail of his eager-made wind. Once she heard his feet pound up the porch steps, she would scatter to the hiding place she had started plotting in the second week of August on the day Leonard had to go back north, his blue eyes teary, his blonde hair cleaned and summer-kissed.

Over the years, summers couldn't come fast enough. She marked the calendar, she shook the hourglass, and began incessantly running with the hope that if she ran fast enough, she could speed up the days. And when June finally came, and she heard Leonard's feet tap up the porch steps, she stopped flipping the calendar, placed the hourglass on its side, and deliberately moved like a slug with the hope she could now slow down the days.

They dove into the wardrobes, the boxes, the chests, and turned the attic floor into their playground. They strung Christmas garlands throughout the rafters. They shuffled through tintypes of their long and gone kinfolks and spent hour upon hour role-playing in the dollhouse. They dressed up with brittle clothes, boas, and feather-pricked hats, and in the afternoons, stripped down to their underwear when the attic got sweltering hot. At night they gazed out of the attic window, counted the stars, and named their own constellations until their eyes grew heavy and their bodies grew limp. The mornings after, they woke sweaty, their mouths sopping with drool, and started it all over again, diving into the wardrobes, the boxes, the chests, both of them fueled with hope that each day would turn over an exciting and new discovery.

One afternoon during a violent storm in the summer of their twelfth year, when they had plundered through every wardrobe, box, and chest, and thought there was nothing new left, Leonard found something shiny.

The attic was dark, and Leonard and Annalee were playing with matches. They had gone through three boxes, struck so many matches their noses had grown immune to the stink and sting of phosphorus. Leonard picked up a matchbox that was strangely heavier than the rest, and when he slid it open, there were no matches, but instead a round and brilliant cut diamond.

"Look," he said, shook it in his palm, and presented it for Annalee's eyes.

"Put it back," she whispered, as if she had already known its forbidden history, as if she could predict its forbidden future.

He had done what she said and put the diamond back in the matchbox, but as she turned her back and walked to the dollhouse that summer day, he slipped the box inside his left white sock.

Another summer passed, another summer came, and in the

attic, Leonard became Annalee's plaything. She could make him do anything she wanted, and took great pleasure in her control. He was a ragdoll she could dress and contort, a game of gin rummy she could always beat, a Simon Says who always did what she said. It was one of the delights of male adoration or perhaps it was Leonard's lot for stealing the diamond. However, the control she was so pleasured by ended the summer she hid behind the gramophone. She was fourteen. Her breasts had changed shape, and her first pimple had pushed through her chin.

She stood at the attic window, looking down at the moon vine her mother planted that spring, it bulging with plump buds, and waited for Uncle Reece's car to turn left on Spivey Street. She watched Leonard rush from the backseat and run up the front porch steps. His shoulders had grown broad, and his throat was bumped with a protruding knot. Annalee held still until the attic flap opened then darted behind the gramophone.

Through an opening, she watched Leonard's loafers, stocked with shiny pennies, come toward her. Her fingers fled to her mouth, concealing her exhilarated smile and the unfortunate pimple on her chin. Leonard's hand reached in a box and retrieved a record. He wiped the record off, the dust falling lightly on his eyelashes, and placed it on its holder. He cranked the handle and positioned the needle in its groove, and from the flower-headed speaker came the most beautiful sound her ears had ever heard.

That summer, they spent all their days and all their nights dancing. He taught her the Charleston, the Shimmy, the Foxtrot, and the Bunny Hug. He made her mind count and her fingers snap. He made her arms pretzel and her feet kick. He made her dip and jump and twirl and rendered her weightless as he threw her in lifts, her hair sweeping the cobwebs from the ceiling. No longer was Leonard Annalee's plaything. She was his.

At night, after their parents stopped yelling up at them to quit all the racket, and after they felt confident the four of them had passed out on gin, Leonard and Annalee knotted the quilts together, threaded them through the attic window, and ran the four miles it took to cross the tracks to Jimmy's Dance Club. Every night at Jimmy's they took center stage. Leonard danced the pennies out of his loafers and Annalee danced the ribbons out of her hair. Come sun up, they raced home salted with sweat and cussing their blisters just as their parents were waking and cussing the empty gin crystal from the night before. They slept most of the day, and started it all over again, threading the quilts through the attic window, running to Jimmy's, and dancing all night.

When August came around and Leonard had to leave, for the first time in her life, Annalee became sick of heart. They promised to write letters every day and did so, wrought with romance and the anticipation of June. When June finally came, and Leonard streaked from Uncle Reece's car and pounded up the porch steps, Annalee, who had spent hours primping in front of the mirror that morning, did not possess the mischief to hide.

The attic flap pried open. A cut of light shone warm on her ankles and traveled up the prettiest Sunday dress she owned—a white eyelet that fit her perfect. From the light crawled Leonard, his shoulders square and broader than the summer before, his eyes hungry, his lips poised. The attic flap slammed shut. Annalee cupped Leonard's face, it void of boy and chiseled with man, brought him toward her, and placed her lips on his, kissing him with the kind of passion the red apple she spent six months practicing on could not possibly stir.

Leonard kept his mouth locked in the heat of hers. He clutched the back of her long slender neck and braced his other hand between her shoulder blades. He backed her against the wall where they

kissed through a hot rainstorm. Annalee lifted her newly shaven
leg, the eyelet lace tickling up her thigh, and wrapped it around
the small of Leonard's back. He lifted her, and with all four of her
willing limbs, she encased him like a spider encases its meal. They
spun around and around the attic's room until they fused into one.

Leonard laid her on the velvet fainting couch and unlocked
his mouth with hers. He reached for his ankle, and from his sock
retrieved the matchbox they had found the summer they were twelve.

"Marry me," he whispered, pulled the matchbox open, and slid
the ring that he had made from the stolen diamond on her finger.

She took him into her mouth again. She lifted her dress above
her waist and fondled his belt buckle until it came unleashed. Her
legs traveled up his calves and hams, her toes eager and grasping,
and tugged his trousers down. His fingers curled inside her panties
and took them past her knees. Her naked pelvis trembled from
the sudden rush of cold only to quickly melt from the weight of
his pressing heat. And there, on the fainting couch, among the
wardrobes, the boxes, and chests, they made love. They took in the
Scriptures, they recited the nuptials, and moved through the songs
and ceremony, and in their bodies and in their souls, they were
married. They lay in each other's arms, their bodies kneaded and
limp. Their breath ebbed and flowed in perfect unison.

The attic flap slammed. Annalee jumped up and covered her
breasts. Leonard grabbed for his drawers.

Towering over them stood Annalee's mother. Her mouth
was clenched shut and her eyes shook with anger. She clawed at
Leonard's collar, yanked him off the couch, and struck his face with
the backside of her hand.

The strings in her neck flexed. "Go downstairs and tell your
father and your uncle what you have done. But spare your mother.
She is too weak to handle this kind of shame." She grabbed

Leonard's arm and made him face Annalee. "Take your last look because you will never step foot in this household again."

"But Mama," Annalee stood up, "I love him."

"Shut your mouth, you silly child. You are not nearly a woman and have no say so in the matter."

"You can't do this!" she yelled, lunging for Leonard. The back of her mother's hand knocked her down on the couch.

Leonard's eyes set deep into Annalee's and stayed there until her mother ripped them apart and shoved him down the attic flap.

Her mother descended down after him and before closing the flap, she stabbed Annalee with her eyes. "You are forever ruined," she said, and she slammed the attic flap shut.

Annalee rushed to the flap and tried to pry it open, but her mother latched it and locked her in. She pounded her fists against the boards and pulled against the flap's handle.

"Leonard!" she screamed. She stood and stomped on the flap, hoping to bust through and fall to the ground. "Let me out!" she yelled, as her feet pounded against the floor. She dropped to her knees and placed her ear to a crack. She heard footsteps and mumbling and then the rise of male voices followed by a hard knock against a downstairs wall.

She pawed at the attic flap and yelled down again, "Leonard!" Her voice echoed throughout the attic walls, its vibration rattling dust from the rafters. She lay atop the attic flap and kept her ear against the boards, listening for Leonard. The house was silent except for the crashing of tears and the beat of her dying heart.

The front door slammed, and she heard Leonard's feet pound down the porch steps. She ran to the attic window and watched Uncle Reece shove Leonard into the backseat of the car and throw their travel cases into the trunk while her Aunt Missy, throwing up her arms, circled in confusion. As they pulled out of the drive, Leonard looked through the backseat window and found her staring down at him. Their eyes hooked. Reaching for each other, they placed their palms against the glass separating them from the world, only to find it unbending and cold. Before the blue in Leonard's eyes, once streaked with hunger, now sinking with tears, began to slip and slide to memory, she removed her palm from the window. She put her wedding finger in her mouth, raked the ring off with her teeth, and positioned it in the warm pocket under her tongue. She vowed then to keep it there forever and never to smile and show her teeth.

"'Til death," she whispered. She watched Uncle Reece's car turn right off Spivey Street while the last bit of Leonard trailed down the inside of her thigh.

Annalee, remembering the dejection of that day, kissed Leonard's wrinkled eyelid. Had he come back for her, an angel finally sent from the turtle-paced God? She had been robbed of what every human being desired most. It had been stripped away, no matter how tightly she grasped, no matter how violently she fought. Why had it taken him so long? For him to return to her this late was an act of the cruelest order, for she had no life left. The damage had been done.

A burning sensation, both foreign and familiar, filled her eyes. She blinked and expressed a tear. It rolled down her cheek and dropped from her chin. She caught it in her palm, stunned it held warmth, stunned it was real. Her hand went to her mouth, and she tasted this little sign of life, and when she did, she heard Gradle weeping from below.

She put her ear on the floor from where the sound rose. It was the quietest thing she had ever heard. No sound came from the girl's mouth, but Annalee could hear the gentle acoustics of her tears.

She pillowed Leonard's head with quilts, came down from the attic, and stood in the doorway of what once was her room. Aglow in the lamplight, Gradle lay on the bed in her bra and underwear next to her green chiffon dress. Blood stained the dress and her underwear, and Annalee could smell the hurt of her wound.

She sat on the bed at Gradle's side. The girl saddened Annalee, and she found herself fighting the urge to hold and pet Gradle as if she was one of her own. She was not at all baffled by the draw, for the girl possessed a type of gravity that would attract many moons, not to mention their circumstances were much alike. If God makes a home for the lonely, they hadn't found it yet.

She wondered who would have told her, who would have taught her about how it happens, how it works. The girl had no mother, no father, and from what Annalee had gathered from their time being here, she had no Leonard either.

A roll of thunder sent the moon vine into a shiver and brought down a hard rain. Annalee remembered how her mother taught her how it happens, how it works. She thought back on that day her mother sowed the moonflowers' first seeds. Annalee had watched her the night before nick their eyes with a knife and drop them one by one in a tumbler of water to soak. Moonflower seed is hard as a rock, and her mother was against the clock. Annalee had just turned fourteen and was beginning to flower herself.

It took three days for leaves, another twenty for blooms. As the hawk worms were turning to moths, Annalee's mother invited her out to the porch for a swing. In the dusk they watched the moon vine creep and bloom. When the first hawk moth drank the flower through its tongue, her mother, pleased with her plan, cocked her chin and said, "You see, Annalee. It's the moth, not the flower, that makes the seed."

Her mother's timing had been profound, but her poetics were not ample warning for what was to come.

Annalee stayed at Gradle's side and offered what piddly little comfort a dead woman could. She felt warmth as she wiped Gradle's tears, yet she couldn't say for certain if she felt her at all. She stroked her head until she fell asleep. When Gradle's breath grew heavy, Annalee removed her cat-eye glasses, kissed her forehead, and covered her with the sheet.

The storm passed. A dark, watery night fell, and hundreds of moonflower blooms starred the ceiling. A hawk moth lit on her ringed finger and stretched out its wings before joining the others in their feast. She watched the moths feed, watched them grow satisfied and flock to the ceiling to roost. She watched the sunrise, and when its delicate pink came in the room, the moonflowers wilted and curled. Night bloomers not made for the sun. She watched every bloom fall to the ground, each making a loud spank as if they carried the weight of wet towels. To serve a purpose and then die. *What a privilege,* Annalee thought.

CHAPTER SEVEN

GRADLE SAT ON the front porch swing reading *The Holy Bible* while she waited for the postman. She had been waiting every day, all day, since she licked the stamp Grandpa had left on her pillow and placed it on the makeshift paper and Superglued envelope she addressed to Delvis Miles. The letter sat in the mailbox for three days because the postman acted too scared to come on the porch and get it. Every day he altered his route by crossing the street before he passed, and crossing back over once he was two doors down, swerving around the old Spivey house like it was a dead animal in the road. The letter would have never been mailed if she hadn't finally chased him down and forced it in his hand.

Each day after, each time he crossed the street and waded through the median's azaleas, she chased after him, yelling out at his back, "You got any mail for me, sir? My name's Gradle Bird!" Every time, the runty postman avoided her eyes and shook his head as he kept walking with his face fixed to the ground. She'd watch him pass on, lift his head once it was safe, and greet the lady down the way with sunshine and smiles, staying there and chatting for a good half hour.

She wondered if her letter had even made it to Delvis. Perhaps it was true what Sonny Joe said. Perhaps Delvis never got mail. Perhaps the mailman was scared of him too or didn't have a key to unlock his box. But until her letter was returned, she would continue to wait and hope. What else did she have to wait and hope for?

She finished reading the book of Luke, turned the page, and entered the Gospel according to John. Her dress sighed in the swing's wind as she read about how the word became flesh, how Jesus turned water to wine, fed five thousand, healed the blind, and rose Lazarus from the dead. The sky darkened and thunder growled in the distance. She came to chapter thirteen and read how Jesus washed his disciples' feet and came to the Scripture that was scribed underneath the stained glass window in Sonny Joe's and Ceif's church. She remembered Ceif with his pitiful limp and bloody arm whispering, "If I then, the Lord and the Teacher, have washed your feet, ye also ought to wash one another's feet."

She clapped the Bible shut, hugged one of the porch columns, and looked down the street in search of the postman. The smell of cigarette smoke moved her attention from the street to where it breathed through the attic's broken window. She had never known Grandpa to smoke, but he had been acting stranger than his strange normal self. He had been working incessantly, more than usual. He worked as if there was no such thing as time, no such thing as night or day, no such thing as a body needing rest. He had stripped the house of all of its paint, replaced all its missing boards, and had fixed most of the leaks in the roof. He hadn't eaten much of the groceries, nor had he bothered to shave or shower, even though he had managed to get the water cut on. When he wasn't working a saw or pounding nails, he was in the attic making all sorts of racket, mumbling to himself and doing God knows what.

She turned her gaze back down the street, and spotted the postman standing two doors down, staring at the old Spivey House. He nervously slapped a letter against his palm, so focused on the challenge at hand that he didn't seem phased by the sudden onslaught of rain.

Gradle jumped the porch steps and ran to him. "You got mail for me?" she yelled through the rain.

The postman held the letter out. She took it from his shaky hand and ran back under the porch, through the door, and into her room. She plopped belly-down on her bed and smelled the letter. There were hints of earwax and body oil buried among a strong scent of cheap cologne. She studied the envelope and found fascination in Delvis's handwriting. Part was written in cursive, and part was written in print. Some of his letters were large and important, others were small and mere, and although there was no obvious pattern, his handwriting almost looked like code. He capitalized all of his Ns regardless of their place, and none of his lines were straight. Everything, even the cross of each *t* slanted down to the right as if the gravity of his black pen was too heavy to bear. Most fascinating of all was the manner in which he dotted the *i* in her last name Bird. Instead of a simple dot, he drew a realistic eye, detailed and precise, with eyelashes and irises and reflections of light on the pupil. As she kept staring at it, she could have sworn it winked.

She opened the envelope and pulled the letter out. It was written on pink paper, like some sort of valentine.

Dear GRaDle,

ThaNk You for YouR NiCE letteR. your A BEAutifuL PersoN. My dog RaiN dieD. I bury-id him iN the back yard aNd MAdE hIm a GRAVE CrOss. He's iN heaveN lickiN' JESUS I kNoW, but I'M STIll sad aND CRY every day STILL. GRadLe LET me Tell you I HAVE a cataract aNd DOUBLE back TROUBLE but they doN't get me DowN. You caN come see me ANYTIME. WheN yoU come HoNk THRee times so I kNow YoUr a True frieNd.

YoUrs Truly,
D-S Delvis MiLes The LoNe SiNger

She folded the letter into her bra and walked around the house to the backyard shed. She pulled the wooden door open, yanked a cotton string leading to a lightbulb, and as sudden as the light snapped on the brittle string broke and a swarm of mosquitoes fled to the light's warm glow.

She emptied water and wrigglers out of a washtub and carried it down the hall through the house, but she stopped and froze when she heard the most unusual sound coming from the attic flap.

††††

Leonard curled in his toes and laughed as Annalee ran her finger down the arc of his foot. They lay on the fainting couch, head to foot, their backs propped by water-stained pillows. The attic was sweltering hot. Leonard felt like a sopping rag; he had already stripped down to his underwear, but the downpour drumming the hawk moths to sleep had begun to make his sweat cool. He could lie like this forever, die just like this.

Annalee inhaled the stale cigarette they'd been trading back and forth and blew smoke from her mouth. The cigarette was from the same box of Chesterfields they had first discovered when they were young, hidden in a sack of love letters written to Annalee's mother, and penned by a man Annalee didn't know. He remembered finding them that day. There had been a thunderstorm much like the one now that helped drown out any sounds of mischief their parents would hear. They had smoked half the pack until Leonard got dizzy and vomited in a box of bone china while Annalee laughed at him and finished off the rest of hers. Although they shared the same blood, hers was always more immune than his, and as he lay on the fainting couch staring at her in perfect peace he believed she had even fought off death.

He pulled a tendril of moon vine through the collar of her dress and unleashed a stream of smoke that crept like a snake in the air.

"That tickles," she said, slapping his hand away and passing him the cigarette.

He sat up, took a drag, and clamped hold of her wrists as his fingers peeked through the cuffs of her black dress, hoping to explore what she kept hidden.

"I want to see the rest of you," he said. He handed her the cigarette and slicked back his hair.

"Why?" she asked, giving the cigarette a pull.

"I want to see your collarbone."

"Is that all?" she asked. She blew out a breath of ice-cold smoke that chilled the sweat in his hair.

"Do you have something else you want to show me?" he said, as he wormed the buttons at her neck through their tight little holes.

Her frock came loose from her bones, but in places it stuck to her skin. He lifted the cloth away, careful not to rip her scabs. When it detached there came blood, tiny beads of it that he dabbed with his finger and tasted to prove it was real.

Annalee pulled her dress off her shoulder and felt her collarbone. "It's still broken."

Leonard rubbed his palm across her bone like a slat of wood and kneaded the spot where it had snapped with his thumb.

"Remember when you dropped me?" Annalee asked.

"You had on a purple dress," he said, as his fingers filed down the splinters of her bone. "It had a rip in it from us sneaking out the window the night before. We were up here practicing the lift we were gonna showcase at Jimmy's that night." He pressed on her bone and hooked the broken pieces back together. "I threw you in the lift too hard and you went flying across the room." He dabbed spit on his finger and stroked the break. "When I got to you, your bone was sticking out and cobwebs were in your hair. I promised you I'd never drop you again, and you smiled back at me like it didn't even hurt. I remember." He sanded the bone with his calloused fingertips until it was smooth. "There. All fixed." He blew the dust from her bone, and a patch of new skin grew over what he had mended.

"I liked it the way it was," she said, smiling. She lifted her shoulder to look at the work he'd done, and her dress fell down to her waist.

A hawk moth escaped from the cave of her chest and Leonard jumped back and ducked. He didn't know what had frightened him most, the barreling monster of a moth or the ruin he was so afraid of finding by coming back here. He stared into her cavity and saw her desiccated skin, saw where rats had nibbled her ribs, and how the moonflower blossoms trapped inside her cage had rotted into a pool of stinking black slime. Annalee had not fought off death completely; she had just done a damn good job of covering it up.

His vision blurred and his head grew dizzy. He felt he would vomit but shook the stars out of his head and pulled himself together.

"I'm in need of more repair than you think," she said, starting to cover herself up.

He stopped her and stared through the hole of her heart at something that caught his eye. His fingers slid through her ribs and tweezed out from a tangle of green vine a piece of paper folded into a square. He unfolded the paper and slowly revealed a hand-drawn portrait of Annalee. Titled at the top in unusual letters were the words *Portrait of.* The artist's signature hid along the scalloped hem of her dress. Drawn in miniature, in the sadness of her eyes, was a reflection of perhaps the artist. The portrait must have been drawn during the same age as her death when most women were ripe with womanhood. But here on the page, Leonard could see her premature withering and grey.

"What killed you, Annalee?" he asked. He saw the fret in her eyes.

She snatched the paper from his hand, folded it up, and put it back in her cavity. She gathered her dress, buttoned it to her neck, and fled to the attic window where she stared out into the rain.

He walked up to her back and reached for her. The sound of feet climbing the attic's ladder made his hands freeze on her cold, stiff shoulders.

"Was that you laughing?" Gradle asked, poking her head through the attic flap.

He let go of Annalee, shook the last cigarette from the pack, lit it, and took a long drag.

Gradle appeared by his side and drew back a piece of his hair to unblock her view. Her eyes were blinding and blue.

"You know every cigarette you smoke takes seven minutes off your life?" she asked, as she swiped the cigarette out of his mouth. She parted the curtains and tossed it through the break in the window. "That man I wrote to wrote me back," she said, reached inside her dress, and showed him a letter. "His name's D-5 Delvis Miles The Lone Singer."

Annalee swiveled her head around and stared at the letter Gradle held. The air in the attic shifted, took on a new charge.

"I'm gonna go visit him. Apologize for throwing firecrackers at his house," she said. "Don't worry if I'm not home before dark." She folded the letter and put it back down her dress. "You got any comments?" She gave him some time to speak before she kissed his cheek and descended the ladder.

He relaxed and let out the breath he'd been holding onto. Smoke ran out of his nostrils and dissipated in Annalee's hair.

"What is it about her that scares you so?" Annalee asked, hooking the lace curtains back. She looked down on Gradle who appeared through the broken glass in a flash of flinching green.

Gradle threw a washtub in the Chrysler's backseat and slammed the car door like she was rushed and enraged. She sat in the driver's seat, placed her hands on the wheel, and bowed her head. She looked just like Veela. Just like the day she tried to run away.

Leonard left Annalee at the window, hurried down the ladder, and ran out to the porch.

"Where you think you're going?" he said, as he marched down the steps into the rain.

"Do you have dementia or something?" Gradle cut into him

with eyes full of tears, eyes that dared him to look at her.

No matter how hard he tried not to, he couldn't help but see Veela, to see her and her teary eyes sitting behind the Chrysler's wheel on what should have been one of the most special days of a girl's life. He remembered that day and heard the thread passing through the chiffon as he finished up the hem of her green prom dress, the one he'd cut patterns out of newspaper to make, the one he'd designed especially for her. It was Veela's first date, he was nervous as a housefly, and a portion of the hem ended up a bit crooked because of it. Maybe Dot would have done a better job, but she'd been out in the yard all day getting drunk.

"Veela," Dot called from the front door. "Your little date's here."

Leonard helped Veela with her dress, zipped up the back, and kissed the top of her head as butterflies hatched in his stomach. He escorted her to the door and found Dot, holding her drink and using the boy's shoulder to keep her balance.

Dot's mouth dropped when she saw Veela walk into the room. "Who in the world did your hair?" she laughed. She pulled Veela's ponytail like it was a tail of a dog.

"Daddy did it," she said.

"Aren't you too old for that?" Dot asked.

The boy walked past Dot and tried to pin the purple orchid corsage on Veela's dress, but Dot snatched the flower out of his hand and gave him her drink.

"Your Daddy never takes me on dates," Dot said, poking Veela with the pin as she tried to fasten the corsage.

"I can do it, Mama," Veela said. She reached for the flower, and Dot slapped her cheek. She knocked her glasses off, and they slid across the floor.

"Can't you see I'm trying to help you?" she said, throwing the flower in Veela's face.

"I don't need your help," Veela said. "Wait!" She yelled after her date, who was already out of the door, rushing back to his car. The boy didn't stop. He got into his car, put it in reverse, and skidded out of the driveway.

Veela ran to her room, locked the door, and crawled out of the window.

Leonard saw her from the window streak across the side yard and climb into the Chrysler's driver seat. He ran through the house, jumped the backporch steps, and caught her in the drive.

"Where you think you're going?" he asked, leaning his head in the window.

"Away from here," Veela said, put the keys in the ignition, and over-cranked the car.

"You wanna go on a date?" he said, as he wiped her tears with his thumb.

"You wanna go fishing?" she asked.

Leonard grabbed his camera, loaded the car with fishing poles, and let her drive down highway 23, over Griffin Ferry's Bridge, and down the dirt roads that led to the sugar white banks of the Ohooppee River. He made her pull over once on the way so he could pick wildflowers for her new corsage.

They drank cold Coca-Colas, strung red and yellow-breasted bream on a string, and stopped a man in a canoe to take their picture. They fished until the whippoorwills started up and twilight set in. Leonard packed up the car with the fish and poles and leaned against the hood as he watched Veela sitting alone on the sand looking up at the stars. He turned on the Chrysler's radio, took Veela in his arms, and danced with her barefooted on the river's barking sand. And as he spun her under a glitter of stars, she rested her head on his shoulder and made him believe it was the most special night of her life.

Leonard came to when lightning cracked near his ear. Gradle stared at him with her broken blue eyes like he was the one who broke them. He leaned in the driver's window and wiped her tears away with his thumb.

She turned the ignition and threw the car in reverse. "I'll see you later."

She backed out of the drive, rammed the Chrysler's rear end into a crepe myrtle, and shook its purple flowers down like confetti. "And go put on some clothes!" she hollered out of the window.

The tires squealed from burning up rubber. He ran after her, but she locked the car in drive, swerved down the road, and sent flowers flying off the hood.

He stood in the road and let the rain beat him down as he watched the purple wounded flowers float past. He thought about Veela, stuck his index finger in his ear, and fished around for leftover river sand.

✝✝✝

Gradle turned onto the dirt road leading to Delvis's house when the rain stopped. The Chrysler's wheels couldn't find their grip and fishtailed in the mud. She rolled down the windows to dry out her tears and get a whiff of the glowing green tobacco fields. She rested her bare foot out the window and wondered how long the grasshopper that landed on her toe would hold on.

She rounded a bend and came head to head with Sonny Joe's growling silver truck. She slammed on the brakes. The Chrysler's hind end whipped forward and T-boned the truck. She slid across the seat, and the grasshopper landed in the bloodstain Sonny Joe had given to her dress.

Sonny Joe revved his engine, threw the truck in reverse, and spun mud all over the Chrysler's windshield. He drove the truck up to Gradle's window. Ceif tipped his hat her way as Sonny Joe took a swig from his brown paper sack and chased it down with cigarette smoke. His glassy and bloodshot eyes stared at her with same kind of hurt they had after she pushed him off of her in the alley.

"You ruined my fucking dress!" she yelled at him and showed him the stain.

"Were you a virgin?" Smoke slithered out of his half-cocked smile.

"Would that make it easier on you?" she asked.

"It was pretty easy," he said. He lit a firecracker with his cigarette and tossed it through her window.

Flaming shrapnel exploded in the floorboard around her feet. She hopped out of the car and rushed toward Sonny Joe. He gunned the truck and slung bullets of mud across her face. "Asshole!" she yelled, grabbed a handful of mud, and threw it at his tailgate.

She walked around the car to inspect the damage. A dent the size of a watermelon gouged the passenger's door. She spat on her hand and tried to rub away the silver spray paint from Sonny Joe's truck, but it wouldn't come off. She wondered what Grandpa would say about it, how long it would take for him to notice. Since it was something she had done, perhaps he would never notice.

She climbed back into the car and straightened it on the road. It had quit raining, but the sky continued to growl and a ring of buzzards soared in thermals high above the pines. She propped her foot in the window and drove real slow until she reached Delvis's house.

Rocks popped under the tires, and she turned off the car without putting it in park. Everything was quiet except for the sound of electricity running through the insects. She pulled her glasses down her nose and stared at the firecracker shreds littering Delvis's porch. She grabbed the washtub from the backseat and started toward his steps.

een a real dragon fly?" Delvis asked. He twisted his
binkie.

d a piece of skin from her toe. "A real dragon?"
them that breathes fires. I seen 'em all the time.
see. They kinda skittish. And they don't come out
no moon and no stars 'cause they real shy and
dy takin' pictures of them or studyin' them 'cept
one in the universe that's ever seen 'em 'cause I got
abilities and laser vision in my eyes." He pinched
de open, scanned the yard with it, and then shut it
aggin'. Just the facts. And around 'bout this time
' their scales. They on different schedules than
mals. I go up to the dump where they nose around
nd I collect the scales 'cause I can get a good price
regions of the state. In fact," he said, holding up
"one flying dragon scale can get me a steak dinner
er if I had a good mind to eat up there."
ou could show me?"
back, and with them came his head skin, shiny
ed from his chair, and his eyes looked like they
paced his porch while he kept watch of his front

de to get 'em. I'll git 'em, but you cain't come
ome through here the other day and turned my
I ain't been able to clean it 'cause I got double
me," he said, sucked in his gut, and slid through

he porch and heard him meddling in his house.
shed on the floor, and in an instant, Delvis slid
or with a wooden box in his hand.

knees of his pants, sat down on the metal chair,

Delvis exploded through the door wearing plaid flannel pajamas and a ratty hat with a brim too short to shadow his rabid eyes. He reached down his side and pulled a pistol from a holster. The metal barrel flashed like a star.

"Damn outlaws makin' my life a livin' hell!" he yelled. He shut his eye and pointed the gun at Gradle.

She dropped the washtub, sprinted back to the car, and tripped over a piece of barbed wire rolled out in her path. Her face hit the dirt and left the imprint of her glasses in the mud.

"I'm your friend!" she yelled over her shoulder. "I wrote you a letter!"

Delvis snapped the cylinder open, thumbed it into a spin, and snapped it back shut.

She rushed to the car, flung the door open, and honked the horn three times. "I'm a real true friend!" she yelled. She honked the horn three more times.

Delvis cocked his head and squinted his eyes. His pistol lowered, and he disappeared through the crack in the door, fast like a skink.

She caught her breath, and three more times she honked the horn.

The door of Delvis's shack creaked open, and he appeared as a transformed man. He wore a white cowboy hat, perfect around the edges, a blue polyester suit, and a pair of worn-out K-Swiss sneakers with fluorescent green laces. In place of the pistol, he held the neck of a guitar. He tipped the rain out of a rusted metal chair, sat down, and tuned his instrument.

Gradle ripped a strand of mud-caked hair from her cheek and watched the man clear his throat and sing, "You Are My Sunshine." She eased toward him, unsure if she should keep moving his way or turn back to the car and blow the horn three more times for good measure.

She climbed the first porch step and crept up the second one, smoothed her dress and sat below his feet. He didn't seem crazy at all. There was something real sweet and real humble about him that made her feel safe.

Delvis played the song two times through. He stopped when he hit the high note of "happy" and cleared his throat. "'Cuse me," he said. He spat off the porch. "Got a frog in my throat. Went down there last month and ain't been able to get him out." He propped his guitar against his chair. "That's the first song I learnt to play. Learnt it on a one string fiddle." He cleared his throat again. "'Cuse me. That frog come back," he said. He spat off the porch again. "Stuff they writin' these days ain't fittin' to sing. Sounds like a bunch of racket."

"I'm D-5 Delvis Miles The Lone Singer." He held out his hand for her to shake.

Gradle stared at his huge hand and the fake gold ring that adorned his pinkie and stained it copper-green. There was something familiar about him. She felt like she had seen his eyes and the dimple in his smile a million times. He looked like he was in his sixties but the K-Swiss sneakers and his scent of too-strong cologne made him seem younger.

"My name's Gradle Bird," she said, as she shook his hand. "I'm sorry about your dog."

"Pleased to meet you," he said, lifting his hat. His hair was skinned dangerously close to the scalp, and blood dried in a razor nick above his right ear.

"D-5's my code name. Ain't nobody been able to break the code since I invented it. The FBI, the GBI, the police, and the county sheriff. Ain't none of 'em been able to break it. It's my special code. Solid, clean, impenetrable code. And if somebody falls into some luck and figures it out, I got it copyrighted up there in the Library of Congress, Washington, D.C. So if they do break it, ain't nobody can ever copy it."

"What do you want
sweat from her upper li

"Delvis. Real true f

"Why do you need

He pinched up th
"People got all kinds c
tryin' to kill me, 'cau
jokin', but I ain't." He
from California, Teni
me. Got some in Pai
'em the same messag
price on me seven n
in his mouth. "Loo
all over his porch.
me. But they in the
read anything in tl
firepopper. I taugh
everything in the r

"They think tl

"It ain't funny
darting past.

"You see tha
asked.

"That's not a

"They spyir
pointing to the
coral geranium
think they call '

"Because tl

"How'd yo

"*Strange St*

"You ever s
ring around his
Gradle pick
"Yes, one o
But they hard to
unless there ain'
don't want nobc
me. I'm the only
special sneakin' u
one of his lids wi
closed. "I ain't bi
they start sheddii
most sheddin' anii
for food at night a
for them in variou
his pointer finger,
at the Western Ste

"You got any y

His ears drew
and taut. He jump
had caught fire. He
door.

"I hafta go ins
inside. A tornado c
house upside down
back trouble. 'Cuse
the door.

She waited on t
Something heavy cr
back through the do

He pinched the l

and opened the box. A breeze stirred the Coca-Cola whirligig into a spin. In the box, mixed with fingernail clippings, was a collection of vibrant colored sequins.

He picked a green sequin, rolled it between the tip of his thumb and pointer, and squinted one eye shut while the other studied what glimmered between his grip. "Like I said, this one could get me a steak dinner at the Western Steer if I had a good mind to go up there and eat." He shoved the box under Gradle's nose. "Pick out your favorite color."

Gradle pressed a green sequin into the tip of her finger, and he violently closed the box shut.

"I better go hide these back." He stood and scouted his junked-up yard and stared the stand of pine up and down. "If anybody finds out I got flying dragon scales, them outlaws liable to raise their bounty price on me and get me killed. Liable to kill you, too." He turned and knelt down in her face. "Me and you's connected now."

He slid through the door once more and was back on the porch before Gradle could swallow. Thunder rumbled in the east and rain broke through the mass of clouds sending down drops that pelted the tin roof like rocks.

"Gradle," he raised his voice over the rain, "there's some things you need to know 'bout me." He wiggled in his chair. "I'm a wanted man. People all over the universe want me dead."

"Why do they want you dead?" she asked, moving her feet out of the rain.

"They just jealous," Delvis snapped. "You see, I'm famous in many areas. Guitar pickin', singin', songwritin', and art. I ain't braggin'. Just the facts. I got twenty-one contracts from music firms, and I ain't hired none of 'em. I can do love, gospel, country-western, rock 'n roll, or mixed my style of rock 'n roll. My type of rock 'n roll is diff'rent. I have my own original songs, invented my own original style, and they all want my stuff, but I got to copyright them in the Library of Congress, Washington, D.C., before I hire any of 'em. You gotta protect yourself 'cause they's a lot of crooks out there."

Gradle side-cocked her head, and as she tightened her ponytail, her eyes snared a small wooden cross with a lei of flowers out beyond the vegetable garden.

She stood up and grabbed Delvis by the arm. "Can I wash your feet?"

He stared into her eyes but only for a flash. He stared down at his grimy fingernails and tried to hide them in his palms. "They stinkin' bad?" he asked.

"No," she said. "I want you to forgive me for making you shoot your dog."

"I done forgave you," he said, clearing his throat.

"So I can forgive myself."

"You cain't," he said, sat down in his chair, and wrung his hands. "I ain't got no runnin' water." He bowed his head and stared at his feet. "But I'm gettin' some next week. Runnin' water and some electricity. I been life savin' for it."

Gradle walked into the rain and turned over the washtub she had dropped in his yard. She stood in the lightning until the tub grew sufficiently full. She set the tub beside Delvis's feet and unlaced his sneakers. His knees began to bounce, and his hands trembled as he tried to figure out what to do with them.

She grabbed Delvis's hands and placed them atop his knees. "I'm not gonna hurt you," she said, as she gently rolled off his socks. She lifted his feet by the heels, placed them one by one in the tub, and sprinkled them with water. She scrubbed the black off his soles, and in between his toes, and after she finished, she dried them off with the skirt of her dress.

Delvis bent down and stared into her eyes. He dipped his hand in the water and cradled her chin. She jumped back, startled by his touch, and knocked her head against the porch rail.

"I ain't gonna hurt you either," he said, and with his thumb he cleaned off the mud Sonny Joe had slung on her cheek.

CHAPTER EIGHT

LEONARD COVERED HIS face to defend the sun as it ripped through the living room drapes like a cleaver of flames. His mouth drooped from the weight of drool, and two feet in front of the wingback where he sat, the television sizzled in a rapid boil. He didn't know what day it was. All he knew was that it had been a while since he'd seen light.

"You're stinking up the house," Gradle said, swarmed through the living room, and split a pair of drapes.

He shriveled up from the sudden rush of sun, raked his hand down his face, and clutched onto what had become beard.

"You got any pressure sores yet?" she asked, splitting another pair of drapes.

He curled into a cannonball.

She grabbed him by the hair and shoved him down the hall, through the front door where she had a chair set out for him on the porch. A green anole skittered across the rail, froze, and fanned his ruby throat. A Schick disposable, scissors, a pail, and a bottle of White Rain set out like surgeon's tools blocked the lizard's way. The lizard barrel-rolled around the rail, leaped into the moon vine, and disappeared into its green.

Gradle shoved him down in the chair. "You need to clean up." She poured the pail of water over his head and soaked his clothes.

He sucked in his breath and let it go, feeling electrified and alive.

She tilted his head back, dolloped his hair with White Rain, and massaged her fingers deep into his brain. He closed his eyes and let her work.

"How'd that dent get in the car?" he asked.

"I wrecked it on my way to Delvis's house."

"I guess I ought to teach you to drive."

"I'm already pretty good at it."

"I can tell," he said as suds tingled his scalp. "Tell me about this D-5 Delvis Miles The Lone Singer character."

"What you want to know?"

"Where'd he come up with that name?"

"It's code," she said, scratching his head like a dog.

"What does the code mean?" he asked. He opened up one of his eyes to take stock of where she was.

"Nobody knows. Not the FBI, the GBI, or the sheriff," she said, rinsed the shampoo out of his hair, and began to rake it flat with the comb.

"D is the first letter in his first name Delvis. Five is the number of letters in his last name. D-5 Delvis Miles The Lone Singer."

"You're talkative today," she said, grabbing the scissors.

"You must be holding your mouth right," he closed his open eye shut. "Don't take too much off."

"I know." She positioned the scissors at his jaw and snipped off a half-circle of hair.

"What about The Lone Singer part? What's that about?"

"He's a musician. And I suppose he's lonely."

"Were you able to apologize for throwing firepoppers at his house?"

"I washed his feet," she said. She lathered his face with shampoo, scraped the razor down his face, and flicked the hair off the blade.

"What'd you do that for?" he asked. He sensed her freeze, and for a while there was no movement, no sound.

He opened his eyes and found her staring at the postman who was stopped a ways down in the middle of the sidewalk, staring frightfully back. She dropped the razor, jumped the porch steps, and ran out to meet him. He handed her a package, and she ran back, sat on the porch swing, and tore it open.

Leonard picked up the razor and walked her way. "Are you gonna finish?" he asked, but all of her attention was dedicated to a letter written by the unmistakable hand of D-5 Delvis Miles The Lone Singer.

His thumb and pointer made an upside-down U above his lip, and he shaved around it, cutting out his mustache, as he watched her transport into a different world, one of which he was clearly no part.

He splashed water on his face, and let it air-dry as he walked back into the house and pulled the attic flap down. He climbed the ladder and found Annalee staring out of the window. She was in the same spot he'd left her however many days ago it had been since he'd found her hidden portrait and they'd gotten into a tiff. She had always been so dramatic, lived her life in a display of symbols and signs. Her blatant silence and disregard proved to him nothing had changed since her death.

"Cat got your tongue?" Leonard asked, as he hugged around her back. "I want to take you on a date," he whispered against her neck.

"You'll look peculiar, Leonard. Going out with an imaginary friend."

He removed her hands crossed over her heart and turned her from the window. "I'm already peculiar."

"I have nothing to wear," she said, turning back to the window.

Leonard opened the wardrobe and catalogued the brittle clothes, boas, and feather-pricked hats he and Annalee played dress-up with when they were young. He dusted mold from a plaid madras suit, changed into the pants, and fastened them with suspenders. He slipped the blazer over his sweaty undertank and topped his head with a straw, red-banded fedora. He stared in the wardrobe's mirror and shook his shoulders to settle the suit. With his clean cut and shave, he had to admit he looked pretty spiff. He spat on his loafers, shined them with his thumb, and flipped their pennies after he was done.

He shopped through the wardrobe for Annalee and stopped on a white dress. He unhooked its hanger and pulled out the eyelet dress she wore that rainy summer day they made love. He drowned his face in its fabric and drew in a whiff. After closeted all those years, it still smelled like them.

"Wear this," he said, and hung the dress on a nail beside her.

Annalee turned from the window and looked at the dress. "I'm too old for that," she said, turning her back to him again.

"I'm sure you'll look beautiful in it," he said, as he gathered quilts from the hopechest and knotted them together end on end.

"Look at me." She whipped around and yanked out a patch of her hair. "Are you blind?" she said. She threw her hair at his face.

He grabbed her by the shoulders and shoved her in front of the wardrobe's mirror. "Look at yourself," he said.

"I'm dead, Leonard."

"There's still life in you," he shook her shoulders.

"How do you know you're not just seeing things?" she asked.

Leonard tore open her frock, and it puddled in a pool of black at her feet. He led her out of it and slid the white eyelet dress up her legs. He kissed her wrists and threaded them through the sleeves, pinched her rear, and zipped her up. He clipped a moonflower with his fingernails and fastened it to the right of her heart.

He squared her in the mirror and watched the bald spot where she had ripped out her hair disappear under shiny thick locks of new growth.

"Maybe I am," he said, and he threw the knotted quilt ladder out of the window for them to escape.

CHAPTER NINE

GRADLE SWUNG ON the porch swing with Delvis's package in her lap and her nose deep in the letter he had written. In the package, there were three envelopes, numbered in sequence. When she had opened *envelope #1*, sequins in a variety of colors fell out like confetti in her lap. She read the contents of *envelope #1* for the third time through.

HellO GRaDle,

THaNK you for washiNg my feet. THEY sqeAK
AND CLeaN. I FORGave you LoNg back. KNOW
your forgiveN cause YOU are a REAL TRUe frieND.

I HopE I didN't SCARE yoU or MaKE YoU mad
Or NoTHINg. SOMe peoplES scARed Of ME buT

That's because THEy aiN'T real TRUE frIENDs. TheM OUTlaWS hadN't BeeN BY here Lately. SO they MuST have hEARd About MY pistol Skills.

ENclosed is a CAsSETTE tape of my OWN origiNal soNgs. ©COPYRIGHTED. BEFORE YOU PLAY THE TAPES REVERSE THEM so the taPes woNt BE LOOSE & taNgle up OK. I WOULD like your OPINIoN ABOUT THEM. GOOD or Bad. WONT mAke me mad if you DONT like them. I HAD My picTUre made for You. I would aPPreciate a PICture of you by yourself. I DO NOT SHOW off PICTURES. I GUARANtee I will treat your PICture with 100% RESPECT.

GRaDk I had a dream last Night ME aNd YOU was walkiNg iN saNdy road = but I woke up before the dreaM. ENDED. GRAdle I WANT NEVER forget about you. YOU IS a Nice persoN: I wish you would COME by to see me. I have a uNbelievable TRUE story of HAPPeNINGS. A REAl shocker. ITS true.

By by ♥ a REAl TRUE frieNd.

Yours TRULy,

D-S Delvis MiLes The LoNe 5iNger

POST SCRIPT: SiNCe You LiKE them FLYiNg DrAgoN SCalES so MuCH. I SENt SOMe mORE. EvERy COLor theRE is. BUT sHHHHH. DoN'T tell Nobody. YOU LIAble to Get KILLED for em. THIS Is miNe aNd yours sECRET.

She read the letter again and studied the realistic eyes that dotted every *i* and the flowers, hearts, and butterflies he had drawn along the paper's border. It must have taken him hours to write the letter and produce its accompanying art, and it made her feel special that he would invest this kind of time in her. She moved on to *envelope #2.* On its front it read:

A PiCTure Of. ME. D-S Delvis MiLes The LoNe 5iNger. RuRal RouTe I Box S6-B. JaNesboro, GA 30431. PICTURE eNclosed.

She turned the envelope over, and on the flap, written in tiny letters, were the words: *JusT a ReaL TrUe FrieNd.* Under the words, he had drawn a heart with a cursive letter *L* in the middle of it. She opened the flap and retrieved a Polaroid of Delvis standing on his front porch in his white cowboy hat, clean and shiny and posing with his guitar. His ears stuck out from his hat, and his eyes were soft and blue. He looked humble and proud.

She wondered how he had taken the photo, what kind of rig he must have made to capture his moment. She suspected he had no friends to take it on his behalf, that she was his only friend.

She placed the Polaroid in her lap and read the front of *envelope #3:*

ITS yoURS TO keEP.
MAKE a COPIE
Of this Tape
AND p.s. KEEp This ~~TapE. TIL I CoME FOR it.~~
NO ~~returN THIS~~
KEEP IT ITS YOURS
Tape please thaNks D-S T.L.S.

She pulled a black cassette tape from the envelope.

ALL rights © rEServed for D-S Delvis MiLes The LoNe SiNger, libRary of cONgreSs WASHINGTON, D.C.

Thunder rumbled behind a dense pleat of clouds. The sky darkened, gesturing rain and signaling the moon vine to tremor with bloom. Preoccupied with Delvis's letter, she didn't hear him coming, nor did she hear him hobble up the porch steps until Ceif pushed a bundle of swamp lilies under her nose.

She folded Delvis's letter and placed it by her side. Her eyes rolled over Ceif. His Bible rested in the crook of his arm, and he leaned on his cane, placing favor on his right leg. His clothes were sopping wet and three red blisters trimmed the leather of his worn-out shoes.

"Did you walk here?" she asked, as she smelled the lilies.

"I don't have a car. And it'd be a sin to steal Sonny Joe's."

"You walked all this way to bring me flowers?"

"And apologize for the other day." His voice cracked, and he smiled an uncertain smile, then slapped and scratched his wrist. "Watch out, that moss might have chiggers in it," he said, pointing to the bundle of swamp lilies and the wet moss he'd wrapped them in to prolong their zeal.

"Did you walk to Delvis's house, bring him some flowers too?" she asked.

"Bringing a man flowers wouldn't go over too well," he said. He pulled a cigarette from his pocket and lit the end.

A loud rumble came from down the street and drew their attention its way. At the stop sign, Sonny Joe sat in his truck. His tailpipe knocked and rock music blared out through the rolled-down window. He peeled out. His tires squealed and blew smoke, and the silver Chevy came down the wrong side of the road toward them, hunting like a hammerhead shark.

Sonny Joe ran his truck sideways into the yard. "Hey faggot!" he yelled out over the cat-screaming voice of Axl Rose blaring from the jam box.

Gradle shot from the swing and stood at the edge of the porch. Her toes curled over the ledge. "Hey faggot!" she yelled back at Sonny Joe.

Sonny Joe took a swig from his brown paper sack and grinned. "I wasn't talking to you," he said. He slammed the truck's door and climbed the porch steps slow. The rain didn't hinder his swagger, but rather over-accentuated his smoothness. His eyes stayed fixed on her, and once he got within sniffing distance, he stopped and leaned into her ear.

"You smell good," he said. His booze-breath was hot and humid.

"You oughta be ashamed of yourself."

"For telling a girl I like her perfume?" he asked. He held out his hand for Ceif to give it skin.

"For throwing firecrackers at Delvis's house. What's he done to you?"

"Other than fascinate the hell out of me, not much," he said. "Appears you find him fascinating, too."

"I don't provoke him."

"I'm sure you do," he said. He sat down on the swing with his legs spread wide and picked up the letter. He snapped at Ceif to give him a drag, and as he smoked Ceif's cigarette down to a pinch he read the words Delvis had put on the page. "Sounds like he finds you fascinating, too." He held the letter out for Gradle, but as her hand reached for it he snatched it away and let it fall to the ground.

She bent to pick up the letter, and Sonny Joe stepped on it with his shoe, causing her to rip the letter in two.

Ceif whipped the back of Sonny Joe's calf with his cane. "Don't be yourself today," he said, as Gradle placed the ripped letter inside its envelope.

"Where you been dick-breath?" Sonny Joe asked. "You hauled-ass at sunrise, and I ain't seen you since."

"He brought me flowers," she said. "Walked all this way to apologize for the other day."

"I didn't realize that needed an apology." He cut his eyes at Ceif, as if questioning his loyalty. "Don't you know when somebody's flirting with you, Gradle Bird?" he asked.

"No," she said.

He took a swig from the brown paper sack and passed it to Gradle.

She took it, turned it up, and passed it back.

Sonny Joe grinned and tossed the cigarette from the porch. "You missed the fight," he said, and slapped Ceif's ribs. "Had to set up, tear down, and collect the cabbage without you." He pulled out a roll of money from his pocket and fanned it under Ceif's nose. "Fifty-two bucks. Enough for us to get drunk off well drinks at Jimmy's and dominate the jukebox."

"Who won?" Ceif asked, as he tapped tobacco in the crease of a rolling paper.

"Same fish she should have bet on last week," he said. "We're still going to Jimmy's, right?"

Ceif licked the paper, rolled the cigarette, and twisted its ends. "Why would we break tradition? You wanna go to Jimmy's with us tonight?" he asked Gradle, tipping his hat.

She stared out into the yard at the jam box sitting in the back window of Sonny Joe's truck. "Can I play this?" She held up the cassette tape Delvis had made.

"You can play anything you want," Sonny Joe said. He nearly jumped out of his skin when he saw Grandpa scaling down the house with a rope of quilts.

Grandpa landed in the bushes and dusted off a pair of plaid pants. He was the most handsome she had ever seen. He was dressed in a suit and hat, and his eyes were almost as shiny as the pennies sparkling in his loafers. He bent his elbow and held it out for someone to take hold and darted from the bushes into the rain. He opened the Chrysler's passenger's side door and held out his hand, as if helping someone inside. He circled around the car to the driver's side, tipped his hat at Sonny Joe and Ceif, and started the engine.

"What in the hell ails him?" Sonny Joe asked.

Gradle chased the Chrysler into the street as far as she could and stared through the rear window at the back of Grandpa's head. His body leaned toward the passenger's side, as if drawn there by the gravity of romance. She didn't know what in the hell ailed him either, but whatever it was, it made him happy.

†††

Cigarette smoke, metal music, and the scent of sugar-loaded booze filled the truck's cab with an air of cool as Sonny Joe cruised the town's main drag like it had his name on it. Gradle sat between the two boys, nestling two bags of blue Crowntail bettas in her lap. One was the victor of the fight earlier that day, and the other was the next victim of the fight Sonny Joe had planned for the evening. Ceif shook out tobacco in a Zig-Zag resting on his Bible and rolled it into another cigarette while Sonny Joe took the occasional swig of Southern Comfort and rewound the Guns 'N Roses cassette to his favorite song, "Mr. Brownstone." The music thundered out loud, so loud Gradle's attempt at suggesting Delvis's cassette was swallowed up by the thundering drumbeat.

"Y'all hungry?" Sonny Joe asked. He swerved across the road as the cigarette hanging from his bottom lip held on. He made a left at a yellow neon sign with letters spelling out: THE WESTERN STEER. "Jimmy's won't be good and wild for a few more hours."

Gradle felt the sweaty heat steaming through Sonny Joe's palm as he placed it on the high part of her thigh. "Me and you are gonna make up tonight," he said. He ran his other hand through his bleached blonde hair and released the scent of grease, fish, and the wooden church pew where he slept, and somewhere weaved between all of this was the leftover scent of her.

Sonny Joe's hand pressed down harder on her thigh. "Ceif," he said, "when's the last time you ate?"

"Been a while," Ceif said, looking out of the passenger window.

"You looking a little poor over there," Sonny Joe said. "He'd starve to death if it wasn't for me."

"I'm the richest boy on earth," Ceif said. He held Gradle's hand and drew her attention to a cluster of swallowtails acrobating through the sky as if they were feeding on raindrops.

"Here's your cut, even though you stood me up today," Sonny Joe said. He reached in front of Gradle and tapped a roll of dollar bills down Ceif's breast pocket, and when his hand came back, he tugged her hand away from the soft pocket of Ceif's palm. "Thou shalt not steal," he said, throwing Ceif a stern eye.

Sonny Joe parked the truck in the lot of THE WESTERN STEER, took Gradle's hand, and assisted her to the ground.

"You stay here," he told Ceif. "Watch over the fish."

He led Gradle through the steak diner's doors where they were met by a fireheaded waitress who seemed put out for having to extinguish her cigarette until her eyes snagged the bright color of Sonny Joe's tattoo. She hiked her tits high in her bra and folded a stick of gum on her tongue.

"Who's she?" the woman, who must have been a decade older, asked Sonny Joe.

"She's new in town. We'll take three specials. One to-go," he said, led Gradle through the dining room, pulled out her chair, and seated her at table in the back corner even though there was a sign at the front that said *Please Wait to be Seated.*

Gradle situated her dress, saw the bloodstain, and tried to hide it with a fold of chiffon that wasn't tainted. She felt out of place as she looked over the dining hall, its dark walls, cheap chandeliers, tables of regulars and transient highway traffic, colored-glass votives, and plastic orange trays that served meat, potatoes, and a choice of vegetable. It was the first time she had ever eaten in a restaurant.

Sonny Joe lit the tip of his cigarette with the candle on the table. He reached under and billowed her dress, exposing the bloodstain she had tried to hide. "I'm sorry I ruined your dress," he said. His eyes were truehearted and hurt. "What's with this dress anyway? Why do you wear it all the time?"

"It's got sentimental value," Gradle said.

"You don't strike me as the sentimental type," Sonny Joe said.

"I'm sorry if I hurt you," she said.

"I don't know what hurt is, Gradle Bird," he said, leaned back, and blew grey mist from his mouth.

"Is that why you hurt everybody?"

A steak dinner tray skidded across the table and stopped sideways in front of him. The waitress smacked her gum as she stared at Gradle and balanced a tray high above her shoulder. Gently, she placed it perfectly in front of Gradle, as perfect as the woman had re-painted her lips with bright red lipstick. "I can see why he likes you," she said, and went on about her other business.

Gradle stared down at her steaming food with one thought in her head—Delvis Miles telling her that one flying dragon scale could get him a steak dinner at THE WESTERN STEER if he had a good mind to go eat up there.

"You gonna eat?" Sonny Joe asked. His teeth scraped a piece of steak from his fork.

"I'm not that hungry," she said, even though hot saliva ran down the walls of her mouth, even though she found the food desirable, even though she had lived off SpaghettiOs and peanut butter and jelly sandwiches for as long as she could remember.

"You can box it up to-go," he said. He snapped his fingers at the waitress. "A box and the check. And the to-go plate," he told her, dismissing her as fast as she was summoned.

After the waitress came back, Gradle transferred her steak dinner into the box, and Sonny Joe led her to the front to pay.

"Sixteen and a tip," the waitress said. She stared at him and popped her gum.

Sonny Joe counted out sixteen bills from the wad in his pocket, counted them out real slow, one by one. When he got to sixteen, he stopped.

"That was some real shitty service, Marcy," he said.

"Asshole," the woman said, as her teary eyes tracked Sonny Joe through the door.

"I thought you did a great job," Gradle told the woman.

"He's gonna hurt you," the waitress said, as Gradle followed Sonny Joe out into the rain.

Sonny Joe helped her into the cab. He held her box of food as she slid next to Ceif who was blessing the steak dinner Sonny Joe had ordered him to-go. Ceif said, "Amen," and scarfed down the food as if he was starved.

"Fish alright?" Sonny Joe held up the bags of fish.

"Didn't say a word," Ceif said, with the last piece of string bean hanging out of his mouth.

Sonny Joe placed the bags of fish in Gradle's lap, lit a cigarette, and put the truck in drive.

"Can we listen to this now?" she asked, pulling Delvis's cassette from her bra.

Sonny Joe took the cassette and inspected the writing on each side. "We need to take the dirt roads and get high to listen to this."

He sped down the town's main drag and when they passed the city limits, he threw an empty liquor bottle at the sign. Wind whistled through the bottle's mouth and the sign received another dent. He drove miles down the highway and turned off on a dirt road that split a field of blooming green tobacco. The rain slowed to a soft drizzle, and the moon rose low over the fields, round and full. Its light seeped through a thin gauze of cloud. When the tobacco fields turned to woods, he parked the truck.

"Roll one up, Ceif," he said, as he broke the seal of a half-pint of Southern Comfort.

Ceif reached into his pocket and pulled out a plastic bag of weed and a pack of empty Zig-Zags. He searched his other pockets, the space around him, and he opened the glove box and searched it, too. "I'm out of papers," he said.

"Are you fucking serious?" Sonny Joe asked. "I ain't riding back into town." He snatched Ceif's Bible from his lap. He opened the Bible and tore out one of its pages.

"You mother fucker," Ceif said. "That's my Bible."

He threw the Bible back at Ceif. "From the beginning," he said, handing Ceif a torn out page from Genesis. "Roll it up, Ceif."

Ceif pinched the marijuana into tiny pieces on the face of his Bible and rolled it into the torn out page. When he was done, Sonny Joe reached for the joint, but Ceif lit it and inhaled it first. "For dust thou art, and to dust shalt thou return," he said, passing the joint to Sonny Joe.

Sonny Joe smiled and took a rip from the joint. "For dust thou art, and to dust shalt thou return," he said, passing the joint to Gradle.

She took the joint from Sonny Joe and sucked in as hard as she could. Smoke burned down her throat, and she could feel it expand in her lungs. She held her breath and could feel their eyes on her. She passed the joint to Ceif and said, "For dust thou art, and to dust shalt thou return." A thick plume of smoke hurled from her mouth and was followed by a series of violent, never- ending coughs that made her eyes feel raw.

"If you don't cough, you don't get off," Sonny Joe said, as Ceif exhaled a purr of smoke and blew out small little rings with his small little mouth. He took the joint from Ceif and inhaled. "You may be new to most things, but seems you get them right the first time," he said. He let smoke creep from his mouth, and snatched it back quick as he handed the joint to her. He rested his arm atop the bench seat, and his fingertips grazed her shoulders and sent a foreign awareness through her body that collected as wet heat between her legs.

She took a drag and stared at him, wondering what it would be like to be with him again. She looked over at Ceif and wondered what it would be like to be with him.

Sonny Joe cranked the truck and pulled out of the woods. They idled down the quiet dirt road. Veiled moonlight waxed the hood. Honeysuckle out-smelled the rain. Gradle felt her body grow gradually hazed, relaxed. Her muscles warmed and melted over her bones, and the blood traveling through her veins carried a cold, ticklish buzz.

"You stoned yet?" Sonny Joe asked.

"It feels like bees," she said. "My ears are breathing." She listened to the amplified sounds of rocks popping under the tires, grasshopper wings vibrating through the air, and the imperfect beat of Ceif's heart. Yet, still, there was a mysterious silence, as if something was blatantly missing. She plundered through her brain, reaching for what it was, finding she couldn't even remember what they were doing out on a dark country road. Finally she grabbed it. Music. There was no music.

She placed Delvis's cassette in the jam box's mouth and pressed play. Loud crackles came through the speakers followed by the sound of a chair being dragged across a wooden floor. She imagined Delvis, could picture him sitting down in the chair, leaning in close to the recorder, all dressed up in his white cowboy hat with his guitar cradled in his arms like a child.

Delvis cleared his throat. "Gradle," he said, his voice like greased rust. "I made this tape for you. One side's titled *A* and the other's *B*. This first song is one of my originals. I got it dated in '79 but it was wrote in 1980. But anyways this here song's titled, "When the Whippoorwills Holler at Night." Delvis led with the guitar first. It was meticulously picked with an unconscious twang. He sang out the words:

I like to hear the whippoorwills holler
When things get peaceful and quiet
I love to hear them whippoorwills holler
When she's in my arms so tight

I love to hold my love darlin'
I love to kiss her lips so tight
I love to hold her in my arms
When them whippoorwills hollers at night

I love to put my lips to her tightly
I love to hold her in my arms tight
When I can hear them whippoorwills holler
When they holler at night

I love to hold my love darlin'
I love to kiss her lips so tight
I love to hold her in my arms
When them whippoorwills hollers at night

"Damn," Ceif said. He turned to Gradle, his eyes glassy and dark. "He's good."

Delvis cleared his throat. "Well, Gradle," he said, "I hope you like some of the songs on here. I deeply appreciate a response from you. Otherwise, a few lines or a letter explaining how you liked them or did not like them. I do want a picture of you if you don't mind. For keepsake. I always like fans' pictures."

Sonny Joe leaned over and twisted the volume knob up.

"This is yours truly D-5 Delvis Miles The Lone Singer," Delvis said. "Gradle, do write me by all means I'd appreciate it. If you say the songs ain't no good, you won't make me mad. If you think I can do better, when my sore finger gets better, I can do better. I'm gonna give you, not *give* you, but give you to *play* my original rock 'n roll of mine which is copyrighted. All rights reserved for yours truly D-5 Delvis Miles The Lone Singer. All my songs on here are copyrighted so nobody else can copyright them." He cleared his throat again. "I'm gonna step out of my complete style into another one of my own original styles, too. I'm gonna try to do this in my own rock 'n roll type style. It's one of my original songs. "I Want All You've Got to Give.""

Delvis belted out a song about a girl who had everything that a man could want. Beautiful legs. Eyes so blue. Lips red. And pretty black hair. The girl had everything to make a man want to live, and this man wanted all she had to give. They kept listening, none of them saying a word, as Delvis sang his repertoire of original songs. His subject matter was mainly about nature, pretty girls, and dancing. Only once he stepped out of his original songs and played "Wildwood Flower" by Maybelle Carter. One song in particular, called "Last Night I Heard You Crying," was about his mama, about how he had heard her crying last night in her sleep. It made Gradle wonder if he had any family. It made her wonder about his mother, if she was anywhere around or if she was gone like hers.

Delvis cleared his throat again and introduced the next song.

"This here song is a sad song. And it's got special meanings to me. It's a blues-type song. A wailing blues-type song. The title's called 'Rain'."

Gradle put her ear against the speaker as Delvis sang.

You was beat and cryin' when I found you
Left in the trash to die
You trembled and shooked, growled and bit
But you couldn't keep me from tryin'

We learned to trust
With peanut butter and love
I mended your wounds and you mended mine
I became yourn and yourn became mine

Rain! Rain! I carry your bullet in me, Rain!
I know your runnin' in heaven now
But them outlaws made my life a living hell
Rain! Rain! I carry your bullet in me, Rain!
Rain! Rain! I carry your bullet in me.

I miss your breath the most
And the sounds you make in your sleep
When I close my eyes I see your wet brown eyes
Starin' right back at me

We'll meet one day up high in the sky
You can teach me to run like you
But 'till then I'll pray and I'll cry
And I'll carry your bullet in me.
Rain! Rain! I carry your bullet in me, Rain!
I know your runnin' in heaven now

But them outlaws made my life a living hell
Rain! Rain! I carry your bullet in me, Rain!
Rain! Rain! I carry your bullet in me.

A tear shed from Gradle's eye as he sang the chorus another time through. She turned to Ceif. His eyes were closed, and his head was bowed in prayer. Sonny Joe had stopped the truck. He stared out of the window at the gauzed moon that had risen significantly higher. He was alone in thought. They were all alone in thought, yet Gradle could sense their thoughts had fused. The day Delvis shot and killed his dog had permanently bound them together. And for the rest of their lives they would be inseparable, even if distanced by years and miles. If decades down the road they saw one another again, that day would be the first thing they recognized about each other.

"Well Gradle," Delvis's voice cut through the heavy silence, "thank you very much for listening to these recordings. Always a *true* friend. I appreciate you coming by the other day. By all means do come see me again. And I still want a picture of you. I don't want a picture just to say that's my girlfriend. Uh, uh! I ain't like that. I ain't that kind of person. Well, I'm just gonna let this tape run out now. Again, this is yours truly D-5 Delvis Miles The Lone Singer."

The tape went silent, except for the crackling of the recorder and the sound of a chair being dragged back across the wooden floor. The tape stopped, and there was a collective and deep breath among them.

Sonny Joe ejected the tape and tossed it on the dashboard. "Are you as in love with him as he is with you?" he asked.

"I believe I am," she said. She slapped Sonny Joe against the ribs. "Can I have some more of that joint?"

†††

They pulled into the gravel parking lot of Jimmy's Dance Club and passed a broken-wheeled kiosk advertising SATURDAY NIGHT CHURCH, $2 COVER and THUNDERBIRD SOLD GOOD AND COLD. The lot was full, and a bundle of barefooted and raggedy children fought each other for turns at the building's only see-through window.

Sonny Joe parked the truck in the handicapped spot in front of the club. A shiny cockroach scampered across the mint green cement blocked wall. It made its journey across a life-size silhouette of a couple dancing and on across two windows that had been boarded up long enough for the nails to rust.

"Hand me my fighters," Sonny Joe said. "I can always draw a crowd in this joint."

"Is there an age requirement at this place?" she asked, handing Sonny Joe the fish she had forgotten were in her lap.

"Ain't no requirements when you're with me. Come on, Ceif. Let's go make some money."

"The prince of darkness himself," Ceif said, slamming the truck door.

They walked around the side of the building and Sonny Joe banged on a handleless metal door until the same man with the lazy eye and misshapen head that sold him liquor at the drive-thru opened the door and greeted them with severely impaired speed.

"Sonny Joe," the man drew out his syllables through the music, while he kept his good eye fixed on something inside. "Ceif," he acknowledged him.

"What's going on, Hammer?" Sonny Joe asked.

"I ain't seen nothing like it," Hammer said. "Started up about thirty minutes ago, and don't look like it's gonna stop anytime soon." The side of his face lifted in a smile, made by whatever he was looking at inside. "Your girl clean?" he asked.

"She's cool," Sonny Joe said, skipped the cover charge, and led Gradle and Ceif inside.

Gradle's eyes cut through the fog of smoke and saw what had kept the raggedy children at the window fighting for their turn and what had captured Hammer's good eye. In the middle of the dance floor, all by himself, was Grandpa. He was dancing so hard the crowd received his sweat, and when he kicked his leg out to the side, a penny flew from his loafer and skated across the floor.

††††

Leonard led Annalee into a tight fast spin. Her dress bloomed out in scalloped waves like the moonflower pinned to her chest. She spotted his eyes with each turn, and each time she came around, her face grew younger and younger as if he was spinning her back in time. He spun her out of his arms into the captive crowd. Her hair was sweaty, her cheeks flush, and her eyes sparked as Leonard signaled to her he was ready. She sprinted across the dance floor and jumped with wild abandon through the air. He caught her by the waist and lifted her high above his head. She was light as air. He could feel nothing but life in her. He lowered her down his body and found her completely restored to the beautiful first cousin he had fallen in love with so many years ago.

Leonard didn't want to let her go. He feared he would lose her. He feared she would revert, but the crowd was clapping them on. He swung her to the left, and then to the right, and as he swung her through his legs, he saw through the crowd and haze of cigarette smoke, a familiar flash of green. Near the entrance, Gradle picked up the penny he had just danced from his loafer.

Gradle moved through the crowd alongside two boys. The tattooed boy led her to a table where he sat with two bags of fish and lit a cigarette. The crippled boy sat down with a Bible on his lap and rested his cane atop a chair while Gradle stood staring out at him, perhaps too stunned to sit.

Leonard grabbed onto Annalee and twirled her across the room, dancing harder and faster in hopes he could dance Gradle out of his mind.

The crowd began to talk.

"Maybe he's nuts."

"But look at him dance!"

"Must be the goddamn heat."

"But man he's got rhythm!"

"Is he hallucinating?"

"I want some of what he's got."

"Maybe he's got an imaginary friend."

The crowd talked louder. Whispers became shouts. They began to point and laugh out loud.

"Freak!"

"Go get your head checked!"

"Go back to the chicken coop!"

"Get a clue, old man! There's nobody there!"

Leonard ignored the hollering and banter. He didn't skip a single beat as he kept bunny-hugging Annalee because no matter what anybody said, no matter what anybody thought, Annalee was there, and he could see her plain as day. He dipped her low until her hair brushed the floor, and when he pulled her up she was no longer there. All he could see was Gradle standing in her place.

Gradle held out her hands for him to take. "Dance with me, Grandpa."

The music stopped. The crowd collectively gasped.

"Take my hand," she whispered. "People are laughing."

Leonard's eyes traversed the room. Not a single soul was laughing. They were all staring at Gradle with their hands over their mouths, as if they were powerless in witnessing a tragedy, like a car about to roll off a cliff.

"Grab my hand, Grandpa," she said.

He began to shake. He clutched his fists, closed his eyes, and went back to the night Gradle was born and he kept telling himself the exact same thing as he watched Gradle's tiny hands rise up, her little arms flail in the air, her little fingers ball up in red little fists, fighting for breath.

"Take my hand, Grandpa!" Gradle yelled.

His eyes snapped open, and he gulped in air.

"We don't have to dance," she said. Her cheeks were slick with tears. "Just take my hand."

A new song started. The crippled boy rose from his chair and hobbled across the dance floor assisted by his cane. He grabbed hold of Gradle's outstretched hands and gently pulled her away. He wrapped his arms around her waist, nudged her cheek down on his shoulder, and led her into a slow and awkward dance.

Leonard walked off the dance floor and went out through the door, leaving Gradle in the arms of a crippled boy who knew how to love her better than him.

††††

Leonard sat in the living room in the dark staring at the TV. His chair was pulled a foot from the screen, and he was lost in an all-night showcase of *Star Trek* episodes. A cat screamed next door and made him rise from his chair. He stared through the front door's beveled glass, switched the porch light on, and went back to his chair.

As he watched the Enterprise crew battle a mysterious contaminant that caused symptoms of alcohol intoxication, the front door slammed. Gradle stumbled into the living room and squeezed between him and the TV. She was drenched in rain and smelled like liquor and smoke.

"Do you love me?" she asked. She stumbled to the side, knocked the TV antenna and her glasses askew, and dropped a Styrofoam box of food on the floor. He wondered if she had been infected by the same contaminant as the Enterprise crew, but after he caught a whiff of liquor on her breath, he knew her intoxication was real.

He stared through Gradle's dress, past her bony silhouette, and fixed his eyes on the TV's flickering light.

"You gonna sit there and stare at nothing?" she asked. She pushed the TV on its side.

The light in the room vanished and reappeared as sudden as it went. She had knocked the *Star Trek* episode out of the TV, and Leonard stared at the black and white horizontal lines traversing the screen.

"Why can't you look at me?" she asked.

"Let me be," he mumbled. He rose and pushed her out of the way with a force that knocked her to the ground.

She crawled on the floor, grabbed him by the hair, and shoved his face into hers. "Look at me."

Leonard stared at her. He focused deep into her eyes and found infinite patterns of blue and saw who he always saw every time he looked at her. He saw Veela on her sixteeth birthday, drunk and crawling through the wet grass in her green chiffon dress.

He had come home late from work, and as he wheeled the car into the drive the headlights cut through the rain and shone on Dot and Veela who slouched on lounge chairs in the front yard. A half bottle of Maker's Mark sat on a little table between them.

"Look what the cat drug in," Dot said, dressed up in her honeymoon frock with a Palmov cigarette hanging from her mouth. She took a sip from the tumbler that looked like it was going slip from her hand.

Leonard slammed the car door shut and saw that Veela was asleep. Her head was slumped, and the straps of her dress hung off her shoulders and showed her bra.

"Where you been, Leonard?" Dot yelled, as if the rain was louder than it was.

"I had some work to finish up," he said. Moths fluttered by the porch light and made eerie shadows against the house.

"You sure do love to work, don't you?" Dot said. She sauntered toward Leonard and didn't stop until her nose touched his. "Why don't you ever work on me?" she asked, her breath sour and gamy from the Maker's Mark.

"You wouldn't remember it if I did," he said.

Dot leaned in to kiss him and nuzzled her smeared red lips against his. When he didn't respond, she bit hard down on his bottom lip.

"You're sick, Dot," he said, shoving her away. Dot tripped over herself and fell down in the grass. Her tumbler rolled and hit the lounge chair where Veela slept.

"Why are y'all all dressed up?" Leonard asked.

"It's Veela's birthday. Sixteen, Leonard," she said, looking around for her glass. "So we decided we'd get all dolled up because certainly you were gonna take us out to celebrate. But we waited and waited. We didn't have anywhere to go and nobody to take us."

Dot crawled over to Veela's chair and jerked Veela's chin from side to side. "Wake up Veela, Daddy's finally home," she slurred.

"How much did you give her?" Leonard asked.

"I don't know, Leonard. I lost count after two," Dot said. "I found out real soon she can't hold her liquor."

"She's sixteen for Christ's sake."

"I know, and she's not even bleeding yet," Dot said, laughing.

Veela's eyes started to wake. Dot slapped her cheek. "Go on,

Veela. Kiss your Daddy hello."

Veela opened her eyes fully, and as her beautiful blues focused on him, she reached out her arms and fell over with the lounge chair. She got on her knees and crawled to Leonard's shins.

Leonard knelt down, she wrapped her arms around his neck, and he carried her toward the house. She looked up at him, her eyes not quite all there.

"You forgot my birthday," she said. Her eyes closed shut.

Leonard felt a quick sting against his face that brought him back to the infinite blue patterns in Gradle's eyes.

"Look at me!" Gradle slapped his face again. She got in his face and forced his eyes on hers. "Who do you see?"

"Veela," he whispered.

"My name is Gradle," she said, backing away. She shoveled the food into the Styrofoam box and slammed the front door.

Leonard raked his hand down his mustache, grabbed the fire poker, and murdered the maimed TV.

CHAPTER TEN

GRADLE WALKED THROUGH the darkest dark she had ever seen. There was no moon or stars to light her path, but she didn't need them to find her way. She made a right down the dirt road leading to Delvis's house and knew she was near after the smell of tobacco turned to honeysuckle. She made another right at Delvis's mailbox, and as she topped the hill, she could see light in the distance. Delvis's house was lit up like ball of fire, like some sort of sun rising.

She stepped on his porch and automatically felt safe. Light pierced through the seams in the door and stabbed through the floor like swords. She knocked on the door three times so he would know she was a real true friend.

"You from the electric company?" Delvis asked from behind the door.

"No," she answered.

"Back up!" Delvis yelled.

She backed up. Maybe the "three times" code only applied to car horns.

"You think I'm gone mess with that box? You think I'm a crook?"

She turned to run but found her feet tangled in rope. The string pulled taut and hammered down a bent fork that pressed the button of a Polaroid camera duct-taped to the porch rail. The camera flashed and spent a square of film from its mouth.

Delvis kept hollering through the door. "I got a Ruger pistol in my hand! A six-speed handgun point-three-five-seven magnum! And it's powerful!"

She had never heard anyone sound that mad. She wanted to run, didn't care if she had to return to all that dark, but the rope had tied a knot around her ankle.

"I'm a volunteer undercover agent! If you want to challenge me to a shoot-out, you know me, D-5 Delvis Miles The Lone Singer accepts all challenges! I will not refuse any challenge! I can draw and shoot within two seconds, ninety-seven percent accurate on target each and every time. If you want to wrestle instead, I'll knee lift you and beat you with an inch of your life. Back up from the door!" he yelled.

The door clicked. She ran down the steps and ripped out the camera and its rig. It trailed behind her like a bumpy ball on a chain. The door opened, and a beam of light shone on her back, so bright she could feel the temperature change. His shadow was a black giant as tall as the stand of pine beyond.

"Don't shoot!" She crouched to the ground, preparing her back to take a bullet.

"Gradle Bird?" Delvis jumped off the porch and ran at her.

She covered her head. "Please don't shoot!"

"Why would I shoot a nice girl like you?"

"I didn't honk three times?"

"Them crooks from the electric company done made me mad. There's somebody up there thinks I'm gonna tamper with his box," he said. "I ain't gone shoot you." He bent his knees so he could be level with her. His eyes were protective and sincere. "You my friend, Gradle. I ain't gone hurt you."

"I'm sorry if I bothered you," she said, unwrapping the rope from her ankle. "I know it's an odd hour."

"I ain't bothered. I'm glad you come to see me. I'm nocturnal," he said, "like the locusts and the deer and the alligators. Nocturnal. N-O-C-T-U-R-N-A-L. Got that word from the *My Big Backyard* magazine. I got my electricity today, and they already done made me mad. Them fools think I'm gone tamper with the box."

"What box?" she asked.

"The electric box. Let me go get my flashing-light, and I'll show you what I'm talkin' 'bout. I got a letter to put to 'em anyway. Wait for me on the porch."

She untied the rope from her ankle and pulled the developing Polaroid from the camera's mouth. The photo had captured her profile, like a sideways mug shot. She wondered why he'd use a camera as a boobie trap, but now understood it was rigged to capture evidence. She was crazy for being here, especially in the dark at this hour. He could've shot her, mistaken her for those fools from the electric company.

Light beamed from the inside of Delvis's shack and assaulted her eyes as he walked through the door and onto the porch. He held a letter and rattled a flashlight in his hand until he could get it to click on. Moths fluttered in the light, their shadows tossing and spinning like disco balls.

"They put the box on the side of the house," he said, leading her to the side of his shack. He shined the flashlight on the electricity meter. "See here." He pointed to the verbiage written on the meter. "It says, 'Do not tamper with this box by penalty of law code 89786.1 section 45A'. That electric man who come up here and installed this, he thinks I'm gonna tamper with the box. He told me he'd be up here every now and then to take a readin'. Next time he comes, I'm gone have some words for him. And if he wants to fight I won't refuse. One thing you need to know about me, Gradle, is I will accept every and all challenges."

He taped the letter to the box, eyeing the box the entire time as if it was questionable and alive. The letter read:

ThÍs *here's* **A ChrÍSTÍaN FOLk whAt** *LÍves* *here.* **I WOULdN't fuCK with YOUr GODDAMNED boX!!!**

YoUrs Truly,
D-S Delvis **MÍLes The LoNe SÍNger.**

Gradle laughed.

"What's so funny?" he asked.

"You," she said.

"Is funny bad?"

"No, it's good."

"Good."

"I brought you a steak dinner from the Western Steer. It's somewhere around here," she said, scanning the yard.

Delvis's eyes pinched together tight. "You didn't trade one of your flying dragon scales in for it did you?"

"No," she said. She picked up the box from the ground and handed it to Delvis. "You hungry?"

Delvis shifted on his feet and looked away out into the dark like he was nervous about something. "I got me a sore tooth. And I ain't able to chew with it much. Been tryin' to get it out. That's why I'm talkin' funny if you ain't noticed. I ain't been able to chew. An' ain't been able to sing right neither. And that's a big hindrance in a songbird's life. I got me some red willow bark I been suckin' on," he said, opened his mouth wide, and shone the flashlight inside for her to see. A wad of bark nested between his gums like a lug of chewing tobacco. "It's a numbin' tonic," he said, and he closed his mouth. "That's what I been doin' inside." He pointed to his shack. "I been tryin' to pull it. If it was one of my front tooths, I could do it, no problem. I've got skills and trainin' for that. But this'ns in the back, and I ain't able to reach it good."

"I'll pull it for you," she said, swatting a mosquito from her shin.

Delvis rubbed his hands down the front of his pants. "I don't know if you want to do that. It might be a little risky."

"If it's hurting you, I can help you get it out."

Delvis stood at the door, contemplating. He rubbed the lobe of his right ear. "Now Gradle, my house is a mess. Another tornado come through here the other day and tore the place up. So please excuse it." He cleared his throat and spat off the porch. "And in addition, I also got a sore throat and some double back trouble and ain't been able to straighten the house up. I'm sorry. It don't bother me none, but for company's sake it might not be the best—" he said, searching for the right word, "environment. Got that from the *My Big Backyard* magazine, too. Environment is what critters live in."

"If you knew the environment I lived in, you wouldn't apologize about the mess yours is in."

"Well, enter at your own risk," he said, opening the door.

The light inside was so bright, it made Gradle's eyes water. She counted forty-two lamps, all with their shades off and their bulbs burning bright. Extension cords and power strips snaked

through the one-foot-wide alleys running and bending in sharp
angles like a maze throughout the one-room shack. The alleys had
walls that touched the ceiling and were made of stacked books,
battery-powered clocks all set to different times, naked baby dolls,
newspapers and magazines, empty shampoo and hairspray bottles
all of the brand L'Oréal, hubcaps, leather shoes with no laces, glass
jars filled with buttons and colored glass, and what looked to be
solidified cooking oil or bacon grease. The walls were chaotically
perfect in their construction. Everything had its place, had its own
purpose in holding something else up. If one piece of it were
removed everything would come crumbling down.

Drawings hung throughout the house, along with spiderwebs
abundant with paralyzed prey. In one corner of the shack, a stack of
toasters, TVs, microwaves, and a jam box tilted precariously to one
side. In another corner, piles of clothes stacked all the way up to the
ceiling. The place was a study in confusion, yet there was an order,
an art about it. Until tonight, Gradle had only been on the outside.
But now she was in. Completely and radically in.

"I like how you decorate," she said.

Delvis stopped wringing his hands and looked down at his feet.
"I appreciate you saying that. It's a bit humble. And like I said, a
tornado come through here the other day, and I ain't had time to
straighten it."

"It's perfect," she said. She couldn't keep her eyes from
wandering over the room. Everywhere she looked there were little
hidden treasures. A Remington noiseless sat on the floor with
its ribbon spooling out of its head. Stuffed animals were tacked
to the walls by their ears—a couple of puppy dogs, an elephant,
and several dirty white lambs. Fake flowers and plants sat on the
windowsills of boarded windows where natural light had never
shone. Tiny figurines of dogs and cats were organized like soldiers
on the doorframe's lip. Christmas ornaments hung from the ceiling

by fishing line, and lying across the back of a ratty orange chair was a snakeskin at least four feet long.

She walked down one of the alleys and turned a tight right. In the corner sat a small twin bed covered with a red threadbare blanket. A cross made of Popsicle sticks kept watch from the wall above it. Atop the bed sat Delvis's guitar, a pack of double-A batteries, a cassette tape, and a recorder.

"I listened to the music you sent me," she said.

"Did you like it? If you don't like it, I can do better. I got sore fingers and a frog in my throat. But I can do better."

"I think you are a true talent." Her eyes tracked a cockroach, the young fast kind, across the wall. "My favorite song was the one about your dog."

"He was my best friend," he said. "But now I got you."

"You ready to pull your tooth? So you can eat that steak dinner before it goes bad?"

Delvis led her through an alley to the left where a small table sat with a pair of pliers, a cracked hand mirror, and a pile of tree bark on its top. He sat beside the table and shined the mirror in his mouth. "It's that'n," he said, pointing to his back-most tooth. He spat out the tree bark and handed her the pair of pliers. "You gone hafta squeeze 'em real hard. 'Bout as hard as you can. And then you just yank," he said, making a yanking motion with his arm. "Don't worry 'bout me. I'm a professional at dealin' with pain. Done this five times." He shot up from the floor, reached into the alley's wall, and retrieved a glass vial holding five of his teeth. "Here's my collection," he said, counting the vacant spots in his mouth. "One, two, three, four, five. Did 'em all myself, 'cause the dentist around here ain't nothin' but a crook and a cavity inventor."

"I'm not a professional." She peered into his mouth, got queasy, and doubled over.

"You got somethin' ailin' you?" he asked.

"My stomach's upset."

"Did the electric man make it mad?"

"No, it's nausea. I think I'm gonna vomit." She felt beads of sweat form on her lip. The room went dizzy.

"Let me roll some bark up in some paper, and you can take a few puffs of it. It'll make your stomach feel better."

Delvis pinched the bark into tiny pieces, rolled it in a rolling paper, and handed her the cigarette. He picked a box of matches from a nook in the alley wall and rattled it to see if it was empty. She found amusement in the fact he knew exactly where the matches were, that he could reach into a wall of chaos and trash and pull out exactly what he reached in for.

"How do you know where everything is?"

"My IQ is off the charts. I was borned with an uncommon mind."

She took a few puffs from the cigarette and waited for it to take effect. Within seconds she felt better. "Alright, I'm ready," she said, grabbing the pliers.

Delvis lay down on his back, tilted his head up, and opened his mouth as wide as his jaws would stretch. He shined the mirror on his sore tooth and fisted his other hand. "Clamp the pliers on the tooth. And yank up hard. Don't worry 'bout me. Like I said, I'm a professional at pain management."

She reached in with the pliers, clamped them hard, and closed her eyes. On the count of three, she yanked. She stumbled back and fell to the floor. She opened her eyes and found Delvis's bloody tooth gripped between the pliers's nose. "I got it!"

The lights in the shack surged, and suddenly everything went black.

"That damn bastard! He thinks I've fucked with the box!" Delvis hollered out in the pitch black dark.

CHAPTER
ELEVEN

MORNING CREPT IN with pale grey light and the soft patter of rain. Annalee stood at the living room window looking out at the sad break of day, while Leonard lay asleep on the floor at her feet. He clutched onto her legs with a grip so tight, she wasn't sure if he had ever fallen completely asleep. She had found him on the floor late last night, curled up in a catatonic C. She had picked the shards of television screen out of his hair, cradled, and rocked him like a child. He didn't cry out or say a word, but she knew he desperately needed help. She listened to his silent transgressions. Her heart overturned with his. She had tried to offer him comfort and hope that he too could somehow be restored. The new morning though, with its early light and silence, made it all a bit bewildering that she had been the one offering solace to him, when this whole time—this lonely and limping time—she had been convinced it was *her* soul that needed saving.

The rain grew heavier, and the ceiling began to leak. She heard raindrops spanking on paper. An envelope rested on the floor, its ink beginning to bleed into the rain. She pried her leg loose from Leonard and picked up the envelope. It was addressed to Gradle Bird. Its sender was D-5 Delvis Miles The Lone Singer, who lived at Rural Route 1 Box 56-B. Annalee closed her eyes, put the envelope to her nose, and lifted the scent of carrots. She hid the letter inside her breast and ascended into the attic, leaving Leonard in an incomplete surrender to sleep.

Back at the attic window, she opened the envelope and unfolded the letter. Inside was a hand-drawn heart creased in threes and a pinch of colorful sequins that fluttered to the floor like wounded birds. She read his words and confirmed what she had suspected. Her hand reached inside her heart and retrieved her hidden portrait. She compared the writer's signature, *D-5*, to the signature that clung in the graphite lines that outlined the hem of her dress.

The attic flap creaked open, and Leonard ascended the ladder as a tear rolled down her cheek. She hid the portrait and the letter inside her dress and turned to meet him face on.

"Gradle's run away," Leonard said, rushing to the window. He looked down on the slick street.

"I'm surprised she's stayed this long," Annalee said, wiping away her tear.

"You want to pick a fight with me?" Leonard jerked his head around.

"Why can't you look at her, Leonard?"

Leonard's hands sprung forward and grabbed her by the shoulders. His eyes drilled into her. "I look at her all the time."

"And what do you see?"

Leonard released her body and started down the ladder.

"You're avoiding the question," said Annalee, who stood at the flap and looked down on him.

Leonard clamped his jaw and climbed back up the ladder. He walked into her, and she back-stepped against the wall.

Leonard turned her chin and made her look him in the eye. "Isn't there a place people go when they die?"

She jerked her chin away, and Leonard climbed down the ladder.

She grabbed a coatrack and used it to smash the dollhouse to smithereens. There was a place people go when they die, and oh, how she had yearned for this merciful place. They say you see a bright light. When death finally fell upon her, after she had smiled at the beautiful rattle it made, she saw nothing but darkness. She rummaged and searched among it, looking for this beacon of Holy Light. Perhaps death had made her blind. But it didn't take long for her to realize her eyesight was perfect all along, and that her new world was the same world she had left, except she was the only one in it. Her very own dark, private heaven.

The front door slammed. She went to the window and watched Leonard walk through the yard, gripping his gun. He folded into the Chrysler and cranked it up. He wouldn't know where to look, but Annalee knew exactly where Gradle was.

She scaled down the knotted quilt ladder and walked down Spivey Street. A pale gray smoked the sky, and a peculiar wind ripped the petals off all the crepe myrtles in town. The petals swirled, drifted, and turned somersaults through the air in her wake. It was the middle of summer, ninety-something degrees, and there was flurry.

She walked down the sidewalk and through the south edge of town, watching the crepe myrtle snow. Petals fell at her feet, swirling like tiny twisters that whispered icicles and spiders in her ears. The last time Annalee saw snow was in 1933 when she went up to that place for those five months, the place way up north where the cold pricks like needles and the snow is not made of crepe myrtle petals.

The morning she left for that place, her mother flitted about the house, singing resurrection-themed church hymns like a songbird thrilled it was spring. Annalee hadn't heard her mother sing in months, and although the two of them had been at odds since she slapped Leonard down the attic flap, it made Annalee happy to hear her mother's measure.

Annalee stood over her bed, doing what she was told, and packed a trunk for the trip. She folded three weeks' worth of dresses, three flannel nightgowns, and her cold-weather coat. She took the white eyelet lace dress from her wardrobe and nestled it in her nose, hunting like a hound for Leonard's trail. He was still there, his carrot scent, clinching tight to the woven threads of cotton. She held the dress against her body, stared in the mirror, and rolled the dress's lap over the abundance in her belly.

"You act like you're proud, Annalee," her mother said, as she entered the room. "Most women earn this right, and you, my dear, have not." She walked to the bed and rummaged through the trunk Annalee had packed. "You need more nightgowns. In a month you'll be too big for any of these." She threw out the dresses one by one. She stood behind Annalee and stared with her in the mirror. "You won't need this one either," she said, removing the eyelet dress from Annalee's body. "It's horribly out of season and needs a wash." She balled the dress in her hands. "What is it with you and this dress?"

A tear went down Annalee's cheek. Her mother would never, never know. She would never understand. It was her engagement frock, her wedding dress, her conception gown. She snatched the dress out of her mother's hands.

"Oh child," her mother said. "Don't be so dramatic. All of this will soon be over. And we can resume our normal lives." She pulled Annalee's hair past her shoulder and cupped it into a ponytail. "You used to have such a pretty smile. Where did it go?" She dropped

Annalee's hair against her back and exited the room, singing a song about life's wondrous ways, as if she didn't care at all to know the answer to the question she just asked.

On the ride up, Annalee stared out of the window while her father drove and her mother sat in the passenger's seat, crocheting and commenting on trivial things like her pound cake recipe and what kind of vacation to take next summer. Her father sat behind the wheel silent, nodding and providing replies when needed, ones that didn't require him to open his mouth. He had not spoken a word to Annalee since he found out what had happened that day in the attic with Leonard, nor had he given her a proper look. When forced to pass each other in the hallways, he looked down and fiddled with his watch. At the supper table, he bowed his head toward his food and asked her mother to pass what he needed, when he had always asked Annalee in the past. And the unwanted times when he caught her eye by mistake, he quickly turned away as if Annalee was too blinding and too bright.

There was a moment though, on the ride up to that place, when their eyes met. Annalee didn't know how long he'd been looking at her through the rearview mirror, but it was long enough for him to catch water in his lids. They stared at each other, and the look was all Annalee needed for her to know that she had succeeded at crushing his heart.

They dropped her off in front of that place, its three-story façade and its great big door looming behind her, like a monster with its mouth open, waiting to eat her alive.

"Nobody ever will know," Annalee's mother said, reaching her hand out through the window. She grabbed Annalee's wrist in a poor attempt at goodbye. Her father drove off, and her mother's hand slipped through her fingertips.

†††

Annalee brushed the crepe myrtle petals from her shoulder as she turned down a country road, making it through the worst of the flower storm. She survived that place. She had survived the vacant walls and cold cement floor, the metal beds lined up like victims of a firing squad. She had survived the endless sadness and shame, the wailing and weeping, the excruciating pains of labor and the unwanted result. She had survived it all because of the diamond ring she kept under her tongue. It was the bullet to bite on and the constant reminder of what always protected, always trusted, always hoped, and what always persevered. No, that place hadn't killed her. What killed her, what sent her spiraling toward death, was where she went and what she did after she left that place.

And here she was, she had arrived at the very spot where she did it. It hadn't changed much since. The junk pile had grown in size and the weeds tangling throughout the throwaways were alive and green. Back then they were dead and brown from the winter. There were three more dumpsters. Back then she remembered only one. A pack of wild starving dogs picked among the garbarge, two of them mothers, their teats swollen and raw.

She remembered back all those years and how she had ended up in the very spot in which she stood now. This was the place that had killed her. To tread on it now might kill her again, if it was possible to kill somebody who was already dead. She remembered the change. It had been sudden, like a strike of lightning, and she felt it charge through her immediately after giving birth to that beautiful blue-eyed boy. The final scream fled her body, she unclenched her jaw, and released the diamond ring from her teeth the moment she heard him crying and saw his hands grabbing in every direction for her. She reached out to hold him, but the woman in white with a face too hardened to wrinkle swaddled him in a blanket and took him away.

"Let me hold him," Annalee said, "Just once."

"It will do you both no good," one of the nurses said. "Now rest, child."

But Annalee did not rest. She lay in bed and pulled at her eyelashes until she pulled the bottom lids bald. She got out of bed and paced the cold long hallways with blood running down her legs, trying to find where they had hidden her son. She opened every closed-off room, and at every locked door, she banged and scratched. When nobody came to the door, she banged harder until her knuckles bled, and still after no answer, she picked the locks with bobby pins. She threw every locked door back, bore her teeth, and raised her claws at nothing but dark emptiness.

In the great big room with the metal beds lined against the wall, she made every girl get up so she could rip through their sheets and search under their bed. She went to the kitchen and opened every cabinet and looked in every pot and jar and searched through every sack in the pantry. She tore through flour and sugar and coffee and oatmeal, slinging them all over the ground. When she couldn't find her son, she harassed the cook. She dumped the soup of the day out on the floor and picked through the vegetables and potatoes, looking for little pieces of her son. She was convinced they had cooked him. She picked out the potatoes and made his arms and then his legs and when she went for the cook with a sharp-blade knife, a nurse in white came from behind and stabbed her with a needle.

She woke in her bed. Her wrists were banded with white straps and secured to the bedrail with chain. *Home. Home. Home.* All she could think about was home. But she wasn't going home without her son.

In the middle of the night, during the worst snowstorm that place had seen in over twenty-five years, she finally twisted and stretched the straps enough to slide her delicate hands through. The great big room was asleep, but down the hallway she heard the wailing and screaming of a girl giving birth. She grabbed her winter coat and the white eyelet dress she had packed with her the day she left for that place.

She tiptoed down the hall toward the soon-to-be mother's sounds. The girl was close. Annalee hid among the shadows, waiting until the labor pain ended and a nurse in white carried the newborn out of the birthing room. She followed the nurse down a dark hallway, and only once did the nurse pause, as if maybe something was tracking her trail. The nursed turned back, and Annalee ducked behind a steel cart.

Lightning lit the dark hallway. The nurse, bouncing the screaming child, went to the window and looked out at the storm.

Annalee followed the nurse around corners and down hallways until she led her to a room, one similar to the room where all the girls slept, except here there were little ones sleeping, boys and girls, in little beds, swaddled in little blankets. The nurse placed the baby in its little bed. There were so many of them. How was she to tell her own?

Her hand turned the knob, and she slid through the door. She crawled through the rows made by the tiny little beds. The lights flickered from the storm outside. She waited until the nurse left, then she rushed through the rows, searching for her son. None of them had names, only dates. When she came to the last bed in the last row, her bosom began to hurt and swell.

She lifted him from his bed and wrapped him in her white eyelet dress. A pair of nurses came through the door chatting about the storm. Annalee ducked. She cradled her son as she crawled through the bed rows in the opposite direction from where the four white shoes went. She slid through the door, ran down the hallways, around the corners, through the corridors, and out of the front door, barely escaping the monster's mouth.

There was a peace and quietness about the falling snow. It made the storm seem less violent and dusted everything in magic. But there was nothing peaceful and quiet about Annalee, nor was there anything calm, and whatever magic she had within her, it was dark. She ripped through the snowdrifts and tore through the woods, the cold a welcomed relief against her hot, sweaty skin.

She walked all through the night, listening to her child wail and scream. Her breasts were on fire, but the baby would not take her milk. It had not come natural, and now that she had him, she had no idea what to do with him. He had inherited Leonard's scent of carrots and his blue eyes, his big ears and hands, but somehow he hadn't inherited whatever it was about Leonard that Annalee loved so much.

She thought of leaving him, thought about hiding him in the snow, but every time the urge came on, she clamped down on the diamond ring, knowing that if she just got home everything would be okay. Everything would get better.

A bright sun came with the morning. She found a road, and she knew the road led south because the farther she traveled it the warmer it became. A truck passed and pulled off on the side of the road. A man with a flat, scarred nose got out of the truck, his lips wrapped around a cherry-smelling pipe.

"Where you headed?" the man asked.

"Georgia," she said, pocketing the diamond ring against the inside of her cheek.

Smoke trailed from the man's mouth. "I'm going that way to buy seed. I'll take you as far as you need to go."

Annalee and the baby got in the truck. The man covered her with burlap sacks. She looked at him confused as to why.

"Your lips are purple," he said, put the truck in gear, and drove down the road.

She did not feel exhausted or tired. In fact, she felt alert, perhaps a little jumpy. She bounced her knee and picked at her eyelashes, collecting them in a fold of her eyelet dress. She kept looking over at the man, thinking she knew exactly what he thought of her.

"You think I'm a bad mother," she said.

The man removed the pipe from his mouth. "No, I think you're a good one."

Annalee looked down at her son and waited for that feeling to come, the one all mothers are supposed to feel. But that feeling hadn't come to her. Something else had. She bit down on the diamond ring.

"What's his name?" the man asked.

"I haven't named him yet," she said. She kept picking at her lashes.

The baby screamed and she offered him her hard and swollen breast, but he thrashed about and writhed his head away.

"I don't think we're meant to be," she said. She looked at the man, her eyes weeping.

"How old?" the man asked.

"A few days. Maybe three, I don't know."

"He's just getting used to breathing air," the man said. "Give it time." He reached over and offered his pinkie to her son. His little lips started sucking it, and for the first time since she had taken him away, he stopped crying, and with the silence they both fell asleep.

It was late afternoon when they got there. Annalee directed the man through town and told him to turn left down Spivey Street.

"Can you stop?" she asked, as they neared her house. Her eyes scoured their pretty, perfect home. The chandeliers were lit. Her father stoked the fire, and her mother was busy arranging flowers in a vase.

"Is this it?" the man asked.

"No," she said. She directed the man back through town and down a dirt country road. "You can let me out here. My house is up a ways."

"I can take you all the way," the man said.

"I feel like walking."

She got out of the truck, forgot to thank the man, and started down the road. The truck's engine and the cherry-smelling pipe faded in the distance. Her son began to scream. She stopped in the road and screamed with him. It wasn't supposed to be this way. She screamed her throat raw and drained her eyes of tears, and finally she moved on down the road to the dump.

Skeletons of weeds, brown and parched and hollow, tangled through the junk. A rusted plow was halfway buried in the ground, its sharp teeth rising up as if trying to bite its way back out. She removed the eyelet dress she had wrapped around him. Her eyelashes that had collected in one of its folds sailed like seeds in the breeze.

He began to shiver. He was cold, but she couldn't bear to part with her dress, to throw it away in the garbage like her mother had done, so instead, she swaddled him in the burlap sacks the man had used to make her warm. She kissed him on his forehead and nested him inside the dumpster between two bags of trash. He stopped crying the moment she put him there, as if all his crying was a need to be out of her arms, and somehow in her twisted-up mind she convinced herself that leaving him here must be right. It wasn't until she made the left on Spivey Street that she realized she hadn't said a single word to him. No hello. No goodbye.

A crepe myrtle petal fell in Annalee's hand, and it did not melt. She had survived that cold, wretched place. She had survived the long journey home. But she never outlived what the weeds tangled through, what the hungry dogs raided, no matter how many times she bit down on the ring, because after what she did that day, the reminder of love was gone.

She moved on, away from all of those abandoned things, down the dirt road, in search of Gradle. She came to a mailbox, rusted and padlocked shut. Written on its side were the words:

NO TResPass-N. FoR FaNS aNd ReaLTrUe FrieENds ONLY. ReTuRN to SENDer if NoT. D-S Delvis MiLes The LoNe SiNger Rural RoUTE 1 Box 56-B

She followed the trail that led to a tiny shack. She walked through the yard among the collection of junk and rage of dandelion, and as she climbed the first porch step, a long ago yet familiar feeling came over her. Even though nothing was there, she felt her bosom swell.

Through the front door a man appeared. He looked around suspiciously, as if expecting an intruder. He had blue eyes, great big ears, and great big hands. She caught a whiff of carrots. Her hand flew up to catch her dropping jaw. My, oh my, how he had grown.

CHAPTER
TWELVE

"WHO'S THERE?" DELVIS heaved in his whispering voice into the hot, muggy morning. He pinched his eyes at something. It was round and sparkly and floated at the foot of his porch steps. He couldn't make it out one hundred percent, but something was there. He could feel it.

He'd been on high alert all night, didn't sleep a wink, waiting up for the Tooth Fairy to come. Gradle told him all about her after she yanked his tooth out with his pliers. She said the fairy was some kind of spirit, like a ghost, who would come in the middle of the night and bring you a gift in exchange for your tooth. All he had to do was put his tooth under his pillow, and she would come. He asked Gradle what she looked like, but Gradle said she ain't never visited her, but she did say the Tooth Fairy was invisible. He wasn't sure he believed that. Ain't nothing in the world invisible. Not even the wind. He would bet all of his flying dragon scales he was looking at the Tooth Fairy right now, even though he couldn't make her out one hundred percent.

He walked to the porch's edge to get a better look. The floating sparkle flew up and froze in the air. He almost peed his pants. It was definitely her, and now he could clearly make her out as plain as day. She was a tiny little thing, half the size of his pinkie nail, and she sparkled bright like a diamond.

"I see you little Miss Tooth Fairy," he said, reaching out his hand to grab her. She zigged left and zagged right. Then POOF! She disappeared just like them ghosts do.

"Come back," Delvis said. "I ain't mean to scare you." He waited for the fairy to come back, his eyes cocked and ready for her bright diamond spark, but she never came back in the three hours he sat on his porch and waited.

He went back inside his house, excited to tell Gradle he had seen the Tooth Fairy, but when he checked on her, she was still in his bed breathing in sleep, her ribs poking through her dress like the gills of a fish. He smiled. She had to be the prettiest thing he'd ever seen.

He didn't want to wake her, although he thought he'd burst from excitement. She'd been sleeping most of the day, and he wondered when she might decide to wake up. It was past one o'clock, and he hadn't seen her wiggle once since she fell over asleep in his bed early that morning. *She must be real tired.* It didn't bother him none she took over his bed. He couldn't sleep anyway, and if he needed to, there was a pile of clothes in the corner that would suit him just fine.

A tingle ran up and down his body as he looked at her. He had never felt so happy. Never in all of his sixty years, had he had a real true friend, one that was human, and to have one as special and pretty as Gradle Bird proved something to him that had never been proved to him before. For the first time in his life, he felt accepted.

It was a feeling he didn't ever want to lose, and he worried that after she woke up, she might go back home and take this feeling with her. He hoped she'd stay right there and sleep forever. If he could, he'd capture her in a Mason jar and never let her out. But he knew he couldn't do something like that, so he decided he would capture her in a different way. Like how he'd captured that unicorn he saw in the woods behind his house. He would draw her.

He tried to remember where he put his drawing pad and No. 2 pencils. It had been a couple of months since he'd used them. Thousands of images flashed on the back of his eyelids like a shuffling deck of cards. His mind threw out half the deck and shuffled through what was left. He threw out another half and shuffled through that and kept on with the task until his mind stopped on the image of his drawing pad and No. 2 pencils. All this, and a second had not even passed. Half a second to be exact. He'd timed it.

He walked to aisle three and stuck his hand into the wall between a box of tea lights and an empty can of L'Oréal hairspray. His fingers stretched and found the skinny drawing sticks and his drawing pad underneath.

He sat in a chair and studied his subject. Through her funny looking glasses, he learned her eyelashes and their thick black curl. A little like spider's legs, he thought. He was one hundred percent confident he could draw them just right because he had a lot of practice at drawing lashes. He might even consider himself professional at it. He learned her triangle nose and her lips, soft and plump like tobacco worms. His eyes wandered along her long neck and the bones of her collar. He learned all of her hollow parts and decided he would shade those with gray. He learned the stones in her knees, the little rocks in her ankles, and the pebbles in her toes. He learned her entire body and all of its young beauty until finally he was ready to make his mark.

He squeezed the handles, and his switchblade knife clicked in position. He sharpened the pencil with the blade and pressed the pencil's tip against the drawing pad, but he couldn't bring himself to go any further. He felt bad, ashamed, as if he was stealing from her. He promised himself if he drew her, he would treat her picture with one hundred percent respect, but he didn't want to make his real true friend mad or hurt her in any way, so he told himself, he would ask her permission first. It was the gentleman thing to do. So, he sat there and learned her some more so that when he did draw her for the first time, he would draw her perfect.

††††

Gradle woke up, blinded by the shiny edge of Delvis's switchblade knife. She jumped and flattened her back against the wall and hit her head on the sill of a boarded-up window. She straightened her glasses. The inside of her mouth felt like a sweater. Her head throbbed.

"I didn't mean to scare you," Delvis said, putting down his knife. "I's just studyin' you."

She took in her surroundings, trying to remember where she was. She spotted the empty Styrofoam box from The Western Steer sitting on the floor, and the night before all came back to her.

"I been waitin' up all night for the Tooth Fairy," Delvis said.

Gradle checked her ear for her earring and found it gone. She rummaged through the bed, stripped the sheets back, and lifted the pillow, but all she found was Delvis's rotten tooth. She picked up his tooth and held it in her hand. She remembered telling herself she would exchange it somehow, even though she had no idea what to exchange it for. The only thing she brought with her to Delvis's house was his steak dinner. She reached in her bra, thinking perhaps she could sneak a sequin from the letter he had written her, but the letter was not there. All she had was the Polaroid of Delvis, and the photograph of Grandpa, smiling beside her mother.

"Maybe she'll come back tonight," she said.

"No, no," Delvis said. "I seen that Tooth Fairy this mornin'. But I scared her away on accident. I heard her magic wand sparkin' outside so I walked out on the porch and saw her in the air right in front of me. She flew up and then stood still for a little bit, like she was surprised to see me, and then she flew off quick-like and disappeared."

"What'd she look like?"

"Like a flyin' diamond," he said. I'm gone try to catch her next time."

"You can't catch her, Delvis. She's a fairy," Gradle said. She put his tooth back under the pillow.

Delvis cleared his throat. He put his fingers to his neck, coughed something up, and spat it in an empty Sanka can. "'Cuse me," he said. "I still got that bullfrog in my throat. I went up to Dr. Smith's office yesterday, and told him just to pull it out with some pliers, but he told me there ain't nothin' in there and all it was, was a figure of speech."

"Maybe he'll jump out on his own," Gradle said, as she remade her ponytail.

"I've had one in there before and that's what happened. He jumped out in my sleep, and I found him hoppin' around on the floor the next mornin'." He cleared his throat again. "You hungry?"

"Starving," she said.

"I got all kinds of eatin' things growin' in the garden. I'll go pick us somethin' to eat."

She followed Delvis out on his porch. Dark clouds threw a hot shade across the yard. A breeze picked up and swept flower petals into a dance along the porch. She wondered where they came from

but couldn't find a suitable home. There were no flower bushes
around except for the hanging baskets of coral geraniums.

"Right there," Delvis said, pointing to where the petals were.
"That's where I seen the Tooth Fairy, right there at the bottom of
the steps. You stay here," he said. "I'll go pick us some food."

Gradle sat down on a bright red pleather booth she didn't recall
being there the last time she was here. She removed the photographs
from her bra, stared at Grandpa, and recalled her fight with him the
night before. There he was, smiling that great big smile, and there
was her mother smiling, too. She stared at her mother, her ponytail,
her thick raven bangs chopped crooked and too short, her chiffon
tank dress, her cat-eye glasses. Gradle went inside Delvis's shack
and retrieved the cracked hand mirror she used to spot Delvis's
tooth. She sat back down on the booth, stared into the mirror and
wondered *Where was Gradle Bird?*

She put the mirror down and surveyed Delvis's junk-littered
yard, and while she listened to his Coca-Cola whirligig spin in the
breeze, she wondered if it was possible to find herself in Delvis's
odd and magical world.

"Look at these rubies," Delvis said, running up the porch steps
and holding up two ripe tomatoes. He sat on the booth's edge where
the foam was coming out and bounced his knees, as if he was either
giddy or gut-sick. "You like my booth? I got it yesterday from the
dumpster. They're givin' the Dairy Queen up town a redo and I liked
the color and the way it sits," he said. He sliced up the tomatoes with
his switchblade knife. "I'm a professional dumpster diver. I'm the
best in the state. Maybe even in the entire Southeast region. Ain't
nobody can compete with me. I'm not braggin', just the facts." He
fanned the tomato slices atop his forearm and presented them to
her as if they were atop a serving tray.

She picked out a slice and bit into it.

"What sets me apart is I can fix anything that's tore up. Give me anything, a broke TV, broke microwave, lawnmower, car, anything broke I can fix it. Once I get it workin' right, I take it up to Rick's Pawn Shop and negotiate price. Some of the stuff I like to keep myself, but stuff I don't want I fix and sell."

"Did you make that?" she asked, pointing to his whirligig that now spun like mad in the wind.

"Yeah. I got a patent on that one. So nobody can steal my design. That one is a mystery. Nobody can't figure out how it works. Like hummingbird wings. Nobody knows how they work neither."

"How'd you learn to do all this stuff?" she asked.

"I was borned into it," he said.

"Was your Daddy a professional dumpster diver?"

"I ain't never known my daddy or my mama. I was borned in the junkyard. They found me when I was a few days old. They had all kinds of people wantin' to adopt me. All over the world. I was a miracle they kept tellin' everybody, so it was natural people wanted me. Hilda Green finally got me. She's this woman who liked to keep children. She had an egg carton full of us. She raised me 'til I was in the third reader, and then she died. And I got it in my mind to go out on my own, and I did, and I been right here ever since."

"I never knew my daddy or mama either." She picked another tomato slice from his arm. "Nobody cared you didn't have anybody to look after you, make sure you went to school?"

"No," he said. Tomato juice ran down the side of his mouth. "They always said I was special. And besides, they didn't have the type of class in school that could work with a brain like mine. I was too smart for all the classes. So they just let me be out here on my own. It's the way I liked it and wanted it and couldn't nobody force me to do nothin' different 'cause I could draw and shoot my Ruger pistol within two seconds, ninety-seven percent accurate on target each and every time."

A hiss of lightning struck the yard, and a loud crack of thunder rattled the **NO** *TResPass-N* and *NO PichtER Tak-IN* signs on the wall.

"We gone get us a mean storm," he said, looking out at the clouds. When his eyes came back, they set on the photographs sitting in Gradle's lap. "Who's them people?"

She held the photographs up so Delvis could see. "That's you," she said. She showed Delvis the photograph of himself. "And that's Grandpa and my mama."

Delvis took the photograph of Grandpa and her mother and put it close to his eyes. He turned his head slightly to the side and furrowed his brows. He put his fingers to his face and patted it, as if comparing Grandpa's face to his own, and then he put his fingers to his ears and traced their gigantic Cs.

He held up his great big hands and turned them over and back over and over again. His eyes honed in on Grandpa's hands, and they stayed there, studying them through and through. Whatever he saw in the photograph rendered him speechless. He swallowed hard, his Adam's apple a greased ball in his throat, and when he finally tore himself from the photograph and looked at Gradle, his blue eyes were calculating. He held the photograph to his eyes again. "He looks real familiar to me," he said, and he handed her the picture.

"He's a real dick sometimes," she said, comparing Grandpa's image to Delvis. There was a resemblance. She must have noticed it before, but hadn't paid it much mind until now, dismissing this familiarity to an imagination warped by her desperation and desire to be the apple of Grandpa's eye. She didn't know why she had run here. She didn't know what drew her so much to Delvis. It was odd, a girl of her age befriending a crazy man in his sixties, much less spending the night with him. Maybe it was leftover guilt.

Pity. Fascination. Heartache. Maybe it was a little of everything combined. But now, as she compared their smiles, she realized her attraction was simple. Delvis reminded her of Grandpa.

"Look at you," he said, pointing to Gradle's mother in the photograph. "That's a big fish you got."

"That's not me," she said. "That's my mama."

Delvis scratched his head. "Sure looks like you."

She did look like her. She looked exactly like her, purposely like her, so much she *was* her. She removed her cat-eye glasses and stared at Delvis. "Do I look like her now?"

"Yes, but without the glasses," he said.

She pulled her hair from her ponytail, felt the weight of it brush her shoulders, and pulled it around to one side. "What about now? Do I still look like her?"

"Yes, but without the glasses and with your hair down," he said.

"Will you cut my hair?"

Delvis's knees bounced. "Why? You got pretty hair."

"I want you to cut it."

"I ain't got no scissors. The pair I had rusted in the rain."

"Use your knife," she said. She banded her hair back into a ponytail. "Cut right above here," she said, pointing to the band.

"I ain't no professional at cuttin' hair."

"You won't hurt me."

He wrung his hands and picked at the foam busting out of the red Dairy Queen booth. "I ain't got no practice at cuttin' hair."

"Just cut right here, that's it," she said.

Delvis fidgeted with his fluorescent orange shoestrings. He looked at her one good time like he was about to take action, but he started messing with his shoestrings again.

"Do you need to suck on some tree bark?" she asked. "Get you over the hump?"

"You know me, I will accept any and all challenges," he said, drew in a deep breath, and let it blow. The shiny blade switched out of its handles with an aggressive click. He grabbed her hair and drew it taut, and with four saws of the knife, her long raven ponytail came loose in his hand.

She felt an oppressive weight lift off her shoulders. She reached back and judged the length of her hair.

"Cut it all off," she said.

Delvis re-banded her ponytail and draped it around his neck like a lady would a stole. He sawed and cut, releasing tufts of her hair into the storm, and with each saw, cut, and release, she felt lighter and lighter. Weightless.

He blew the last bit of hair from his fingertips. "That's 'bout as close as I can get it without cuttin' you," he said.

She reached to her head and had nothing to grab. "What about now? Do I look like her?"

"You look like you." He folded the blade gently back in its frames.

He walked to the edge of the porch and looked out at the rain. His heel nervously tapped against the sagging boards. It grew louder and louder as if he might explode. He spun around and stabbed her with his eyes. "Can I draw you?"

"What for?"

"'Cause you're pretty," he said. "I like to draw pretty things. I'd like to draw you for keep sake."

She brought her knees into her chest, an effort to shield her sudden insecurity. She looked at the sagging porch floor and raked her fingers through her inch-long hair. "You think I'm pretty?"

"I'm sorry," he said, bowing his head. "I didn't mean to make you mad." He wrung his hands and stared down at his fluorescent orange shoestrings. "I'm a plain person, Gradle. And I don't know how to talk right sometimes."

"You're not plain," she said. "You can draw me if you want."

He rushed into the house and came out with a pad and a pencil and samples of what he had drawn before.

"This here's a unicorn," he said. He sat on the edge of the booth. "I saw it back behind my house a little over a year ago. It stood in the woods long enough to let me draw him. No, I couldn'ta drawed that if I hadn'ta seen him. At the time, I didn't have no picture camera, so I couldn't take a picture, so I drawed him for proof. I submitted to the newspaper, but they was too scared to print it. Might cause widespread panic. I make replicas, two drawings of everything I draw for security reasons. In case one of 'em gets lost or stolen I got a backup."

"Wow," she said, marveling at the skill it took to draw something so imaginary and make it look so real.

He took the picture away and switched it for another. It was a portrait of his dog, Rain. He had drawn a teardrop rolling down the side of Rain's face, and in it was Delvis's reflection. It looked so real; she touched the teardrop with her finger, expecting it to feel warm and wet. He showed her three more pictures, all of a woman in a dress. Each portrait progressed in skill and detail, as if the woman was something that required a lot of practice. She was thin and frail like the threads of spiderwebs, and although it was possible to see that at one time she possessed an incredible beauty, she was aged beyond her years, wasted away with what looked like grief. Gradle knew the look all too well. She had lived with it, memorized it without any effort. Just like Grandpa, the woman's sadness was everywhere, in the hollows of her cheeks, in the creases of her eyes, and even in the smile on her face that seemed to struggle not to show teeth.

"Who's she?" Gradle looked closely and found Delvis's reflection in the sadness of the woman's right eye.

"I don't know. She wouldn't ever tell me her name. I thought she didn't like the picture I'd drawn of her, so I kept practicin' at her portrait, hopin' I'd see her again. But I only seen her once."

"Why's she so sad?"

"I reckon she was lonely."

Gradle studied the woman again, wondering if loneliness could eventually kill a person, if it would eventually kill her. "Where'd you learn to draw?"

He leaned back into the booth and popped his knuckles. "Boys made fun of me at school. I was in the second reader. It was Thanksgivin' and the teacher said, 'ever-body draw a turkey'. I drawed a turkey for the teacher and the boys made fun of me. I will admit it was a little grizzly. So I sat up for six weeks trainin' myself. And now I'll give anybody a twenty-dollar reward if they make a mark, a letter, a dot, what have you, that I can't make a picture out of. No sense braggin', just the facts." He clasped his hands in front of his belly. "God shows me what to draw. With his help," he pointed to the sky, "there's nothin' I will fail at. But there's one thing," he said, pausing to allow his eyes to grow mean, "I will not, no matter how nice somebody asks me, I will not draw a picture of Jesus Christ. I refuse. 'Cause in the Bible it says make no false images of me. Anything with Jesus Christ I won't draw."

"You won't go to hell for drawing me," she said.

"I promise you, Gradle. I'll treat it with one hundred percent respect."

He laid his drawing pad on his lap and skinned the pencil's tip with his knife.

She dropped one leg from her chest and tucked her cheek against her upright knee. Her wrists hooked around her ankle, and the fingers that could reach cupped the undersides of her toes.

His eyes caught her. He pinched down his view and magnified

something within her she could feel but couldn't see. He made a mark. His pencil let loose like something wild from a cage. She felt powerful and guilty, a little bit erased. Exposed, yet free.

When he was done, he titled the portrait, **POrTɾAIT** *of* **GRɑDle B̊iRd**, and signed his code name in the lobe of her ear: **D-5**. He handed her the portrait and pointed out his reflection nested in one of the many diamonds that formed her iris. "That's my trademark. I put me in everything I draw." His eyes were assured, yet desperately sought her approval.

She studied the drawing, and it made her eyes hurt. "That's me."

"That's you, Gradle Bird," he said, hooked his thumbs together, and motioned his hands like flying wings.

CHAPTER THIRTEEN

SONNY JOE WOKE on the wooden church pew with a brown-liquor hangover and a hard-on. He sat up, adjusted his groin, and picked the nuggets of sleep from his eyes before he took down what was left in the half-pint of Southern Comfort. He looked around the dark sanctuary for Ceif and found him in the pulpit, preaching from his Bible to an audience of one. He had listened to Ceif preach a hundred times, his sermons always following on the day after a long booze bender or an all-nighter steeped in nothing but no good. It didn't matter how much sin they'd wallowed in the night before, no matter if they still stunk of it, Ceif kept his faith. And while Sonny Joe didn't believe in angels, he always found his crippled friend preaching from the pulpit a bit angelic. But today was different. Ceif didn't look like an angel. In fact, Sonny Joe found him a bit devilish. Ceif had danced with Gradle last night and still, even in the morning, it was eating him up inside.

Ceif's Bible hissed as he turned the pages. He bowed his head and prepared. "Love is patient. Love is kind. It is not jealous," he said. He bore his dark eyes into Sonny Joe. "Love vaunteth not itself, it is not puffed up or arrogant. It does not act unbecomingly. It does not seek its own. It is not easily provoked. It thinketh no evil," he said, aiming right at him as if his little mouth was a barrel and his words, bullets. "It rejoiceth not in iniquity, but rejoiceth in the truth. Love beareth all things, believeth all things, hopeth all things, endureth all things,"

"I know, preacher boy," Sonny Joe said. "You want to save my soul if it becomes the death of you." His words were hollow and echoed off the sanctuary walls. "Maybe you ought to put an ad in the paper about your church out here so you can get a real flock, and be a real preacher, and preach to some people who'll actually give a damn."

"You are my flock," Ceif said, closing his Bible shut.

"Why do you worship me so much?"

"It ain't worship."

"What is it then?"

"I pity your soul."

A smile cut up the side of Sonny Joe's mouth. He slid to the end of the church pew, got on his hands and knees, and crawled down the center aisle. He knelt at the altar and sprawled his arms down the warped wooden railing like the crucified Jesus himself, and stared up at Ceif, his eyes posed in the most willing and helpless position they could find.

"Save me, motherfucker," he said.

Ceif hobbled down from the pulpit and laid his hands on Sonny Joe's shoulders. "Father God," he said, "we come to you right now in the name of your most Holy son, Jesus Christ, asking you to accept Sonny Joe."

Sonny Joe's arm started to shake. The more Bible words Ceif let loose from his mouth, the more Sonny Joe shook.

"If you confess with your mouth that Jesus is Lord and believe in your heart that God raised him from the dead, you will be saved," Ceif said, laying his hands atop Sonny Joe's head.

His entire body shook now, and he could hear the passion in Ceif's voice rise, as if his physical reaction was fuel for Ceif's heart. Sonny Joe stood up. His body convulsed. His eyes rolled back into his head.

"Say it!" Ceif yelled.

Sonny Joe writhed around on the floor like a serpent in hot ashes.

"Accept Jesus Christ as your Lord and Savior. Say it!"

His body went still. He closed his eyes. The sanctuary was silent. Ceif nudged his ribs with his shoe. "Say it."

He opened his eyes and found Ceif standing over him. A halo of light lit up his crown and his dumb, innocent expression of suspense. He had turned back into a little angel.

"I had you going, man," he laughed. He backslapped Ceif's thigh.

"Dick-wad," Ceif said.

"I admire you. You're a persistent little fucker. One day you might get lucky and catch me in a weak moment. But it ain't today." He sat up, proud he had put the hurt on Ceif, and punched him in the arm. "Come on man, let's blow this joint."

Sonny Joe lit a cigarette and cranked the truck while Ceif slid in the passenger's seat and punched the rain out of his hat. Sonny Joe slung mud all the way down the road with one thing on his mind—Gradle Bird.

Ceif flipped the visor down and looked at himself the mirror. He finger-brushed his teeth and combed his hair to the side before gingerly placing his hat back on his head.

"What you primping for?" Sonny Joe coughed in his hand, checking for bad breath.

"Gradle Bird. I think she likes me," Ceif said, and tipped his hat. "You might wanna spit down that cowlick you're sporting." He nodded at Sonny Joe's head.

Sonny Joe looked in the rearview mirror. "Fuck," he said. He looked like shit. His eyes were bloated and bloodshot, and the stubble on his face made him look dirtier than usual. He spat on his palm, and the whole way to town he tried to iron the cowlick down. He stopped at the Rite Aid, lifted a bottle of gel, and used it to finally get his hair to go flat.

He parked the truck in front of the Old Spivey house and got that feeling he always got when he came anywhere near that girl. His stomach hollowed and filled up with a thousand beating wings. He wasn't scared of much, but there was something about Gradle that spooked his nerves.

"You gonna get out?" Ceif asked. He pulled the handle with the hook of his cane and pushed Sonny Joe's door open.

They walked to the porch. The swing, decorated like a grave with wilted swamp lilies, creaked and swung in a wind that wasn't there. But it wasn't the home's creepiness that scared him, it was rather the thought that when Gradle came to the door, she would look at Ceif first.

His palms began to water. He grabbed the bundle of swamp lilies from the swing, shook the rain from their petals, and held them against his heart as he positioned himself in front of the beveled glass door.

"Don't you think that's a little desperate?" Ceif asked.

"I should've left you at home." He knocked on the door. A hawk moth fluttered past his ear, and he flinched as it tickled his lobe and left wing-dust on his shoulder.

"You nervous?" Ceif asked.

"Shut up midget," he said. He nudged Ceif's cane, forcing him off balance.

He cupped his hand and stared through the glass. Darkness flooded the long hallway except at its end where a square of light shown through the back door's window. He knocked again, but nobody came.

"She must be hungover," he said, and as he walked down the porch steps, the front door creaked open.

"Where is she?" Grandpa came out on the porch with a shotgun in his hand. He looked beat up. His wifebeater was dirty and stretched, and his suspenders hung down to the knees of the same funky plaid pants he wore at Jimmy's the night before. A bruise yellowed one of two swollen eyes. His hair was like a rat's nest.

"We thought she'd be here," Sonny Joe said.

"She's not here," he said, walking down the porch steps. The man grabbed him by the front of the shirt and shook. "Where is she?"

"If I knew she wasn't here, I sure in the hell wouldn't be here." Sonny Joe ripped his shirt out of the man's hands. "No wonder she's all fucked up," Sonny Joe said, and got into his truck.

Ceif climbed into the cab and lit a cigarette. "You're fucked up."

"We're all fucked up." He threw the swamp lilies on the dash and revved the engine. "I bet I know where she is," he said, punched Delvis's cassette tape in the jam box, and skidded out of the yard, flinging blades of grass at the old man who probably would have kicked his ass or killed him if he'd stayed a minute longer.

†††

Sonny Joe rolled the truck to a slow stop and took a rip from his cigarette. Its tip glowed russet like the sun setting behind a stand of pine. Smoke snaked from his mouth as he watched Delvis's door, hoping Gradle might pick up his scent and walk out any minute to greet him.

"How you reckon we get her to come out?" he asked, inhaling his smoke.

"Firecrackers," Ceif said, and tucked a cigarette behind his ear for later.

"We ain't got to worry 'bout his dog no more," Sonny Joe said. Smoke filled his lungs as he stared at the empty doghouse and the white cross that marked a grave.

A gun fired in the distance. They jumped, and the cherry of Sonny Joe's cigarette broke off and singed a hole in the knee of his jeans. He saw Gradle in that green dress appear from behind the house, and it gave him the tickles. She walked to a wooden sawhorse topped with Coke cans and mason jars, one of which a bullet had just busted through. She picked up the busted jar and smiled back at Delvis who was walking her way with three jars in his hand.

Sonny Joe revved the engine, and it drew her attention as designed. She signaled Delvis to wait and moved through the weeds in his direction. Tufts of dandelion floated above her bare feet like some kind of magical fume. She wore a holster and had a gun in her hand. She was natural with it.

"What're you doing here?" she asked.

His groin swelled. "Hunting you," he said, trying to figure out what was different about her. She had always been beautiful, but he had never seen her beauty so flagrant.

"I like your hair," Ceif said, removed his hat, and handed her the wilted bundle of swamp lilies Sonny Joe had tried to steal as his own.

Sonny Joe got a whiff of the flowers and Ceif's stink. He wanted to smack the shit out of him.

"Thanks," she said. Her hand caressed the back of her naked neck. "Delvis cut it."

"He cut off your good luck charm too?" Sonny Joe asked, nodding at her ear.

She thumbed the naked lobe of her ear. "I lost it," she said.

"Lucky you," Sonny Joe said. He took a rip off his cigarette. "What's with the gun?"

She popped the chamber open, spun the revolver, and snapped it closed. "Delvis is giving me lessons. In case I need to fend off dirty outlaws such as yourself."

"I'm through takin' this mess from you outlaws!" Delvis yelled from the backyard. He ran toward the truck, stopped halfway, jumped in the air and did a twirling kick. "This is private property! Ain't no trespassin' allowed!" He sprinted toward Gradle, scooped her in his arms, and carried her like a bride to the porch. He laid her on the red booth, grabbed the pistol from her hand, and came back through the yard, his legs lunging and his arms frozen straight out in front of him as if pretending to be some kind of movie spy.

Sonny Joe didn't know whether to laugh or run.

"Let's get out of here, man." Ceif slapped Sonny Joe's ribs.

"That gun ain't loaded."

"I'm sure he's got plenty of bullets in his pockets."

"If you're scared, preacher boy, start praying."

Delvis approached Sonny Joe's window. His eyes quaked. "Don't make a move! I can draw shoot this Ruger pistol within two seconds ninety-seven percent accurate on target every time. I don't wish to shoot nobody, but I will if I'm forced to." He leaned in the window, and got a look at Ceif who was whispering in silence into the Bible pressed against his lips. "I'm a God-lovin' person too, but if you reach down and draw a gun, I'll take you out before you can count to one." He cleared his throat and spat to the side. "I'm that fast. I ain't braggin'. It's just the facts. You know who I am? I'm an undercover FBI agent, and I'll have you two put under the personal protective act if I have to."

"Delvis!" Gradle yelled, as she ran through the yard. She grabbed him by the arm. "They're my friends."

Delvis looked at Gradle as if she'd punched him in the gut.

"That's Ceif and this is Sonny Joe," she said.

Delvis stuck his head through the window. The room between their eyes was crowded, and Sonny Joe could smell pepper and mouthwash on his breath.

"I know you boys. You always comin' up here puttin' harassments on me. Throwin' rocks and firepoppers. I know you," he said, putting his pointer finger on Sonny Joe's nose. "And I know you." He pointed to Ceif. "You ought to be gracious I can shoot on target."

"We're big fans of yours," Sonny said. He pressed play on his jam box, and Delvis's music blared loud through the speakers.

"How'd you get that music? You know it's copyrighted in the Library of Congress, Washington, D.C."

"Gradle left it in my truck last night," Sonny Joe said, smiling. "Been listening to it ever since. 'Bout to wear it out. I don't understand why you ain't all over the radio waves."

Delvis lowered his gun and shoved it in the band of his pants. "Which song you like best?"

"When the Whippoorwills Holler at Night," Sonny Joe said. "What about you Ceif? Which one's your favorite?"

"I like the one about your dog, Rain," he said.

"Them's all my originals. I invented that type of music," Delvis said, cleared his throat and spat on the ground. "I got contracts from music firms all over the world wantin' my original music, but I ain't signed with one of them."

"Why not?" Sonny Joe asked.

"I'm lookin' for the right break. Timin's got to be good."

"Will you play something for us? I bet you sound real good live," Sonny Joe said.

"Well, I don't know. I got sore fingers and a damaged throat, so I don't know how good I'll be."

"If you ain't up for entertainin', we'll come back later," Sonny Joe said. He flicked his cigarette out of the window.

"I always satisfy my fans," Delvis said. "And I accept any and all challenges. Get out of the truck."

Sonny Joe and Ceif got out of the truck, and Delvis patted them down.

"Got to make sure y'all ain't got no recording devices, 'cause everything I got's copyrighted."

They followed Delvis, who walked toward his porch with violent momentum. He whipped around twice on the way there to give Sonny Joe and Ceif the once-over. It was the first time Sonny Joe had ever been this close to the man. The intimacy made some of his prior opinions change. This man was wilder and cooler than him, and he couldn't help but smile.

"Y'all sit on the Dairy Queen booth. I'll get my guitar," Delvis said. He raked his throat and spat out something that held his attention for a while. His chin rested on his shoulder, and he looked at Gradle and smiled. "I just got the frog out," he said, and he slithered through his door like a pissed-off snake.

"He's intense," Sonny Joe said, grabbing the cigarette behind Ceif's ear. He motioned to Ceif for the lighter.

Ceif sparked the flame and held it in front of Sonny Joe's eyes, a little too close, as if to warn him of something. He lifted his cigarette to the flame then blew the fire out.

He sat beside Gradle on the booth and opened up his body for her to see. "What're you doing here, Gradle Bird?"

"Me and Grandpa got in a fight."

"And this is where you run to?" Sonny Joe asked, drawing in her scent.

"I don't have anywhere else."

"What about me?"

Sonny Joe stared at Gradle, inhaled his smoke, and when he let it out, the door swung open and out came Delvis wearing a blue polyester suit, a white cowboy hat, and his guitar. Draped around his neck was a tail of shiny raven hair that no doubt once belonged to Gradle. He wore it proud, like a prize. "Who give you them flowers?" he asked, staring at the dead lilies in Gradle's lap.

Sonny Joe pointed to Ceif. "He did."

"You don't belong to be givin' her no flowers," Delvis said.

"It was a gesture of respect," Ceif said.

"You belong to be respectful," Delvis said. He gave Ceif an unpredictable eye. "Them flowers is dead. Gradle, I can get you some real live livin' ones, some real special ones." He sat in a chair and tuned his guitar. The gold on his fingers flashed like fire. "These flowers I got are secret 'cause nobody in the universe can smell 'em except me. Not the police, the FBI, or the GBI. I was borned with nose holes that were 'specially designed to pick up that particular smell."

"What do they smell like?" Sonny Joe asked.

"Flowers," Delvis said. He reared his head back, strummed his guitar, and made the kind of music built of hillbilly bones. He stopped his riff and announced, "This is one of my originals. It's a boogie-oogie-type style, my style of boogie-oogie invented by me in 1983. It's called, 'Over to Me'."

"I went to a dance one night," Delvis sang out the words.

Sonny Joe laughed when Delvis's voice severely cracked on the word "night."

Delvis stopped playing and cleared his throat. "I'm sorry. My voice got rust in it. And I had that frog caught up in there so my throat's a little damaged, and I don't sound right."

"Take your time, Mr. Miles," Ceif said. "Do what you need to warm up."

"Light that lighter near my throat," Delvis said.

Ceif flipped his lighter and kneeled at Delvis's feet. He moved the flame back and forth under Delvis's chin. His hand was steady, but his mouth quivered like he was about to cry.

"Forgive me," Ceif said, "for ever being mean to you."

Their eyes made contact, and their union was amplified by the flame's light; holy, Ceif would say, like something out of his beat-up Bible. "Mind if I pray?"

"No, I don't mind," Delvis said, as Ceif took his hands.

"Dear Heavenly Father. Forgive us of our sins. Have mercy on us. And bless Delvis's throat and tongue so that he may sing the music you want him to sing. In Jesus's precious name we pray, Amen," Ceif said. He unbowed his head.

"By all means, thank you. My throat's pretty warmed up now." He belted out the first line of the song. "I went to a dance one night!" He leaned back in his chair as if the power of his voice had blown him that direction.

Ceif hobbled over and sat beside Gradle, who stared at him with some sort of adoration.

"Queer," Sonny Joe said, kicking Ceif's cane. "I didn't realize you were gonna turn this into a church event."

Ceif ignored him and clapped his hands to the beat of Delvis's song.

I went to a dance one night
What I seen was a beautiful sight
It was a beautiful raven doin' her thing

She was dancin' the bibble-bobble-boo
Pretty as could be
Her diamond eyes looked right on me

You could hear them guitars
Sounding out a strange kind of boogie
Just right to dance to
She danced over and gave me a kiss
Winked at me then started to twist

I's so glad as you could see
That beautiful raven going out with me
Oh, do it baby
Twist it over to me, baby

She was doing the bibble-bobble-boo
As pretty as could be
Her diamond eyes looked right on me

Sonny Joe paid careful attention to Delvis's lyrics as he sang the song another time through. There was no doubt in his mind Gradle was the beautiful girl with raven hair and diamond eyes, and there was no doubt in Sonny Joe's mind that he wasn't the only one in love. All three of them were in love with her.

Gradle and Ceif hooted and clapped together after Delvis finished the song. Their coupling made Sonny Joe feel he was losing his gain. He felt on the outside, trying to intrude his way in.

"This one's a slow type," Delvis said. "Wrote in 1991. Copyrighted. This one's a good song to dance slow with a girl to. It's got a short title. It's called 'Moonlight'." He strummed the guitar slow, closed his eyes, and sang, "You're pretty in the moonlight. And the moonlight is pretty in you."

Ceif rose with the support of his cane, removed his hat, and held out his hand for Gradle to take.

Sonny Joe kicked Ceif's cane from under him and pulled Gradle to her feet. "My turn," he said, and pressed her body into his. He hooked his arms around her back and felt the blades of her shoulders and her timid breath letting go by his ear. He moved his hands down the bumps of her spine, and held her tight so she wouldn't run away from him again.

The music stopped. Suddenly, she was torn out of his arms.

"Don't touch her like that!" Delvis said. He bumped his chest against Sonny Joe's. "You ain't treatin' her with one hundred percent respect. I can tell."

"Fuck you, retard." Sonny Joe slammed his hands into Delvis's chest, knocking his cowboy hat off his head.

Delvis came back at Sonny Joe fast. He knee-lifted him in the gut and tackled him to the ground. Sonny Joe's fists flailed wildly and pounded against Delvis's ears. He cracked his hand against his jaw and felt it give, but it did more damage to him than Delvis. He broke free of Delvis's hold, rose to his feet, but he couldn't stand straight due to the pain in his gut.

Delvis jumped to his feet, swiped Sonny Joe's legs from under him, and when Sonny Joe's back hit the floor, his breath left. Delvis grabbed one of Sonny Joe's legs, hugged it between his groins, and wrapped his other leg across his knee into the figure four. Delvis threw himself down to the floor and applied pressure that made Sonny Joe scream out like a girl. In the background he heard Gradle laugh.

Sonny Joe faced Delvis. The man was wild-eyed and crazy.

"Tap out!" Delvis yelled.

Sonny Joe looked to Ceif for help, but he was leaned against the porch railing, smoking with a smirk, silently and thoroughly enjoying the entertainment. He looked for Gradle to help, but she too appeared to be enjoying the show. Her hand was over her mouth, but he could see both sides of her smile grinning from ear to ear. She thought all this was funny.

Delvis reared his head back and put on the pressure until Sonny Joe had no other choice but to submit. He slapped his palm against the porch, tapping out as best he could.

Delvis unhooked Sonny Joe's legs, and they collapsed, stretched out and spent.

He straddled Sonny Joe and spat blood from his mouth. "That's my signature move. Ric "The Nature Boy" Flair stole it from me even though I got it copyrighted in the Library of Congress, Washington, D.C. That'll show you not to mess with me, boy. And don't be messin' with Gradle neither. She's my friend and deserves one hundred percent respect at all times."

Sonny Joe brushed himself off, ashamed he had become unmanned in such a way. At least he had made Delvis bleed, but it was not nearly enough damage. He shoved Delvis aside, unzipped his pants, and pulled out his wand. He pissed all over Delvis's porch, all the while staring at Gradle, letting her know she had done him harm.

"You're an asshole," she said, as Sonny Joe shook off his stick.

He pinched her chin and jerked it up toward his mouth. His pelvis pressed against hers. "You," he said, staring into her endless and cruel blue eyes, "are fucking crazy."

He kicked Delvis's guitar out of his way, walked toward his truck, and looked over his shoulder to make sure Ceif was following not too far behind.

††††

The insects were loud and electric. They deafened the night and so did the frogs whose throaty dialogues warned of rain. It was sticky and suffocating hot, but on occasion a little breeze would come up and bring currents strong enough to make the Coca-Cola whirligig whine and spin. Gradle sweated as she scrubbed Sonny Joe's urine from Delvis's porch. She could still smell him. Dirt. Fish. Church pews. And her.

Delvis sat on the red Dairy Queen booth and sliced petals out of a Sprite can with his switchblade knife. He had been working quietly, had not said anything since Sonny Joe and Ceif left, but she could tell he was talking loud in his head by the way his brows almost mumbled when he stopped his work and stared out into the dark and lonesome night.

She wanted to apologize, but the silence between them was too perfect to disturb. She felt responsible. She could have stopped everything. She could have stopped Sonny Joe from ever getting out of his truck. But she didn't. She went along and was lured like everybody else into the snares of Sonny Joe's seductive games. And while Delvis had managed to overpower him and make him admit out loud his defeat, Sonny Joe still won.

Delvis cleared his throat. It shut up the insects and frogs. He stabbed the Sprite can with a coat hanger, inserted washers on either side, and bent its cutout petals into a flashy-green flower. He rose from the booth and hung the Sprite-can whirligig on Gradle's finger.

She lifted it up and it spun in the breeze.

"I don't care one bit that boy pissed on my porch, but I ain't no retard," he said, picked up his guitar, and walked inside his shack.

CHAPTER
FOURTEEN

A TENDER RAIN TAPPED against the tin roof. Its raindrops clung to the attic window like crystal magnets. Annalee stood still and cold, stoned by the encounter with her son. She hadn't moved for over a day, didn't flinch as the moonflower burst into bloom or shift with the soft sunrise. There was a place people go when they die. But she had not gone there. She was not dead yet. And now she knew why.

She gripped the window's lever, and pulled it to, severing the moon vine's green veins, stopping its green blood. She secured the lock, closed the curtains, and shoved furniture over the attic flap, sealing its seams with boxes and bricks. She wanted no light, no draft, no sound, no Leonard. All she wanted was to die.

Against the far wall she went and lay upon the fainting couch. She removed the portrait from over her heart, stared at her reflection, and remembered when she was alive and the day Delvis drew her.

It was almost summer. Of all things, it was the acute craving for a tomato that brought her out of the house that day. Her parents had been killed in a car wreck and ever since she didn't have much reason to go out. Most days she kept to her bed, didn't put on make-up or bother to take a bath. The days she didn't keep to her bed, she kept to the house, wandering around the attic caught up in aimless make-believe. But on that particular day, her tomato craving snapped her out of it. She popped out of bed, took a bath, and applied red stain to her lips. She combed the matted knots in her hair and moisturized her skin. She wanted to be pretty again, the prettiest she'd ever been. So, she went to her closet and put on her white eyelet dress. So much time had passed, and it still smelled like Leonard.

She looked at herself in the mirror. The dress still fit, but since she last wore it, sadness had stunted her growth and aged her prematurely. But she was still so ungodly pretty. She slipped her purse on her wrist and turned the front door's knob. The sun blinded her eyes as the door broke through a seal of spiderwebs and a pile of mail collecting by the door.

In the town square, she moved through the bundles of people who stared and whispered at her back. She could only imagine what they said. How could a young woman with so much beauty be so shut-in? Was she coo-coo? Had she been dented in the head? The poor child; what a tragedy about her parents.

Annalee went from farmer to farmer asking for a tomato. They all estimated another two weeks, but still she waited all day under the shade of an oak, hoping a farmer from the next county south would show up with an early crop.

When the farmers began packing up, a slight wind blew and carried the soft sound of chimes. She rose from under the tree, walked toward the sound, and found another tree with limbs decorated with wind chimes. Some were made of forks and spoons, others with bottle caps and colored glass, another with sparkplugs and fresh water shells, all of which made their own original sounds. A ratty quilt spread out under the tree and was weighted down with all sorts of trinkets and framed artwork for sale. She ran her fingers through a wind chime and picked up a music box from the quilt. It had been stripped, painted yellow, and layered with shellac. Instead of a ballerina, there was a tiny porcelain cat with a broken tail in her place. She wound the box and allowed the music to crawl in her ear, losing herself in the sound as the broken-tailed cat pirouetted on its stem. She hadn't heard music since the day she made love to Leonard in the attic. Her eyes closed, but tears streamed down regardless, and when the music slowed and dwindled, she felt a tap on her shoulder.

"Ma'am, I see you like my creations," a voice said.

Annalee flinched. She turned around and found a young boy, all of perhaps twelve, with a pair of blue eyes that already seemed to know her.

"They're my own originals, made out of stuff people throw away and don't think ain't no good no more. I shiny 'em up and mix and match 'em with other things to make my own creations. They're copyrighted in the Library of Congress, Washington, D.C. so ain't nobody can copy what I do. You can't find this type of art work anywhere," the boy said. "Not even China. I put my signature on every one of 'em. It's in a hidden place so ain't nobody can mask over it." The boy turned over one of the shells of a wind chime. "See it?" he asked, pointing to the inside lip of the shell. Scratched in the shell's mortar were two letters: D-5.

"I can sell you this for a decent price," he said. "And it comes with a one hundred percent guarantee ain't nobody in the county will have a duplicate. Nobody in the universe for that matter. One hundred percent guaranteed. Or, if you like, I'll do your portrait. I got me a stool over there you can sit on for the posing. I like to

draw pretty things," he said. He took her by the hand and led her
to the stool.

His touch felt like electricity. It made her wonder if the feeling
was there because it had been so long since she had felt someone,
or if indeed there was some mysterious current between the two
of them. She situated herself on the stool while he tore a sheet of
paper from his book, secured it to his easel, and chose a pencil from
his jar. He inspected the pencil's tip and skinned it with a knife from
his pocket. He handed the pencil to Annalee and moved his easel
in front of her.

"Make a mark," he said. "You can draw a dot, a line, any kind
of mark, and I'll draw you from it. I like my subjects to participate
in my artwork. You can do a circle for your eyes. An *M* for your lips.
Anything you want."

A breeze picked up. It tickled her face and the chimes in the tree.
She hovered the pencil over the blank canvas unsure of how to start
her portrait. One of her eyelashes blew onto the canvas.

"Can you start with this?" she asked, pointing to her lash.

"I can work with anything. That's my talent. I'm especially good
at drawing lashes," he said, licked the tip of his thumb, and sealed
the lash to the paper with spit. "In fact, I'm semi-professional at it.
Not yet professional. Four more years at practicin' drawin' lashes,
and I'll be a professional."

He took the pencil from her hand and began to sketch her face,
starting with what people always said was the most perfect line of
a forehead. As his fingers bridled the pencil, as his wrist moved
across the canvas, she caught traces of his scent. Carrots, sweet,
sweet carrots. She looked around for the farmer that must have
been nearby with a crate full of them, but the square was empty.
The sky had turned twilight, and they were all alone.

"Can you look forward ma'am?" he asked. "My memory ain't

photographic yet, and I need to make sure I get the angle of your cheeks right."

She was scared to look at him, but she had to validate what in her gut she feared was true. She studied the boy with as much intensity as he studied her. He was mostly Leonard. He had his ears exactly, his butterfly-winged ears. He had his hands, his long-fingered hands, musician's hands, artist's hands. His eyes were Leonard's, too. Sparkling blue marbled mazes one could get lost in for days. And he had his smile, his magnetic, dimpled smile.

She searched for herself in him, but it had been so long since she had seen a mirror she had almost forgotten her own face. It wasn't until he finished the bones of her cheek and the heart of her chin that she found evidence he was hers. She shivered as if it was the dead of winter.

He got close to her face and began to count her lashes. "Hold still," he said. "Try not to blink."

She couldn't help it. She couldn't control it. Her eyes kept blinking, her lids like cloths trying to blot away her tears.

"One hundred twenty-five plus thirty-six," he said, moving on to her other eye.

After he counted her lashes one by one, he drew them on his page, adding company to the real lash of her eye. With each pencil stroke he made, she felt her lashes being plucked out, three hundred and four times, as she remembered the ride home from that forsaken place and the man with the cherry-smelling pipe that had picked her up alongside the road.

"Can you smile?" he asked.

Her fingers went to her mouth in an effort to prevent it from wailing. She bit down on her ring as his hand moved her fingers away so he could study the mouth that had kissed his tiny little forehead once, once and never again.

He drew her mouth, shaded her temples, and sketched her nose. As a final touch, he went back to her eyes, the right eye, and worked there for a little while, detailing something small, something intricate. When he was finished, he titled his work: "*POrTrAIT of.*" He removed the paper from his easel and presented it for her review.

"If you don't like it, I can do better," he said.

He must have seen her breathlessness and thought it was a result of his art.

"I put two signatures on this one. My typical style signature using my code name. And then I put a special signature on this one. A little experimentation I ain't never done before." He pointed his finger to the right eye he had drawn, and there in her bottom lid, he had sketched a reflection of himself wading in the pool of her gathering tears.

She stared at her portrait in awe of the detail and artistic rendering. He must be some sort of genius. It was a perfect mug shot. All these years, she had gotten away with her crime, escaped a jury, a long sentence in prison, until now. He had captured his perpetrator, his attempted murderer, his mother, down to every last lash.

"Do you like it?" he asked. "If you don't like it, I can practice some more."

Annalee reached in her purse and handed him all of her money.

"I ain't finished with it yet ma'am," he said, pushing the money back at her. "I don't take money until it's complete. What's your name? I need to put your name in the title."

She dropped the money at his feet. "I'm sorry," she said. She ran off clutching the portrait against her chest.

When she got home, she went up to the attic, locked the window, and pulled the curtains. She pushed every piece of furniture and stacked every heavy box atop the attic flap to secure her prison door, to seal up her grave. She hung her white eyelet dress in the wardrobe, clothed herself all in black, and swallowed hundreds of poisonous moonflower seeds. She lay on the fainting couch, holding the portrait against her chest. She took a deep breath, crossed her heart, and hoped to die.

And now after reliving it all, she found herself in the very same place, in the very same spot, except now she was a ghost. She lay her head back on the couch's rest, popped moonflower seeds in her mouth, and clutched the portrait now decades old against her chest. She took a deep breath, crossed her heart, and hoped to die again.

CHAPTER
FIFTEEN

DELVIS WOKE AT the split of dawn and immediately checked under the pillow to see if the Tooth Fairy had come. There was no sign of her, just his back molar and the bare floor on which he had slept. She must have had too many teeth to collect last night. If there were five billion people in the world and last night half of them lost their teeth, she would be busy. Maybe she was like Santa Claus and had reindeer to help out her speed. But he didn't remember seeing any reindeer the last time he saw her. She was all by herself. All by her sparkling diamond self. He wondered if she would come back tomorrow, but maybe he had scared her so bad the other day she had no mind to come back anytime soon. He scared people all the time. He didn't know why. He just knew he did. Maybe she had decided to let him keep his tooth and had hidden his gift somewhere else. Maybe she had forgotten. But something with that kind of magic must have an extra special memory. He would ask Gradle what she thought about it all once she woke up from her peaceful and pretty sleep.

He unlatched the front door bolt and stepped out on the porch to see if maybe the Tooth Fairy was waiting for him outside. He always kept his doors locked up tight in case somebody like George "The Animal" Steele tried to get inside and put him in the Camel Clutch. A wild grey cat scared from the woodpile and ran up under one of his old fixer-upper cars. Its hood was ajar like an alligator's mouth collecting rain. Along the horizon, a pink sun shredded the clouds and began to scare away the mist that looked like a ghost hovering over the hairy balls of dandelion weed. He walked to various places on his porch, stood still, and sniffed the world suspiciously. He grabbed an old rake that was propped up against the wall and raked the porch, concentrating in the area in front of the door. He looked for footprints and fairy dust. He looked for any sign, any clue somebody had come during the night.

Somebody had. But the evidence didn't appear in a footprint or with fairy dust, but rather it appeared on a handwritten note taped to the screened door. He snatched the note with his hand and read it out loud, "*BE AT THE PIGGLY WIGGLY PAY PHONE AT 12 NOON SHARP TO ACCEPT A VERY IMPORTANT PHONE CALL.*"

Delvis grinned from ear to ear. It was a note from the record company. He had waited all his life for this to happen. Gradle's friends must have gone out and spread the word about his singing and guitar talents, and now the record companies had caught wind of it. They must want to talk to him about recording some of his original songs and copyrighting them in the Library of Congress, Washington, D.C. He twitched with joy. They had driven all the way from Nashville, Tennessee, so excited about his music that they couldn't wait until the morning. They had come in the middle of the night to deliver the note and didn't knock on his door because they wanted to be polite.

Maybe they had scared off the Tooth Fairy. He walked to the porch steps, pinched his eyes, and surveyed his property.

"Wherever y'all are, y'all can come on out now!" he hollered off the porch. "I'm awake and we can talk business! We don't have to wait 'til noon at the Piggly Wiggly! I can set me up a table on the porch and we can draw up the contract right then and there!" He waited for the bushes to rustle, and when they didn't, he scanned the woods, waiting for the music men to come out dressed in fancy suits and shiny boots, cowboy hats, and bolo ties.

"Don't be shy!" he yelled into the woods, thinking they may be nervous about meeting a music man with the biggest fan club in the universe. He waited around for another half hour, watching the woods and bushes for signs of the record company people, but the woods and bushes remained as still as the mist hovering in the morning. Then he thought better of it. These were big shots from Nashville, Tennessee. They'd have enough money to rent a room at the Magnolia Motel in town. He figured he'd have to wait until noon to talk to them. By the height of the sun, he figured he had over four hours to prepare. If he was going to sign a music contract today, he better dress and look the part.

He walked inside his shack and found Gradle awake and making up his bed. She was so pretty in that green dress with the short hairdo he'd given her. It was like she had never slept, like she was a constant dream.

"Who are you out there yelling at?" she asked.

He showed her the note he had found on the door. "Record company wants to meet me at the Piggly Wiggly at noon. They gonna call me up on the pay phone to talk some business," he said, as Gradle read the note. "Will you come with me?" he asked. Gradle would help calm his nerves if they got too out of control. She would also help make him look like a genuine music star since genuine music stars always had pretty girls wrapped up in their arms.

"How do you know this is from the record company?" she asked. She read the note again.

He pointed to the word *IMPORTANT.* "'Cause it says it's a very I-M-P-O-R-T-A-N-T phone call I need to take. There ain't but three things important in my life. My music, my art, and you." He paused for a moment and contemplated her question. "You think that note might be from some art man wantin' to see my sketches?"

"I don't know what to think about this note," she said. "Do you get notes often?"

"Not like this one. This is a once in a lifetime note. I need to get prepared," he said. "It's important I stick out my best foot forward."

He went to his clothes pile and selected his blue polyester suit and a white button-up shirt. Before he put it on, he worked on the stains with some baking soda and vinegar and then masked up the smell with several sprays of a half used bottle of Old Spice he'd found at the dump. He dry-shaved his stubble with his knife and massaged some second-hand Vitalis in his hair. He spit-shined his K-Swiss sneakers and tightened his bolo tie he'd made out of a piece of leather shoestring and a silver dollar. He slipped his gold rings on his fingers, situated his white cowboy hat on his shiny slick head, and presented himself to Gradle. His pants were a little tight in the thighs and his jacket was still damp where he'd worked on the stains, but other than that, he felt like a real live country music star.

"You look real nice," she said, and that made him smile.

It was nine-thirty in the morning, and although he didn't have to be at The Piggly Wiggly until noon, he wanted to leave now. If he ran into trouble on the way, or if some outlaws trying to make his life a living hell ambushed him from the trees, he'd have plenty of time to kung-fu them off or challenge them to a duel. There were a lot of people out there jealous of his many talents, and he anticipated them trying to get in his way of signing a music contract.

"We need to leave now," he said, grabbing his guitar and his collection of sketches. "This could be a dangerous operation, and I might have to put on my World Wide Wrestling Federation outfit. You don't know this about me, but I'm the Masked Man. Nobody knows my identity. I've saved Hulk Hogan on many occasions. I've wrestled "The Nature Boy" Ric Flair and George "The Animal" Steele, and I've slammed metal chairs into Brutus "The Barber" Beefcake when he turned bad. But shhhh," he said, "don't tell nobody."

He rushed out of his shack and stood by the passenger door of his 1970 Opel Kadett. He'd found it a few years back at the junkyard gutted clean to its skeleton. He spent six months fixing it up to what it was today, a turquoise and rust speed rocket that he'd fine-tuned not to be stingy on gas. He removed his hat and opened the car door for Gradle. The Opel Kadett knocked and roared to life. He rolled down the window to let the air swirl inside, and they were on their way to the Piggly Wiggly. He was so excited he couldn't keep his knees from bouncing.

The Opel Kadett skidded into the Piggly Wiggly's lot. Over a dozen cars were parked in the lot, and people came in and out of the store, buying groceries before the day got too hot for anybody to move. He parked the Kadett in front on the pay phone and almost pinned the man who was talking into the receiver between his dented bumper and the phone booth.

He got out of the car and circled the phone booth four times while he stared down the overall-wearing man with the best threatening eye he had. He paced back and forth, popped his knuckles, and practiced his fast draw and kung-fu moves, but his strategy didn't seem to scare off the man who just kept talking about how his truck broke down up the road, so Delvis tried another tactic.

"Hey mister," he said. "I'm expectin' a very important phone call and if you don't get off the phone in two seconds flat, I'll put a flyin' knee kick to your face before you can say tid-bit."

"Jesus, Delvis," the man said, "just give me a minute."

Delvis pushed his face into the man's eyes. "How you know my name?"

The man hung up the phone. "Everybody knows who you are," he said, wiping the sweat from his upper lip. "You're damn near a celebrity in this town."

"You want my autograph?" Delvis hollered at the man as he walked off.

Gradle got out of the car, sat on the hood, and waited for two hours straight, while he protected the phone booth. He crouched like a badger when anyone came within three feet of his territory, and when an old lady with blue hair and dark glasses approached, he told her the phone had been possessed by aliens and that he was working on sending them back to Jupiter, so she better stand back—way back.

After a while, the butcher stomped out of the front doors, wiping his bloody hands on his apron.

"Delvis," he said, "you can't hog the phone. It's a public phone, and my customers have the right to use it." He looked at Gradle sitting on the hood of his Opel Kadett and stared at her for a long time. It made Delvis shifty and uncomfortable.

"Listen here you hog-slayer," he said, narrowing his eyes. He put his finger to the butcher's nose and pressed it down like an on-button. "I got me a very important phone call waitin' for me. And I promise if you try to ambush me like I think you're tryin' to do, I will put you in the Boston Crab."

"Do you want me to call the sheriff?" the butcher asked.

"Go ahead and call the sheriff," he said. "Half the law enforcement men around here ain't nothin' but a bunch of crooks anyway. Y'all think they're protectin' you? It ain't them, it's me that's keepin' this town safe. I work undercover 24-7, under the radar, and no type of monitoring device can find me."

The butcher walked through the front doors, shaking his head, and ten minutes later, Sheriff Hill pulled up beside Delvis's Opel Kadett with his blue light flashing. Delvis was no stranger to this blue light. He'd seen it flash at him many times, like the time he refused not to drive past the stop sign at Roundtree and Lewis until the sign changed its words to *GO*, or the time the weather called for hail, and he spent all day in the park yelling at anyone who passed by to get down on their knees and repent before the Devil came to take their souls, or the time he wouldn't let anyone use the diving board at the public pool, convinced the lifeguard on duty would drain all of the water out while the diver was mid-air. Citizen complaints is what the sheriff said they were, which Delvis supposed was what the sheriff was responding to now.

The sheriff got out of his patrol car and shifted his chewed up cigar to the other side of his lip. "Hey, Delvis," he said, rattling the change in his pocket. Sheriff Hill had eyes black and shiny as a bat's and a strawberry birthmark that splotched his right cheek. Delvis had read all about birthmarks in a doctor's magazine while he waited for Dr. Smith to get the frog out of his throat, so he knew all about them and half-way felt sorry for Sheriff Hill having to live with one so colorful and big on the side of his face, even though he was nothing but a crook on the inside.

"Got a call from the butcher. Said you're up here harassing the customers and won't let anybody use the phone," Sheriff Hill said.

"I ain't puttin' no harassments to anybody. All I'm doin' is guardin' what's mine," Delvis said. "Ain't that right, Gradle?"

"He's waiting for an important phone call, sir," Gradle said, sliding down the car hood.

"Are you with him?" Sheriff Hill asked Gradle.

"Yes sir," she said.

The sheriff hung his eyes on Gradle, looking like he was sizing her up, trying to figure her out, and after he was through with that, he kept on staring at her, but in a different way. He looked bewildered. *Bewildered* was the word of the week in the town paper three months ago. Delvis made a point of adding all the words of the week to his vocabulary.

"You that girl that moved into the old Spivey house earlier in the summer?" the sheriff asked.

"Yes sir," she said. "My name's Gradle Bird."

"Moved in with your grandpa. He's your grandpa, right?" the sheriff asked.

"Yes sir."

"I'm glad somebody's finally fixing up the place." The sheriff finally got his eyes off Gradle and put them back on Delvis. He shifted his cigar to the other side of his mouth. "So Delvis, what is it that you think is yours?"

"You tryin' to trick me up? Tryin' to get me to say somethin' wrong so you can arrest me? You part of the trick?" Delvis shouted out the words.

"What trick, Delvis?" he asked.

"Don't lie to me, 'cause I'm trained at readin' minds."

Sheriff Hill rested his foot on the Opel Kadett's bumper and took his time to relight his cigar. "What am I thinkin', Delvis?"

Delvis looked at his gold-plated watch. It was five minutes 'til twelve. His palms started to sweat. "I'm not authorized to say right this minute."

"This is what I'm thinking, Delvis. I think if you don't move your car and let people use the phone, I'm gonna have to impound your vehicle and arrest you for disturbing the peace."

Delvis spat next to the sheriff's shiny black shoes, moved into him, and seriously thought about putting him in a death-hold. "I know what you're tryin' to do. You and the butcher and everybody else who come up here tryin' to get me away from this phone. Y'all jealous. Don't want me to sign a contract with the Nashville music men 'cause y'all wouldn't know how to swallow it." He loosened his bolo tie. "Now listen to me, Sheriff Hill. I know you ain't nothin' but a crook. I know 'cause I'm an undercover agent working for the FBI, and we got our eyes on you. If anybody's arrestin' anybody, it's me arrestin' you. I got my cuffs in the trunk."

"Blocking traffic. Disturbing the peace. Assaulting the county sheriff," Sheriff Hill said. "Why don't you and Gradle go on home. Town's not the best environment for you. We've discussed this before. Now move your car and get on."

"I done had enough of you! You dirty outlaw, tryin' to make my life a livin' hell." He rushed at the sheriff with his guitar and cocked it behind his shoulder. Before he could swing, Sheriff Hill put him in a wrist hold, spun him around, and cuffed his hands. His face slammed into the patrol car, and his white cowboy hat fell to the ground, crumpled and out of shape.

"Don't be so rough with him," Gradle yelled, charging the sheriff. "He wasn't hurting anybody!"

"He was about to whack me upside the head with his guitar," Sheriff Hill said. "All I'm trying to do here is make sure nobody gets hurt."

"He's not dangerous. He's just different," she said, picked up his cowboy hat, and put it back on his head.

"In this town, different is dangerous," the sheriff said.

"Uncuff him, and we'll go home," she said. "Won't we, Delvis?"

Delvis couldn't tell if she was making a statement or if she was asking him a question. She sounded like there was no option, but he answered anyway. "After I get my phone call," he said.

As Sheriff Hill reached for his key chain, the pay phone rang. Delvis plowed forward. He bumped the sheriff out of his way and rushed from the patrol car to the phone. His hands were still locked up behind his back, and he couldn't wiggle them free to pick up the receiver. The phone rang again.

Gradle ran to his side, lifted the phone from its hook, and held it up to his ear. She looked as excited as he did.

"D-5 Delvis Miles The Lone Singer speakin'," he said. He put one eye on the sheriff to make sure he didn't make any crook moves, but he didn't look like he was going to make any moves anytime soon. Delvis had put the freeze on him.

"Did you get my note?" the voice on the other end said.

"Yes sir," he said, smiling at Gradle. "I'm standin' right up here at the Piggly Wiggly and can play you some of my originals whenever you get up here. Got my guitar and everything."

"I ain't interested in your music," the voice said.

"Well, I brought my art up here too for you to take a look at it."

"I ain't interested in that either," the voice said real slow, like the grey clouds that moved like slugs across the sun. "What I'm interested in is that pretty little girlfriend of yours. I'm gonna steal her away from you."

"No, you ain't you son of a bitch!" Delvis shouted. "I'll hammer drop you in half a second flat. Besides, she ain't my girlfriend. Uh-uh, I don't look at her like that. She's a real true friend, not no girlfriend."

"I already know she likes flowers. I gave her some the other day, and she couldn't keep her nose out of them."

"Listen here you crippled hobo-monkey. I don't 'preciate you talkin' 'bout her like that."

"I may walk with a cane, but that don't matter. I'm gonna take her away from you," the voice said. "And you won't ever get her back."

"Listen here you dirty outlaw. Now we can handle this like a couple of gentlemen. Or if you got the guts, meet me face to face, and we can draw up a contract for a clean and honest duel, Western style."

"Who is that?" Gradle asked.

"That crippled boyfriend of yours."

The voice started talking again. "I'm gonna come in the night and take her right from under your nose." There was a click and then silence.

Gradle put the phone up to her ear. "Who is this? Ceif, is this you?" She listened for something from the other end.

Delvis counted to ten, and she gently placed the phone back on its hook.

"You satisfied, Mr. Miles?" the sheriff asked. "Was that them music men you were expecting?"

"Hell no!" Delvis yelled. "Just some other crook tryin' to sabotage my fame and take away what is mine."

"Come on Delvis," Gradle said. "Let's go home."

"I gotta stay up here 'til those Nashville men call," he said. His eyes stayed glued to the phone.

"Delvis." Her voice was low and sweet. She placed her hand on his bicep and gave him a little squeeze. "They're not gonna call."

"At noon they said they would."

"The music men didn't write that note," she said.

Sheriff Hill walked through the cloud of his cigar smoke and unlocked Delvis's handcuffs. "Go on home, Delvis," he said. He got in his patrol car, rolled down the window, and looked at Gradle real stern. "Be careful," he told her, shut down his flashing lights, and drove off.

On the ride home, Delvis's mind was at war. His thoughts fired off like a machine gun spitting bullets. He thought about the boy's plot to take Gradle away from him and how he might execute. The boy would probably pick the night to ambush him. He'd probably stake him out up in the oak tree right by the house. He wouldn't be alone. They'd be two of them. Delvis was too much of a match for just one. Especially one that was crippled. No, he'd have his tattooed friend with him. They'd be hooded with masks so he couldn't identify them. He thought about turning around and going back up to the Piggly Wiggly pay phone to call up Hulk Hogan to see if he'd be interested in tag-teaming with him like they had done against "The Nature Boy" Rick Flair and the Iron Sheik.

He put the brakes on his thoughts and looked over at Gradle. She had the window rolled down. Her check was resting against the door like she was tired. Her eyes were closed and the wind pressed down her lashes. They wanted to take her away because she was his. She was his real true friend—not theirs.

He almost ran off the road from looking at her too hard. He swerved and it startled her to lift her neck. She petted her dress down and rested her hands in her lap.

"I'm sorry if you're disappointed," she said.

"About what?" he asked.

"The music men."

He swung the Opel Kadett into his yard and bumped into a pink plastic flamingo.

"One day they'll find me," he said, and he put the Kadett in park. He walked around the car, removed his cowboy hat, and opened the door for her like a real genuine country music star would.

SIXTEEN

"GRADLE!" DELVIS YELLED, as he busted through the front door and startled Gradle awake.

Gradle peeled her cheek from the Dairy Queen booth's sweaty red vinyl. "What is it, Delvis?" Gradle asked, rubbing the sleep from her eyes.

After Delvis laid his eyes on her his entire body sighed. "You weren't inside, and I thought you was gone for good," Delvis said. He surveyed his yard. "I thought somebody might have took you in the night."

"No, I just slept out here," she said, sat up, and smoothed down her dress.

"Why ain't you sleepin' inside?" Delvis asked.

"I needed some fresh air, Delvis," she said. "And a little privacy."

"Inside is private," he said. He spat off the porch.

"I needed to be alone," she said.

"You don't like my company?" Delvis asked. "If you say no, it won't make me mad. I can improve in that area."

"I love your company, Delvis. I just needed to be alone," she said. Last night was the first time she had been alone since coming there, and to achieve her solitude, she had to sneak out, tiptoe around Delvis who lay snoring atop his bed pile of clothes with his pistol within arm's reach. If she woke him, he would be right at her side, watching her and the air around her as if at any moment she would get whisked away. His attention to her was extraordinary in the same way as Grandpa's lack of it.

"We gotta go divin' before it gets picked over," he said. "Splash your face and do your business if you have to. I'll be waiting in the car."

Gradle cupped her hands in a bucket of rainwater, careful not to scoop out a wriggler in the process, and splashed her face. She splashed her armpits, rubbed them free of their stink with a scrap of rag, and went behind the house to take a pee. When she came back around, Delvis sat in the Opel Kadett, warming its engine.

He opened her car door and she sat in. He slammed the door, put the car in drive, and sped down the dirt road to the county dump.

Delvis rolled the Opel Kadett to a gentle stop. The dump was beautiful, how the sun blushed the trash mounds in pink, how wild morning glory twined through rusted car cadavers and farm plows, and how a pair of glistening buzzards sat atop a dumpster spreading their wings to dry off the dew. A tricycle sat apart from the rest of the junk, as if its child had missed it, come back in the middle of the night, and taken it for a ride.

Delvis's eyes glistened as he surveyed the dump's precarious landscape. The abandoned and thrown-away seemed to appear as precious jewels in his eyes. He was excited, borderline jittery, which

made Gradle even more tired than she was from staying up most of the night, wondering how Grandpa was getting along, if he was happier without her.

He killed the engine, got out of the car, and handed Gradle a pair of gloves. "Since this is your first mission with a professional dumpster diver, I gotta teach you how to do it right. This is serious business here, and if you go in untrained, you're liable to get hurt. First thing, you gotta be on watch out for is snakes and rats. They have all sorts of hide-ee holes, and if you run up on one, don't, I say don't, under no circumstances try to pet it. They might look cute and pretty but don't be fooled. And there are other things, not critter-type things, that'll bite you just as hard. There's nails, torn tin, and barbed wire all over the place lookin' for victims." He gloved his hands and stretched his body. "Next," he said, as he performed a forward lunge, "you gotta get your body warmed up and taffy-candy-like 'cause this type of work is stressful. You don't want any Charlie-horses or muscle tears."

Gradle imitated Delvis's stretching exercises, and when he gave her the signal, they both stopped.

"Your body feel loose and warm?" he asked.

"I feel like taffy candy," she said.

"What flavor?"

"Banana."

"I'm feelin' blueberry," he said. "Now, I'm gonna teach you my very own divin' techniques. These are professional techniques only I know. They are copyrighted in the Library of Congress, Washington, D.C. along with all of my other materials. You cannot under any circumstances tell anybody about these techniques."

"Cross my heart and swear to God," she said.

"You ain't supposed to swear to God, Gradle. It says that in the Bible."

"Swear to Jesus."

"They're the same. Pick somebody else."

"I swear to the sun."

He scratched his head, turned back to the rising sun as if to determine if it would mind. "The sun ain't a somebody," he said.

"I swear to you, then."

He smiled and led her to the dumpsters where a pack of mangy dogs nosed the dirt. He ran back to his car, popped the trunk, and scattered a bag of kibble on the ground. The dogs waited for him to get out of range, then gobbled the food down as they growled at each other for position.

"None of 'em will let me touch 'em," he said. He lunged to the left and then to the right. He touched his toes twice, leapt on the dumpster's lip like a cat, and scared off the buzzards.

"First," he said, as he walked along the dumpster's ledge, "you gotta scope your dive. Check for hidden stumps under the water and what have you. People who ain't professional don't do this and end up gettin' bad hurt. Break their necks and some get paralyzed. It's a dangerous job, I'm tellin' you. Most dangerous job in America."

He walked the dumpster's perimeter one last time and stopped on one of the corners. "Now you gotta prepare for your dive. Nonprofessionals don't do this either. It's important to take one deep breath in." He breathed in and raised his arms over his head, bringing his hands together to a point. "And breathe out," he said. He brought his arms back down to his side. "Do that twice, but only twice. If you do it more than that, you'll start thinkin' too much about possible underwater stumps even though you've already checked for them in the scoping exercise. Now, it's time to determine the dive type. Again, nonprofessionals do a straight dive. Some of them better-than-nonprofessionals, but not as good as professionals like me, might try to get fancy and do a jack-knife type dive. Me, on the other hand, I do what's called the swan dive. I invented it and it's copyrighted, too." He paused long enough to catch his breath. "Are you ready?" he asked.

"Ready," she said, having no idea what she was ready for.

"You ain't got nothin' to worry about. I'm a true professional."

She held her breath as Delvis's arms rose above his head. His arms fell back down to his thighs, and he repeated the rise and fall. He rose on his tiptoes, and after counting to three, he dove from the dumpster's edge. He flew through the air, his arms spread wide open, his body arched. His legs were straight and glued perfectly together. He looked beautiful, more beautiful than his abandoned junk backdrop she had thought so beautiful only minutes before.

Gradle climbed up on its edge after he disappeared in the dumpster and looked inside. He lay flat on his back, his eyes fixed above on the bluing sky.

"Are you okay?" she asked.

"This is where I was borned. Right here. Just like this. On a bed of trash. That's how divin' got in my blood." He popped to his feet. "Let's get to business," he said, picking through the trash. "I'm lookin' for metal door hinges, chains, deadbolts, and padlocks," he said. "If you find any on your mission, I'd appreciate you savin' 'em for me."

"What's my mission?" she asked.

"Whatever you want it to be," he said. He hopped out of the dumpster and went hunting atop a junk mound.

Gradle bunched her dress above her knees and wandered through the dump, finding it curious what people chose to throw away. She picked up a pink pacifier and wondered if she ever had a little girl, would this be something she could ever part with. She wondered if she had one when she was a little baby, and if she did, had Grandpa kept it. Was there a box hidden somewhere with all of her keepsakes, and if so, did Grandpa ever bring it out, stroke a lock of her baby hair or roll her baby teeth between his fingers? Or had he just thrown it all away? Was her baby hair in some dump, decomposing alongside her sixteen-year-old diapers? Were her teeth fossilizing beneath a sedimentary layer of trash? She cleaned the pacifier off with some spit and kept it cupped in her palm as she sifted through more trash.

The sun rose higher, got hotter, and started cooking all of the smells: souring watermelon rind, motor oil, crayons, car metal, and rust. Gradle picked through the trash and found two dried leather belts and a brand new pack of red and white shoelaces still marked with a price tag of sixty-nine cents. She decided to use them to make a guitar strap for Delvis so he could wear his instrument around his neck.

On her way back to the car, Delvis appeared over a trash mound draped in metal chains. He carried deadbolts, metal hinges, and padlocks in his arms, and dragged a roll of rusted barbed wire behind him like a train of a wedding dress. He dumped his loot in the Opel Kadett's trunk. It sagged from all of the weight.

"What're you gonna do with all that?" she asked.

"Booby-traps for intruders," he said.

Perfumed with fruity-smelling trash, they drove down the dirt road, through the green country, and into the deep woods back to Delvis's shack. The sun had disappeared behind a canvas of creamy steel. They unloaded their findings and set them out on the porch. A bouquet of swamp lilies with a note rested against the front door.

Delvis grabbed the note and read it out loud, *"I CAME TO CLAIM WHAT'S MINE. I'M READY FOR A WESTERN STYLE DUEL IF THAT'S WHAT IT WILL TAKE TO GET GRADLE BACK IN MY ARMS. SINCERELY, CEIF 'THE ELECTRIC GUNSLINGER' WALKER."*

"That boy done come up here to try and steal you away," Delvis said, handing her the note. "He better be glad we weren't here 'cause I don't need no advanced notice for a duel. I can fire and shoot within two seconds, ninety-seven percent accurate each and every time." He gently lifted the flowers and placed them on the red Dairy Queen booth. "Maybe we can get us some fingerprints off those so we can nail that hobo-monkey real good." He grabbed the rake propped against the wall and raked in front of the door. "I'm seein' if I can find any footprints of his so we can nail him double time."

Gradle read the note and a hot wave of anger surged through her body. "This is a joke, Delvis," she said, wondering how on earth she would describe something as tricky as a joke to Delvis. "Do you know what a joke is?"

"It's when somebody's tryin' to be mean to somebody else," he said. "Like them boy's laughin' at me at the way I drawn a turkey that one time."

"Yeah, jokes are supposed to be funny. Ceif doesn't want to steal me. It's Sonny Joe. He's trying to poke fun at you. It's a game to him."

"It ain't that boy," Delvis said. He spat off the porch. "It's the other one. The crippled one my dog Rain got after. See," he pointed to the note. "He even put his signature on it." He resumed raking in front of the door. "I can't let him steal you. I won't let it happen."

Gradle paced the porch. If Sonny Joe were here now, she would strangle him. "I have to go somewhere," she said. "I'm taking your car." She hurried through the yard, cranked the Opel Kadett, and spun the tires onto the dirt road.

Delvis sprinted after her, yelling, "Where're you going! You can't be out alone! That boy'll steal you!"

She stared through the rearview mirror at Delvis running after her and shaking the rake. It made her sad to leave him behind without an explanation, but no matter how thorough and deep she explained all of this, she knew Delvis would never understand the facts.

"I'll protect you Gradle!" he hollered.

She pressed the gas pedal to the floorboard and left him in a swarm of glittering dust as she fishtailed down the road.

The Kadett shot out on the highway like a burst of fire. An oncoming storm faced her. It churned a wicked grey and started to spit down on the windshield as she sped down the road. When she arrived at the abandoned church, she parked the Opel Kadett sideways, blocking in Sonny Joe's truck.

She ran through the rain, inside the church, and found Ceif sitting on the front pew, reading his Bible, his little mouth mumbling the verses out loud as he ate with his hands from a can of sardines.

"Where's Sonny Joe?" she asked, as he scarfed down a sardine.

"Four pews back," Ceif said. "He's hungover."

She found Sonny Joe with his hand shoved down his jeans and his mouth hung open like it was snagged by a hook. His T-shirt and a half-pint of Southern Comfort sat on the floor beside him, and one arm reached out toward the bottle as if he had passed out in the middle of reaching for one last sip.

Gradle poured what was left in the bottle on Sonny Joe's face. "Rise and shine," she said.

He came up spitting. "What the fuck?" He grabbed his T-shirt, wiped his face, and finally removed his hand from the front of his pants. He wadded his T-shirt and threw it at the back of Ceif's head. "What're you laughing at?"

Gradle leaned into Sonny Joe's face and received an unwanted whiff of his sour breath. "Leave Delvis alone."

"What're you talking about, crazy girl?"

"The notes on his door. The phone call at the Piggly Wiggly. The flowers left on his porch. You're pretending to be Ceif. Don't play dumb." She wadded up the note and threw it into Sonny Joe's face. "Leave him alone. Save your bullshit games for your pretty little fish."

"Come on, Gradle Bird. I'm just having a little fun," he said. He licked the liquor from his shoulder's skin.

"He's dangerous," she said.

Sonny Joe walked into her space. She could feel his heat, his magnetism.

He lit a cigarette. "Is that why you like him so much?" he asked. He blew smoke in her face. "I'm not dangerous enough for you?"

"Leave him alone," she said, and she walked out of the church into the storm.

†††

Delvis crouched, put his nose down on the rain-splashed road, and took a big fat sniff. He couldn't find it. All he picked up was the asphalt and rain, a little bit of car oil, and a little bit of blood from the opossum he saw lying dead on this very spot of road four months back. He crawled up and down the road, sniffing, as the rain spanked his back, but still he couldn't find it.

He had tracked the Kadett down the dirt road, but when the road let out on the highway he had nothing to follow, except his nose. Typically, he could find it, her girlie green scent, because he was born with special nose holes that were designed to pick up her smell. But today the best he could smell was the leftovers of that opossum that got killed here four months ago.

He blew his nose hard, thinking perhaps it was clogged, and sniffed the road again. Still he couldn't find it. Maybe the rain had something to do with it. He paced up and down the road. He had no idea which way Gradle had gone. He didn't know why she had run off so quick or where she was headed, because when he hollered after her she didn't holler back. Maybe her heart had changed, instantly, like how a cricket all of a sudden decides to stop chirping with no warning. Maybe she had gone to visit that crippled boy so she could be back in his arms so tight.

He fell down on his knees in the middle of the road, locked his fingers together, and prayed in the Christ name of Jesus. He prayed Gradle's heart hadn't changed and asked God to bring her back soon because he didn't know if he could bear his life without her. She was the only real true friend he ever had. He prayed in the middle of the road until he had backed up a line of three cars. They honked their horns and the drivers cussed out of the window, trying to make his life a living hell. When he couldn't take the honking and cussing anymore, he stood, performed some kung-fu moves for effect, and then directed the traffic to go on their way as if he were a professional traffic cop.

With no scent to track, he walked back home. He thought he'd wait until the rain stopped, and then he'd try out his special nose holes again, because he was now convinced the rain had something to do with it.

The rain kept on, but within minutes of him getting back home he swore he started to smell the color green. He threw his nose up in the air. Not only could he smell her, but he could hear her breathing, almost panting, because he had special ear holes for that, too. He ran through the rain and stood in the yard. His body felt like it was crawling with ants.

And just like that, she appeared. She parked the Kadett in the yard, and before she could get out on her own, he offered her his hand, and before she could stand, he pulled her into him and hugged her as tight as he could. She hugged him back. He wished they could stay like that forever and wondered if that Medusa lady with the snake hair he'd read about in a booked called *Mythology* was anywhere around, because if she was, he would make it a point to look in her eyes so he and Gradle could turn to stone.

"Delvis," she mumbled into his chest, "you're hugging me too tight. I can't breathe."

He released his grip, but once Gradle caught her breath, he hugged her as tight as he could again. He'd never hugged anyone in his entire life, nor had he ever been hugged back, and it was the best feeling he thought he would ever know, even better than when his dog Rain would lick him on the neck.

"It's okay, Delvis," she said, wiggling her way out of his grip. "Nobody's gonna take me away from you."

He leaned in to hug her again, but she moved away. He wasn't yet a professional hugger, but he was smart enough to know she didn't want to be hugged again.

"Where'd you go?" he asked. He followed her through the rain and onto the porch.

"I went to tell Sonny Joe to leave you alone."

Delvis sat on the Dairy Queen booth and fiddled with the piles of chains and padlocks and metal door hinges he'd picked from the dump. "Did that crippled boy try and trap you?"

"No," she said, shaking the rain from her dress. "Ceif doesn't want to steal me. Nobody wants to steal me. Sonny Joe is playing with you for his own entertainment."

"If that boy wants to be entertained, he can come up here and I'll play him some of my original rock 'n roll style music," he said.

She sat beside him on the booth and touched his hand. "Don't let him drive you crazy," she said. "Relax. Enjoy the rain."

He stared out at the grey rain and tried to do what Gradle had asked, but he couldn't turn his mind off. He had searched his head for an off button, a knob to turn, or a switch to flip when his mind started sparking the way it was now, but every time he hunted for the off lever, he never found anything of the sort. He figured it was something God had forgotten when he made him. As much as he wanted to forget about that crippled boy writing all of those nasty notes and leaving Gradle flowers and threatening him to a duel, he couldn't. Although Gradle had told him nobody wanted to steal her away, he didn't believe it one bit because he had seen it written in plain ink and had heard the boy say it when he called him on the Piggly Wiggly pay phone. There was no way that boy was going to take her away from him. *No way. No how. No sir. Not under his watch.*

All of a sudden his senses stood on high alert. He could hear the rain screaming as it fell, and along with the screaming rain, he heard rocks hitting against his tin roof. That boy had done come up here, trying to distract him and make his life a living hell. He shot up from the booth and ran out into the yard. He turned his laser vision on and saw the boy limping toward his house carrying a bouquet of flowers and his cane, but when Delvis ran to the place he saw him, he wasn't there or anywhere around. He sniffed the air. His special nose holes smelled the bouquet of lilies, even through all of the rain, so he knew that crippled boy must be around somewhere.

He walked the perimeter of his house three times, looking for the boy. He shook the bushes and the chinaberry tree.

"Delvis!" Gradle called from the porch. "What're you doing?"

"Enjoyin' the rain," he said, lying to make her feel better because that was what she wanted him to do. He squatted and crawled up under the house. He heard the boy whispering out at him in the darkness, but Delvis's laser vision couldn't find him. He crawled to all four corners, through the cobwebs and hornet's nests, and in and out of the holes his dog Rain had dug when he was alive, but he couldn't find that boy in any of them.

"*I'm gonna steal her away from you. She's mine,*" he heard the boy whisper behind his back. Delvis spun around, arched his back, and hissed like a cat, but the boy must have hid again in one of the dark corners because Delvis didn't see him when he turned around. He plotted the area under the house and crawled over every square inch of it, front and back, side to side. When he finished combing the area, he went back over it a second time, and then a third time to be safe because he wasn't going to let that boy take his one and only real true friend under his watch. *No way. No how. No sir.*

When he crawled out from under his house, it was twilight. The rain fell soft. A whippoorwill hollered in the distance and the bullfrogs burped like drunks. The early night was loud with sounds, but quiet and hollow, too. He felt something missing. He patted all of his pockets then raced to the front porch. He couldn't find Gradle anywhere around. His heart got a Charlie-horse and cramped up inside him. He had kept his eyes off Gradle for too long, and that boy had figured out a way to sneak up on her and take her.

He ran inside to get his pistol, but he couldn't remember where he had put it. Thousands of images flashed on the back of his eyelids like they always did when he couldn't remember where he put something. He tried shuffling through the images and throwing out the ones he didn't need, but his brain couldn't evict them. He grabbed his head, squeezed, and started over. The images flashed up again, but he couldn't figure out which ones were important and which ones weren't. He shook his head and tried again, but again he couldn't sort out the images because the images were not the images he needed to sort through in order to find his gun. On the back of his lids he saw: Gradle screaming, Ceif laughing, lilies, Ceif's cane, notes with mean writing, the Piggly Wiggly pay phone, Gradle crying, Ceif grabbing at her, Ceif's Bible, lilies, Ceif's cane, notes with mean writing, the Piggly Wiggly pay phone. The pictures kept repeating, and he couldn't shuffle them out. He grabbed his head again and squeezed and squeezed until all of the images blurred and his world went black.

"Delvis, are you okay?" he heard Gradle's voice, pure and sweet, reaching down for him.

He couldn't pry his eyes open, but his mouth seemed to work just fine. "Are you safe?" he asked.

"Yes, I'm right here."

"That boy didn't come take you away did he?"

"No," she said. He felt her padded hand cradle the back of his neck and lift it off the floor. "I'm right here, Delvis. I'm right here with you."

Delvis's eyes busted through the bricks weighing them down. Gradle was kneeling beside him, looking down at his face with a troubled look on hers. She petted the rain and sweat out his hair.

"You must have fainted," she said. "Probably from the heat."

He propped himself on his elbows. "Where'd you come from?" he asked.

"I've been here the whole time," she said.

"When I got done under the house, I came back and didn't see you on the porch. I was afraid that boy snatched you up from right under my nose."

"Don't be afraid, Delvis," she said. "I'll always be with you. Even when I'm not here."

His brows pinched. In his mind, he tried to understand what Gradle said. How could she always be with him if she wasn't always there? For her to always be with him, she had to be here, here so he could smell her, see her, touch her, talk to her. He tried to solve Gradle's puzzle in his mind, but it kept getting more confused. The pieces didn't fit clean in their cutout spaces. He knew she wasn't trying to trick him because she was his real true friend. His eyes stung and clouded with tears. He didn't understand and didn't trust that his mind could ever grasp what Gradle was telling him. They always said he was special. They always said they didn't have the type of classes in school that could work with a brain like his. Delvis always thought he was too smart for the classes, but maybe, just maybe, he was too dumb.

†††

Delvis couldn't sleep. He felt as if the same electricity making the stars sparkle and the porch light shine ran all throughout his veins. He could even hear his skin buzzing like locusts in the trees. It was a quarter past two in the morning, Gradle was asleep, and he had just finished busting the guts out of the last padlock he had found at the dump. He picked the guts out of the lock with a pair of tweezers and replaced them with some spare guts for which he had keys. He had stored the spares away in a shoebox between an old car alternator and a sack of women's hosiery, knowing one day they would be of use.

He lined the padlocks up in a straight row and tested their keys twice. Satisfied they worked, he hid the eleven keys in one of the hanging flower baskets on the porch, pushed down in the dirt where his coral geraniums grew. It was a hiding place nobody would suspect. In the star-punched night, he fastened metal hinges on all four of his windows, but instead of using them as hinges he used them as locks. He spread them flat across the window's cracks and locked them down with screws. After all four windows were properly secured, he unrolled the rusted barbed-wire fence and wrapped it around the porch railings. He weaved the wire through all of the empty spaces between the porch steps and the front door, and when he was done it was safe and tight, something even a starving fox couldn't wiggle his way through. From the barbed wire, he made a special door at the porch entrance and clamped it locked with seven of the salvaged padlocks whose keys germinated in the hanging basket's dirt.

Quietly, and careful not to wake Gradle, he opened the front door and walked inside his shack. Gradle was almost safe, but not quite. He installed four deadbolts around the front door, one at the top, two on the right, and one on the left, gently clicking each locked before he started on the next. He pushed on the door. It wouldn't budge. She was almost safe, but not one hundred percent.

The sun would soon rise, and he had one last task to do before he could say for sure she was protected. He grabbed the pile of chain from the floor and stood over the bed. She was hard asleep. Her mouth was open and singing pretty whistling, nighttime songs. She was full of beauty, full of last week's word of the day S-E-R-E-N-E. He didn't know how he would do it without waking her up, and he knew if she did wake in the middle of it, she wouldn't let him finish what he needed to do. He was stronger and could hold her down if he had to, but he didn't want to scare her because she was his real true friend. He wouldn't ever, never do nothing to hurt her. Maybe if she woke up he could explain it to her in plain, simple terms.

He threaded the chain under and around her wrist and strung it through the headboard and down around the bedpost, locking it with a padlock. He did the other wrist the same, then moved down to the foot of the bed where he wrapped the chain around both of her ankles. She stirred, but she did not wake, just stopped her pretty whistling and singing for a minute. He waited for her to start up singing again, and when she did, he moved swiftly, finishing the job one padlock at a time.

He knelt beside her bed. He wanted so badly to pet her, but instead he whispered in her ear, "You'll always be with me."

And he hoped in her dreams she would find a way to understand.

CHAPTER SEVENTEEN

LEONARD SAT BEHIND the Chrysler's wheel, stalking the Fireside's truck lot like a creep. He hadn't slept for two days, and his eyes felt blistered and full of sand. The night was slow. There were no cars parked at the motel and only two rigs in the lot, and the only things that had moved in the past three hours were the cockroaches and the sphere of moths fluttering near the polelamp's head, dazzled and confused by its bright neon light.

His head nodded and whipped back. He downed the last sleeve of Goody's headache powder, rubbed his eyes into focus, and squeezed his fist around Gradle's gold-cross earring to help keep him awake. He'd found it on the floor after their fight and had been holding onto it ever since. She had been gone for three days, and he'd been gone for two. He'd driven miles looking for her. He'd driven the town of Janesboro's grid so many times it made him sick to the point he had to pull over and vomit up an empty stomach.

He'd driven up and down the four highways leading out of town with his eyes trained for a certain shade of green, and early last night he had come here, wondering if she had run back. He'd looked in the windows of all fifty-two rooms, banged on the doors, and checked if she was lounging by the dried-up pool.

He put the Goody's sleeve to his mouth, tapped its end, and remembered it was all gone. He opened his fist and traced the cross of Gradle's earring with the tip of his finger. Where in the hell had she gone? That little girl who used to walk around in his loafers, who used to wear his undertanks as nightgowns to sleep. He squeezed his fist around her earring, and at the corner of his eye he saw a girl climb down from the cab of a black Peterbuilt.

He ran from the Chrysler, leaving the door wide open, and into the lot toward the girl who struck a match and brought it to a cigarette.

"Gradle?" he whispered. He kept running until he realized it wasn't her.

Loretta the lot lizard shoved a wad of money in her bra and startled when she saw Leonard standing in front of her.

"Jesus Christ," she said. She took a pull off her cigarette. "You scared the shit out of me. What're you doing out here?" she asked with her dark silvery smile. "You got the urge?" She hiked her breasts in her bra and strutted up to him. "I always wondered what you'd be like," she said, twirling her finger in the sweaty hair of his chest. "I bet you've got a lot of experience."

He slapped her hand away. "Have you seen Gradle?"

"Not since y'all high-tailed it out of here. Duck's let the place go to shit," she said, dabbing her neck with perfume. "Gradle's finally done run off from you. That sad girl, I always wondered what took her so long. Good for her," she said with a slack laugh that made him want to punch the silver teeth out of her head.

"If you see her, tell her I'm looking for her."

"She ain't comin' back here." Loretta tightened the strap of her high-heeled shoe and took another drag from her cigarette. "Why in the hell would anybody wanna come back here?"

Leonard walked across the lot, cranked the Chrysler's engine, and drove back to the old Spivey house, fisting Gradle's earring the entire way. He wheeled into the drive, put the car in park, and idled there, staring at the attic window in a daze. The pane was closed, its glass dark. He waited for Annalee's mirage to appear, but in his gut he knew not a single soul was home.

He cut off the engine, walked through the moonflower bloom, and turned the front doorknob. The door sighed open. His footsteps echoed throughout the hollow house as he walked down the hall. He went into Gradle's room to check if she was there, but her room felt more abandoned now than it had when they first came.

He walked into the hall, flipped on its light, and stared up at the attic's entrance. He grabbed the poker from the fireplace and tapped it against the flap.

"Annalee!" he yelled. He couldn't say for sure if she was up there.

He reached for the string and yanked it down. A chest fell through the flap and splintered into kindling on the floor. Bricks and boxes came divebombing after and exploded into dust. He couldn't say for sure if she had ever been up there.

He trotted the ladder, shoved a teetering box from the ledge, and knocked the iron sewing machine over on its side. The air was hot and stunk of death. He threw open the window to keep the vomit from rising up. Morning was on its way in, blue-white and delicate.

"Annalee?" he whispered, searching the room. "Annalee!" he yelled. He found her through the blur, on the fainting couch completely entombed in spiderwebs. He slid in moonflower ooze as he rushed to her side. She was still, and he started to imagine the worst.

He shredded the webs to get at her, afraid at what he may find. He ripped the webs draped in her mouth, and as he did, she drew in a breath so strong it pulled him down.

"There is a place people go when they die," she whispered, as she rose up out of her webbed cocoon. "But I am not dead yet. And I need to tell you why."

Leonard had to cover his eyes she was so bright. But suddenly her light dimmed and she grew mute, like a waterpainting faded from the sun.

He scratched his eyes, hoping they were just tired from no sleep, but when he put her in focus again, she was not clear.

"I know where Gradle is," she said.

He pulled her into his chest. "Tell me," he said, and he closed his sandy, blistered eyes.

†††

Gradle woke to something tickling the inside of her thigh. A black snake ribboned down her leg. She screamed, but she couldn't move to slap it away, which left her confused if the snake was real or if she was still stuck in a dream. The snake thumped on the floor, writhed a bit, and slithered away into the wall, between a hubcap and a decapitated babydoll's head.

She tried to sit up, but her body was anchored to the bed by what appeared to be more snakes coiled around her ankles and wrists. She jerked and wormed, and when she heard the melody of metal she realized she was anchored down by the chains Delvis took from the county dump.

"Delvis!" she screamed. Her ears cocked, but she heard nothing but muted songs of morning birds and the snake disturbing the junk as it slithered deep within the walls.

She thrashed again, only to be jerked back by unbending chains. She looked around for help, and her eyes fell on a letter from Delvis suspended in the atmosphere above the bed. It hung from the ceiling, stuck to a strip of fly tape, and twirled slow in the hot suffocating air.

Dear GRaDle,

ThAt OUTLAW boY doNe comE up HERe aND left aNOthER THREAT. He FIgureD oUT how TO geT tHRouGH . . .

The letter twirled and turned its back, but she couldn't reach up to grab it, so she blew air from her mouth to make it face forward again.

mY BOObie traPS I SET out For Him. ThAt boY's SPECIAL. AiNt NoboDY iN the uNIVerse BeeN Able to StEP aROuNd ONe of MY 100% gARauNteed-tO-Be-CAUGHT BooBiE trAPs I iNveNted for THE Viet-DamN war.

The letter turned again. Gradle blew steady streams of air and kept the letter forward until she read it whole.

HE left A NoTE. It SAID: Go TO thE PIggLY WIggLY toDAY aT 10:00 A.M. sHaRP to disCUss coordiNATES foR our Duel. GRaDle BIRd IS miNe TO claiM. I will AT LASt HAVe her Back iN MY arms.

HE WROTte a P.S. aNd put it iN ALL CAPS. "DO NOT UNDER ANy CIRCUMSTANCES BRING GRaDle WITH YOU. You WILL PUT HER IN SERIOUS DANGER!"

I'M sorry I hAd chaiN YOU up. I doNT WANT to make YOU MAD. I'M a plaiN persoN aNd doNT KNOw how to PUT it iN the RIGHt Words.

YoUrs Truly,

A REAL trUe FrIENd
D-5 Delvis MiLes The LoNe SiNger

Gradle's eyes began to burn. She twisted and jerked, trying to find slack in the chains, but they had nothing to give. Panic set in.

"Grandpa!" she screamed out, hoping he could somehow hear, hoping he could somehow help.

CHAPTER EIGHTEEN

LEONARD'S KNUCKLES STRETCHED tight and white as he gripped the wheel and barreled the Chrysler down the dirt road. Rocks clanked against the tirewalls, and rows of tobacco sped by in bands of psychedelic green. He gripped the wheel tighter, felt sweat and the gold cross of Gradle's earring jab his calloused palms.

Annalee sat beside him in the passenger's seat, turning vague and cloud-like. He wanted to grab onto her, to stop her from fading any further, but he was too scared he'd reach out and find nothing to hold.

The tobacco thinned and turned to woods. The shade smelled of honeysuckle and cooled the black leather seats.

"Turn right at the mailbox," Annalee said, pointing at a slanted mailbox that was rusty and padlocked shut.

He should have known Gradle would come here, but how on earth would he have ever found this place, how on earth would anyone know it existed? He drove slow past the mailbox and stared at the writing on its side. He'd seen this writing before. He'd seen it in the letters this man had written to Gradle, and it hadn't struck him until now, that he had seen this writing on the portrait Annalee guarded so closely to her heart. Not only did Gradle have a connection with this man but so did Annalee.

He looked over at Annalee, and what little he could see of her, he could still tell she faced forward down the wild overgrown drive.

When he saw the shack, the hair on his arms rose. Junk scattered the yard with both chaos and order. The windows were boarded, and the only sign something wild didn't live inside were the baskets of coral geraniums hanging from the porch.

He put the Chrysler in park and killed the engine.

"Gradle!" he yelled, as he ran toward the shack.

He raced up the porch steps and ran into a barricade of barbed wire. "Gradle!" he yelled again. All he heard in response was the squeak of a Coke can whirligig starting up in the breeze.

He tugged at the barbed wire and thought he heard Gradle whimper. He put her gold-cross earring in his pants pocket and gripped the barbed wire with both hands. He yanked and thrashed and squeezed his way through the barricade. With his bloody hand, he turned the doorknob, but it wouldn't come free of its seal. Locks bolted the door shut from the outside like a set of metal teeth. He pulled and pushed against the door, but it would not give. His eyes searched the junked-up porch for an object to help bust open a window and found the handle of an axe sticking out of a box filled with railroad ties and rusted circular saws. He sliced into the first lock, jolted by the hit of steel on steel. He moved to a boarded up window and hacked away at it, gouging into the wooden flesh. He tore away the boards, busted out the glass, and climbed through.

Inside it was dark. The clutter and chaos confused him. He felt dizzy, as if he wasn't in this world. He didn't know which way to go, which aisle of junk to take, until he heard her whimpering again.

He stumbled toward the sound and found her chained to a bed, her wrists and ankles raw and bleeding.

"Grandpa." Tears coated her face like wet glass, and the blue in her eyes shook with fright.

The shack's door flew open. A sword of sunlight blinded Leonard. He raised his hands over his eyes, and when he lowered them, they revealed a tall silhouette of a man standing in the doorway with a cowboy hat on his head.

"Freeze and put your hands up, mister," the man said. He leaped forward, bowed his legs into a straddle, and drew a pistol from his holster.

Leonard turned back and looked at Gradle and the chains that held her captive. His stomach grew sick, and his vision darkened into a screen of bursting black dots.

"Are your ears broke?" the man said, pointing the gun at Leonard. His gold rings rattled against the pistol's handle. "I said freeze and put your hands up, mister!"

Leonard shook the dizziness and sweat from his head. He grounded his feet and choked the axe.

"Back up mister," the man shouted. "I will shoot you."

"Don't shoot, Delvis!" Gradle yelled.

"I can shoot on target with ninety-seven percent accuracy each and every time and can pull this trigger faster than the bullet can fly."

"Delvis! Don't shoot!" Gradle yelled.

"Drop the axe mister."

"Let Gradle go," Leonard said.

"I'm protectin' her. There's people out there wantin' to steal her from me. I already organized a duel with one of 'em this morning at the Piggly Wiggly for tomorrow in the A.M., A.M. means before midday. And you just might be one of 'em. How do I know you ain't one of 'em?" Delvis asked.

"Drop the axe, Grandpa," Gradle said. The chains rattled on her wrists. "He's my friend. He doesn't mean to hurt me."

Leonard squeezed the axe's handle tight, let out a roar, and charged Delvis. With the axe's blunt end, he clipped the back of Delvis's knees. The gun flew through air and Delvis hit the floor.

Leonard spun around, hacked the axe against Gradle's chains, and freed one of her arms. He hacked the other chain and freed her other hand.

A pair of arms grabbed Leonard from behind and put him in a chokehold. "Come up here tryin' to make my life a livin' hell," Delvis yelled in Leonard's ear. "Do you know who you're messin' with? I'm a professional in the WWF."

Leonard felt the life in him dwindle as Delvis applied more pressure.

"Did that Ceif boy send you up here? 'Cause if he did I ain't got no regrets giving you a swift kick to the nuts and puttin' you in the figure four."

Leonard kicked to find his breath, but the man's grip was superhuman strong.

"Since you're now good and frozen, I'm gonna read you the lady named Miranda and the rights that go along with her. You have the right to remain silent and refuse to answer any of my questions. Do you understand?"

Leonard couldn't speak. As he watched Gradle racing to free her legs, his vision turned black. The axe fell from his hand and landed with a thud on the floor.

"Do you understand?" Delvis yelled in his ears again. "Are your ears broke? I said, do you understand?"

The man's words echoed and rang inside Leonard's ears. He began to slip, to cross over into unconsciousness. He heard Gradle next to him, urging the man to let him go. Her words were fragile and sweet, like the song of birds. Leonard dug his heels in and used what life he had left to flip Delvis over his back.

Blood rushed back in. Leonard coughed for air, and his vision blurred back into focus. He jumped on Delvis's chest, pinned his arms with his knees, and punched his face. The man's eye split and blood ran from the slit, bright and red. Leonard punched the man's face again and again, mopping it with blood to the point he didn't know what the man looked like anymore.

"Stop!" Gradle yelled. Half of her body moved off of the bed. "He's my friend!" She grabbed Leonard's hair and yanked him back.

Delvis's hips popped and bucked Leonard forward. The man's legs rose high in the air, wrapped around Leonard's head, and yanked him onto his back. Delvis squeezed Leonard's head between his thighs. Leonard's eyes bulged, and his head felt as if it would explode.

"Do you know who I am, mister? I'm The Masked Warrior from the WWF." Delvis released the pressure, jumped up in the air, and came down on Leonard's chest with his elbow.

Leonard punched Delvis in the throat, grabbed him by the front of the shirt, and lifted him to his feet. Delvis socked Leonard in the nose. A flood of red warmth drained from Leonard's nostrils. He blew blood from his nose, grabbed Delvis by both ears, and gave him a headbutt. Delvis wheeled back into the wall, and a mountain of junk came tumbling down upon him.

Leonard grabbed the axe from the floor. He waded knee-deep through the junk, stood over the man, and waited for him to make a move. Delvis's legs kicked. The head of a babydoll flew up in the air and rolled along the floor. Leonard cocked the axe over his shoulder, ready to bring it down.

"He's your son!" Annalee screamed.

The wind of her voice blew Leonard back. His head banged against the wall. The axe slid through his grip and balanced on its head before tipping over and hitting the floor with a clap.

Leonard shook his head, and through the strands of fallen hair, squinted at a sphere of light. The light burned bright, dazzled with a million facets. He narrowed his eyes and focused the light to the diamond of Annalee's ring. Annalee stood in front of the man, protecting him with her misty light.

Leonard walked to where Delvis lay and knelt at his side. He took off his undertank and wiped the blood from Delvis's swollen face. His eyes pried opened and their pool blue penetrated Leonard with a shocking intimacy.

"Who are you?" Delvis whispered with all the energy he had left.

Leonard touched Delvis's face in the place he knew would dimple if his son was to smile. "Smile," Leonard said, tapping the side of his face.

"My face is broke," Delvis mumbled.

"I'll break it some more if you don't smile."

"You don't know me, Mister," Delvis said, struggling to get the words out. "My name is D-5 Delvis Miles The Lone Singer," he said and spat blood from his mouth. "And I will accept any and all challenges." Delvis stared deep into Leonard's eyes and smiled a half-dimpled smile.

Leonard's hand moved to Delvis's ear, traced it, and moved on to his shoulder, down his bicep and wrists. He grabbed Delvis's enormous hand, felt the callouses on his fingertips and palms, folded it into a fist, and brought it to his lips. He was his. There was no question Delvis was his.

Leonard cupped Delvis's armpits, drug him from the junk, and situated him against a wall where he remained slumped and motionless. Leonard took the axe, raised it in the air, and hacked at the chains around Gradle's ankles. The chains split. Leonard dropped the axe and opened his arms for Gradle.

Gradle kicked the chains off her feet and ran from the bed over to Delvis. She knelt by his side and cradled his bloody chin.

"Why'd you have to hurt him so bad?" she asked.

An emptiness overcame Leonard. His legs couldn't hold his hurt anymore. They bent, and he collapsed on the floor where he rested his back against the bed rails. Gradle petted Delvis's hair, and did her best to stop the trail of blood running from his split eye. Leonard's jaw went slack, as he stared at Gradle and watched her love and nurse her captor, his son.

"I'm sorry," Delvis mumbled. He touched Gradle's hand. "I didn't mean to make you scared. I ain't got the right words for it." He licked blood from the corner of his mouth. "I told you I'm a plain person, Gradle. I don't talk right sometimes," he said, leaned to the side, and spat out red. "I chained you up so you wouldn't never leave me. So nobody could never steal you away."

"It's okay, Delvis. I understand," Gradle said, holding him tight in her arms.

Thunder cracked the sky, and as a hard rain pelted the tin roof, Leonard watched her hold Delvis and Delvis hold her. Where did all their beauty come from, he wondered?

"I have something to give to you," Gradle said. She crawled under the bed and retrieved a strap made of leather belts and red and white striped shoestrings. "I made this for you from the trash I found at the dump," she said. "It's a guitar strap." She grabbed the guitar from a wooden chair sitting beside the bed. "It'll help you carry your guitar around. Free your hands up for autographs when you become a real live country music star." She helped Delvis to his feet and placed the guitar in his arms as she fitted the strap.

She stepped back and looked him over, as if trying to memorize who she saw. When she was done, she leaned in. "I'll be listening out for you on the radio waves," she said and kissed Delvis's cheek.

"Come on Grandpa," she said, taking his hands. "Let's go home."

She looked around the room, as if it was the last time she would see it. Her eyes scanned the stuffed animals tacked to the walls, the fake flowers sitting on sunless windowsills, the porcelain figurines lining the lip of the door jamb, the Popsicle stick cross keeping watch over Delvis's bed.

Leonard rose from his feet and stood eye to eye with Delvis. Delvis walked in closer and looked him up and down.

"I know who you are," Delvis said. "I know where I got my good fightin' skills."

"I know who you are too," Leonard said back.

"But shhhhh," Delvis said, putting his finger over his swollen lip. "Don't tell nobody."

Delvis turned his attention back on Gradle. "I got somethin' to give to you, too." From the wall, Delvis untacked a hand-drawn portrait of Gradle. "I done drawn me a replica of this one, so I have one for keepsake," he said, handing her the picture. "I ain't never gonna forget you." He gave Gradle a swift hug and walked them to the door.

Leonard and Gradle stepped out of the shack onto the porch. Hard rain pounded the roof, and a roll of thunder vibrated in the distance.

Delvis zipped his palm up the guitar's neck and cleared his throat, and then his fingers picked the strings and produced a sound that was familiar, yet unlike any Leonard had ever heard.

Leonard and Gradle walked down the steps, and while they walked toward the Chrysler through the rain, Delvis belted out from his porch a true original song.

†††

Gradle sat in the backseat and watched raindrops tremble off the ends of Grandpa's hair as he drove the Chrysler down the muddy road. The wipers sucked back and forth, and if it weren't for their sound and the seat separating her from Grandpa, their world would have been unbearably quiet and close. She smoothed her dress and stared at the portrait Delvis had drawn of her, the cut of her jaw, and the hundreds of diamonds in her eyes. She could see herself completely, and wondered if Grandpa ever would, too.

A mosquito whined at her ear. She shooed it away, and when she looked up, she caught Grandpa staring back at her in the rearview mirror. His bloodshot and bruising eye held onto her like a hook, and she didn't know how to look back at him—if he was her enemy or her hero.

"What're you looking at?" She looked away through the window into tobacco's passing green.

"You look different," he said, reaching in his pocket, and stretching his arm and a closed fist into the backseat. He opened his fist, and on his calloused and bloody palm rested her gold-cross earring.

She took it from his hand, and stared at this lost little piece of her, where the gold had turned green and where it had worn pale. She straightened the cross's chain, ran her fingertip down it, and closed her fist around it, wondering if it was something she had outgrown.

Her temple rested against the backseat window. She closed her eyes and wondered to what world he would bring her back and if their time apart had made him different, too.

The ride put her to sleep. When her eyes opened again she found herself lying down in the Chrysler's backseat. It was still and twilight. The Chrysler's windows were rolled down, and the air smelled of moonflower and hot leather. She peeled her sweaty cheek from the seat, got out of the car, and faced the old Spivey house.

She remembered the day they first came here and feeling the hope and possibility in its abandoned beauty, the belief that this place would be different. But now, as she stood before the house, she felt afraid to walk back inside a life from which she had already run.

†††

Leonard sat on the porch swing working his pliers, bending a coathanger into a bird. The Chrysler door slammed. He pushed his black-rimmed readers up his nose, looked out in the front yard, and saw Gradle walking his way. She climbed the porch steps and stood in front of the door for a long time, like she was scared to walk through it. She didn't see him sitting on the swing. He bowed over his work, and cleared his throat to get her attention. He could feel her looking at him as he curved the wire to make the bird's head.

"Were you gonna leave me in the car all night?" she asked.

Leonard switched his pliers for a pair of wirecutters and snipped three pieces of coathanger into equal lengths.

"Cat got your tongue?" she asked, and he could feel her walk up on him.

He bent a piece of wire into a coil and picked up another piece to do the same.

"You know it's not my birthday," she said. "It was back in July."

He could feel the twilight get darker and the last of the moonflower blooming near his ear.

Gradle picked a moonflower bud off the vine, cradled it in her palm, and watched it slowly open without any lifeline at all. "Why won't you look at me?" she asked, staring into the flower. She closed her fist around it and threw it over the porch rail.

Gradle turned to walk off, and his swift hand grabbed her wrist.

"Sit down," he said. He pulled her down beside him with a force that gave her no choice.

He picked up the third piece of wire, bent it to a coil, and held it up for his eyes to inspect. "The night you were born, a little bird flew in my house," he said, trimming the wire's end and connecting the three coils to make the bird's wings. "There's an old wives' tale about that."

"About little birds flying into people's houses?" Gradle asked.

"They say it's a sign of death."

Gradle pulled her knees into her chest. The chiffon of her dress whispered to him and brought him back to that night she was born—July 10, 1976. It was late afternoon and he sat at the kitchen table, sweating over copper wire and conduit, trying to run electricity to a socket that had blown. A summer storm had blown in, and he opened all the windows in an effort to cool down the house.

A knock came at his back door. He closed the blade of his pocketknife and walked down the hall. Her face was so sunken and lined, like somebody had taken a black inkpen and scribbled all over her, that at first he didn't recognize the young woman slapping the glass.

He turned the knob, and Veela rushed in. She smelled like a sour rag and had the jitters.

"I can't go to the hospital," she said. She paced his hall, scratching at her needle-tracked arm. "I need your help." She clawed into his bicep like a wild animal and looked at him with a pair of painful, half-mast eyes.

She bent over, grabbed him around the waist, and moaned as something overcame her body. Her shoulder blades stuck out like shark fins, and he could see every vertebra in her back. She was so skinny, it wasn't until she made it through the contraction that he realized she was pregnant.

He brought her head into his chest, and when he did, it felt like a hammer hit his heart and busted it up into a million tiny pieces.

"Can I go to my room?" Veela asked.

Leonard led Veela to her old room and calmness seemed to set in as if the room she hadn't seen in over four years provided her sanctuary. She sat down on her vanity stool, wound her old jewelry box, and stared at herself in the mirror while the plastic prima ballerina pirouetted to "Somewhere Over the Rainbow." She grabbed the picture frame from the vanity and wiped off the dust that had muted the photograph of her and Leonard on the banks of the Ohoopee River. Her hand gripped her mouth, and her forehead pinched together in an effort to hold back something that desperately needed to come out. She took a deep breath, and tears tinted with mascara rolled down her cheeks. She bowed her head and placed her hand atop her belly. As another contraction crashed upon her body, she stared at the photograph, as if it was the only thing that could help her make it through.

"Look how happy we were," she said, as her body came back to her and the music died.

She rose from the vanity's stool, walked to her closet, and pulled out the green chiffon dress Leonard had designed and sewed for her. The wildflower corsage he had picked for her that day was still pinned above the dress's heart, their petals desiccated but still bright. She held it to her body and stared in the mirror.

"It's a girl. Maybe one day she'll get to wear this," she said. Leonard felt his breath go missing. "I'm gonna name her Gradle."

††††

Leonard pulled himself back into the present and found that his eyes were lost inside the chiffon of Gradle's dress. He brought his eyes back to his work, clipped off another piece of coathanger, and bent it in a triangle for the bird's beak.

"I was piddling around with some copper wire and conduit when your mama came knocking on my door. She was pregnant and in trouble." He worked his pliers and attached the bird's beak to its face. "Your mama had troubles."

"What kind of troubles?" Gradle asked, handing him the three coils he had hooked together for the bird's wing.

"Addiction," he said. He attached the bird's wing to its body. "While your mama was in labor I kept piddling with that wire. Stripped the conduit from it, and started shaping it into a bird. I don't know why I picked a bird," he said, looking up from his work to try and solve that puzzle. There really was no reason. It was just where his hands and fingers had led him. He shook his head and bowed it back down. "I thought I might make you a mobile out of it. Something your mama could hang over your crib."

A hawk moth whirred past his ear, hummed above the last of the moonflowers, and stuck its tongue inside. "Your mama named you Gradle," he said. "I don't know where she got that name from, but I always thought it unusual." He shaped the wire into the bird's breast, and clipped off pieces to make its legs. "She didn't have a last name for you."

"Where'd Bird come from?" Gradle asked.

Leonard cleared his throat and felt a quake starting up in his hands. "I named you Bird."

"I've always thought Bird was unusual." She watched him make a hook on each of the bird's legs.

"It is," he said, attaching each leg to the bird's body. "I've had a bird fly into my house once before. When your grandma who you never met was pregnant with Veela. But it was daylight then. What was strange about the bird that appeared when you were born is that it appeared in the night. And this little bird wasn't a night bird."

He pushed his glasses up his nose and bent the wire with his pliers, making curls in the bird's tail. "That's unusual." He held the bird in front of his face, thumped its tail, and the bird swung on the hook around his finger.

"Here," Gradle said, handing him her gold-cross earring. "Use this."

Leonard took her earring and held it in his hand, surprised she would surrender what she had worn and loved for so long. He positioned the stud to serve as the bird's golden eye. The chain looked like a trail of gold tears, the cross a gold teardrop.

"You named me after that bird?" Gradle asked.

"That bird flew through the window right after I had caught you into this world. It lit right on you." He felt his throat burn and his voice begin to crack. "I didn't care what the old wives thought. I took it as a sign of life. And I made a promise to you right then and there that I wouldn't let anything ever hurt you."

Leonard clamped his jaw in an effort to hold back tears. He could feel Gradle's stare burning his cheek. "Your mama was real tired after you came," he said. "So I held you, danced around the room with you all night." He stared down at the bird in his hands, and remembered the steps he waltzed with her. "When your mama woke up, I didn't want to let her have you. But you were hungry. So I let you go and gave y'all some privacy."

Leonard closed his eyes and drew in a staggered breath. His hands began to tremble, and Gradle grabbed hold of them. "I went back to the kitchen and started piddling with that wire again. I made two more little birds for your mobile. When I was finishing up the second bird I heard one of the sweetest sounds I've ever heard. Your mama was singing to you."

Hush little baby don't say a word, Mama's gonna buy you a mockingbird. Leonard heard the words in Veela's voice.

"It made me so proud to know she had taken to you. That she was loving you. It was something I wanted to see," he said. "So I got up from the table and tiptoed down the hall with your little birds in my hand. And I looked in on you and your mama."

Leonard remembered walking down the hall that day, and how that board he'd put off fixing creaked under his foot, how the rain sounded on the roof, and how Veela singing to her newborn child gave him such hope. He peeked inside Veela's bedroom door. A used needle sat on her bed, and Veela was trying to suffocate Gradle with a pillow.

"She was trying to hurt you," he said. "She wasn't in her right mind. I grabbed hold of her and tore her off you. And she kept clawing at me, trying to get back at you."

Leonard stopped and tried to get the vision of Veela out of his mind so he could finish what he needed to say out loud. He closed his eyes hoping the darkness would erase it all. "I grabbed her by the neck," he said, opening his eyes. He swallowed and felt rawness in his throat. "And I squeezed it too hard."

There was silence. He felt as if his body was drained of blood.

"You killed her?" Gradle asked.

Leonard nodded. "I told the law she died in childbirth." He clenched his jaw and bit the inside of his cheek. "Not long after, I packed up some things and ran away with you."

He could feel Gradle's eyes all over him, but he couldn't bring himself to look at her. He stared out into the night, and suddenly Gradle's body lunged into him. Her arms wrapped around his neck and she buried her head into his chest. He had never felt her hold him so tight.

"Thank you for saving my life," she said.

Blood rushed back through his veins. He buried his face in her shorn hair and held her tight. His body tensed, and he clamped down his face in an effort to hold back tears.

"It's okay to cry," she said.

He clamped down harder, but he didn't have the muscle to hold it together anymore. He looked up at the ceiling and felt light for once, and wondered if this was what it felt like to die and go to Heaven.

CHAPTER
NINETEEN

CEIF USED HIS cane like a blind man as he hobbled to the pulpit in darkness. "And God said, 'Let there be light,' and there was light," he shouted at the empty sanctuary. He struck a match and lit a candle.

"What the fuck you think you are? Some kind of magician?" Sonny Joe appeared like a black beast at the altar. Ceif jumped and sucked the flame out of the candle.

Ceif reignited the flame. "How long you been kneeling there?" he asked.

"That Jesus character is fucking mute," he said, throwing a tin of sardines at Ceif's crotch. He popped a white cross from its bottle and turned the halfpint of liquor on its head. "I been sitting in the dark all night, getting still and quiet, trying to get him to talk to me." He peered into a jar sitting on the altar containing every fighting fish he owned and picked out one of the dead. "You say he talks to you all the time. But guess what, Ceif? I ain't heard a peep," he said. He smoothed the blue fins of a fish against the altar's wood, next to several others that were scattered like flower petals along the altar rail.

"Maybe you're the deaf one," Ceif said. He peeled back the can of sardines and scarfed them down.

Sonny Joe's stomach convulsed. He leaned to the side and vomited all over the altar's bench. After he was done, he spat out the remnants, and wiped his nose. He turned the bottle back on its head and let the liquor rush down his throat.

"You haven't had enough?" Ceif asked.

"Just making more room," Sonny Joe said. He threw the empty half-pint, and it skated across the floor. He peered inside the jar of colorful chaos and watched the fish fight. Perhaps they were reflections from the candle, but Ceif could have sworn he saw bright red flames burning in Sonny Joe's eyes.

"I got that crazy fucker thinking you're gonna steal Gradle from him," Sonny Joe laughed. "I got him believing you're gonna challenge him to a duel. A real bona fide Western duel with leather straps and gun holsters." He picked out another floater from the jar and splayed it on the altar. "Delvis is like a fighting fish. He goes ape-shit when something intrudes on his territory."

"Why're you killing your fish?" Ceif asked.

"To breed the pussy out of them," Sonny Joe said. He fisted a Royal Red he had named Sin in his hand. "It's called natural selection."

"There's nothing natural about what you're doing."

Sonny Joe doubled over and vomited again. The white cross he had popped earlier landed atop his spew in one whole piece.

"Why doesn't she like me?" he asked.

"You need to go to bed," Ceif said. He threaded his arms under

Sonny Joe's pits and dragged him down the aisle to Sonny Joe's sleeping pew.

Ceif lay Sonny Joe down on the pew, placed his head on his lap, and stroked his hair. He stayed up with Sonny Joe and tilted his cheek to keep him from choking each time he vomited. Ceif stayed awake long after the candle melted, after its wick burned down, and its flame dwindled to darkness.

"Owe no man anything but to love one another," Ceif whispered into the crown of Sonny Joe's passed-out head. His breath was holy and hot and stunk of canned sardines and cigarettes. "Thou shall love thy neighbor as thyself. It is high time to awake out of sleep, my friend. For now our salvation is nearer than we believed. Let us therefore cast off the works of darkness, and let us put on the armor of light."

Sonny Joe had gone too far with Delvis, and in the quiet, in the dark, Ceif made the decision it was up to him to put on the armor of light.

"Watch ye therefore, for ye know not when the master of the house cometh, at even, or at midnight, or at the cockcrowing, or in the morning; lest coming suddenly he find you sleeping. And what I say unto you, I say unto all. Watch," Ceif whispered to his sleeping friend.

He hobbled to the pulpit, lit another candle, and wrote a letter to Delvis. He approached the letter like a sermon, poured over it, making sure the words were convincing and clear. He finished the letter at daybreak and folded it inside his Bible among the book of Romans.

Ceif limped from the pulpit, paused at Sonny Joe's pew, and took one last look at his friend before leaving. Sonny Joe's body was still, sedate from his all-night communion of Southern Comfort and white crosses. A blue bottle fly dipped in and out of his mouth, and in his hand he palmed the dead red fighter, whose tattered finnage was dried up and glued to its padded, pulsing grave.

As he pointed his cane in front of him, Sonny Joe grabbed a fistful of Ceif's shirt and pulled him back.

"What was all that love one another and armor of light bullshit?" Sonny Joe asked, his voice a mouthful of gravel. He coughed up a wad of phlegm and spat it on the floor. "You trying to save me again, preacher boy?"

"Save yourself." Ceif moved forward, breaking away from Sonny Joe's grip.

"Where you going?" Sonny Joe yelled after Ceif.

"To tell Delvis you're nothing but a joke."

"Life's one big joke," Sonny Joe said. "But I'm glad you think I'm funny." He removed his vomit-stained shirt and peeled the dead fish from the skin of his palm. He tossed it at Ceif. "He probably needs a funeral, preacher boy. They all do," he said, nodding at the altar confettied with dead fish.

"Bury them yourself," Ceif said, cupped his Bible, and drug his lame leg through empty liquor bottles and cigarette butts. He hobbled down the center aisle and stepped out of the fetid-smelling church into a morning that was lively and new. A symphony of birds chirped in the tree heads whose leaves were made blinding green by a happy yellow sun. He had not heard the birds sing this way all summer and couldn't recall if that summer he'd heard a single bird sing at all.

He walked through the churchyard and hung a right on the road leading to Delvis's place. He found himself so consumed by the day's beauty that when he rounded the last bend, he had walked at least seven miles, but it seemed as if he had barely walked one. He felt like he was strolling in a garden, one abundant and lush and lit with a pure quality of light. White morning glories cloaked the trail banks and bloomed the size of dinner plates. He saw prints of deer, heard the coos of doves, and stumbled upon a snake that ribboned across the sand in a shock of green. There were orange monarchs and blue swallowtails and the yellow kind that looked like flying pats of butter. Ceif knew they all must have been born today because on any other day that summer the sun would have singed their wings, the rain would have drowned their tongues. Long ago, he had claimed to have found his Eden when he jumped into the South from a fast-moving train, but Ceif had never seen the South like this, so as he hobbled down the winding trail, he kept a lookout for Adam tending the fields and for a fertile, naked Eve.

He turned down the drive, and when he saw Delvis's shack in the distance, he was struck with an overwhelming sense of clarity and felt the armor of light. It was as if the breath of God was breathing down upon him.

†††

Delvis sat in the yellow morning on the Dairy Queen booth, listening to the birds sing. He had been sitting there all night with the whippoorwills who hollered off and on in the trees. He had watched a spider weave an entire web, trap some supper, and wrap it in thread for later, and he had watched the sky turn from light blue to black to light blue again. His guitar had rested against the booth all night, but he didn't feel like playing. He didn't feel like singing. All he felt like doing was thinking and being quiet. He had thought about Gradle and wondered if he'd ever get to see her again. He remembered the first time he laid eyes on her, how she looked like an angel all dressed in green. He couldn't stop thinking about her then. And wouldn't stop thinking about her now. He'd never stop thinking about her. He supposed when he got sick from missing her so bad, he could always look at the copy he'd made of her portrait and see her that way. Maybe if he imagined her with his best imagination, her portrait might move, her lips might smile, she might even talk back. But he wasn't missing her real bad yet. He felt like she was still there, still sitting beside him somewhere. Maybe that's how real true friends felt. They didn't never go nowhere. They were always just there, even when they weren't.

He had thought a lot about Gradle, but he had thought even more about her grandpa and used up most of his brainpower on him. They always told him after they found him in the dumpster that people from all over the world wanted to adopt him. What he couldn't put right in his mind was why Grandpa would want to throw him away, especially if he was so precious in the world's giant big eye. Grandpa was his daddy. He'd never been so certain and clear about anything in his life. He'd had his suspicions when he first saw him in that photograph Gradle always toted around with her and stared at. He thought then that some of the dots in his mind that never had lines drawn to them started to connect. But he wasn't for certain-certain until Grandpa appeared in his shack, his way of wrestling, and the point when he out of nowhere dropped the axe. The truth was in his eyes, in the diamond part of them. When Delvis stared into them he saw his reflection. He saw how much Grandpa loved Gradle, and for a minute, maybe even two, he saw that Grandpa loved him, too.

Once the sun's head rose higher, he got up from the Dairy Queen booth and walked the aisles of his garden. He cut the last blooming sunflower stalks, placed them in a bundle over Rain's grave, and knelt down on his knees in the pillow-like dirt.

"I'm sorry I ain't been out here to visit you like I ought to. Don't let it have no bearing on our friendship. I promise to do better from here on out. I appreciate you being a real true friend," he said, rubbing the scar below his ribs where he kept Rain's bullet. "I know you're up in heaven. But I know you got good ears. I miss you, boy."

He wiped away a tear and rose from his knees. The crows were rattling and cawing in the trees like a bunch of wild Indians. It made him suspicious, like they were warning him of something. He started back to his porch, and his spine started tickling. He got the feeling he wasn't alone. Somebody was at his back, watching. He spun around faster than lightning. There in the distance, he saw him, backdropped by blue sky, Ceif "The Electric Gunslinger" Walker, hobbling toward his shack.

Delvis reached for his gun, but it wasn't there. He ran inside, retrieved it from his bedside table, and shoved it in his holster. He stood in front of the mirror and practiced his fast-draw over and over. He was a little rusty. The last duel he had was way back years ago when George "The Animal" Steele challenged him over the TV at the Soap 'n Suds laundry mat up town. Once he reached his fast-draw record of two seconds flat, he walked bow-legged out of the shack. He spun his six-speed Ruger like a windmill around his finger and shoved his pistol back home.

When Ceif saw him, he stopped in the middle of the road. Light gathered all around the boy, like a shield, blinding and bright. He looked like an angel. He even had a halo. But Delvis knew Ceif wasn't any of God's kind of angels, and this light and the halo, giving Ceif the advantage was nothing but the Devil's doing.

Ceif hollered something, but Delvis couldn't make out what he had said for all of the crows screaming in the trees. The boy reached out his cane and took the first step. Delvis braced himself. His hand hovered over his holster, and took his first step, too.

"I'll give you one chance to surrender!" Delvis yelled out, knowing the rules of dueling allowed the challenged a chance to surrender if they wanted to avoid blood.

Ceif yelled something back, but again, Delvis couldn't hear

because of the birds. He wanted to fire a shot in the air to get them to hush, but the rules of dueling didn't allow any dumb shooting or firing in the air either.

The boy took another step forward and then another. He didn't wait for Delvis to take his turn. Ceif was two paces ahead of him, and when he took another two paces without waiting on Delvis to take his, Delvis knew Ceif was not honoring the rules. He was a true outlaw and couldn't be trusted. Delvis's hand trembled by his gun as he tried to get even with Ceif, but the boy kept coming at him, paying no mind to any kind of rules.

Delvis knew he could be a dead man in a matter of seconds if Ceif had his ability to draw, so he kept his eyes focused on Ceif's hands, watching for them to twitch. The boy paused and opened up his Bible. He reached inside and started to draw something from it.

Delvis drew his pistol and pulled the trigger.

The shot popped and tore through the air. The crows hushed and flew away in a flock of black, leaving the whole wide world silent. The boy stumbled backward as the color of his heart bled through his shirt. His cane snapped in two, and Ceif "The Electric Gunslinger" Walker collapsed to the ground.

Delvis ran to the boy with caution. He could still have his gun in his hand, and so he needed to be careful. Ceif lay on his back, and his arms and legs made the shape of a cross. His eyes, like two black marbles, glassy and bright, looked up and beyond Delvis at something that made him smile. The boy mouthed a word that started with an E, but that was all Delvis could make out because the rest was drowned with gurgling, as if there was a bubbling red spring inside the boy's throat.

He knelt beside Ceif and patted his clothes, trying to find his holster and pistol. They weren't where they were supposed to be. He scanned the surroundings, thinking Ceif's gun had flown out of his hand, but all he found was Ceif's broken cane and his Bible laying in the dirt with its pages whispering in the breeze.

Delvis got confused. He would swear to God he had seen Ceif reach for his gun even though he wasn't a swearing-to-God kind of man. As he patted Ceif down again, he noticed a square of paper resting in his outstretched hand. He took the paper, unfolded it, and read the words written on the page.

Dear Mr. Miles,

I am writing you this letter to apologize and beg your forgiveness of my friend Sonny Joe. Like all men, the Devil sometimes enters his heart. It is Sonny Joe, not me, who has written you the mean letters, and it is Sonny Joe, not me, who has called you at the Piggly Wiggly threatening to steal Gradle from you. There is no need to fear, for it is all a joke, a game in which Sonny Joe finds amusement at your sake. He does not want to steal Gradle. He's hurt she doesn't love him the way she loves you. He does not want a duel. His affliction are idle hands, which they say are the devil's playground. Please forgive him, Mr. Miles, for he knows not what he does.

Sincerely,

Ceif Walker

Delvis read the letter twice through, trying to grasp its meaning. The letter didn't contain any foreign names, but some of the words he didn't understand. He didn't understand at all what idle hands being the Devil's playground meant. He had heard of riddles before, but even after they were explained, he wasn't any good at making sense of them. He grabbed his head and squeezed. He squeezed out all of the words he didn't know and read the letter with only the words he did. He read them out loud, slow and focused on pronunciation. When he finished, he grabbed his heart because he felt like he was the one shot and bleeding.

He lifted Ceif's shoulders, cradled his head into his chest, and rocked him like a baby. "Don't die. Please don't die." He looked into Ceif's eyes. They were glassy and bright.

"I done did a bad thing," Delvis said, as tears puddled up in his eyes.

He lifted the boy in his arms. He felt Ceif's heart beat against his. It was warm and wet with blood. He turned toward the shack, and when he did, there was a truck coming at him, silver and mean like a bullet. The truck slammed on the brakes and fishtailed to the left before it stopped.

Delvis stared through the windshield and watched Sonny Joe's smile vanish and his eyes turn afraid. With Ceif limp in his arms, he ran toward the truck. Sonny Joe shifted the gear column and sped in reverse down the drive before Delvis could yell for help. He watched the truck disappear around the bend, realizing Sonny Joe didn't want anything to do with him or what he held in his arms.

He turned in all directions, looking for help, but there was only the road, a broken cane and a Bible, and the crows that had come back to scream in the trees. He grabbed Ceif's cane and Bible and rushed Ceif inside his shack. He waded through the swamp of junk, wanting to bury Ceif under it, to hide him deep beneath his treasures so no one would know where to find the boy except him. But Ceif was still breathing, and maybe he could save him.

He situated the boy on the bed and stripped him from his shirt. Blood pumped from Ceif's heart and drooled down his ribs, coloring the sheets the brightest red he had ever seen. He snapped open his switchblade and poked the tip into Ceif's wound until he heard the clink of metal. His finger dug in beside the blade. He lifted the bullet from the wound and placed it on his bedside table. He worked fast and gathered cobwebs from the ceilings and high corners. After packing all of the spiderwebs and all of the sugar he had in the house into Ceif's wound, he tore the sheet with his teeth and wrapped it around Ceif's ribs.

Ceif grabbed Delvis's arm and pulled him toward his lips. The boy tried to say something, but no sound came out of his mouth.

"I'm sorry," Delvis said. "I didn't know it was a game."

"Eden," Ceif said, and gently his bright black eyes went still while a river of blood ran down from his frozen smile.

"You can't die," Delvis said, shaking his head. "If you do I'm the one who done it to you."

He listened for the boy's breath, but it was gone off somewhere. He sobbed over Ceif's body, quitting long after its warmth had turned cold, long after its skin had paled. He dried his eyes and stared at the bullet he'd plucked from Ceif's side. He lifted the bullet from the table and unbuttoned his shirt. With his switchblade, he slit his chest and lodged the bullet into the same spot where he had shot Ceif. He found the duct tape, tore off a piece with his teeth, and patched it over his heart.

"Please forgive me. I didn't know what I was doin'." He lay down with his body heavy from the weight of two spent bullets, one that had saved Ceif's life and one that had taken it away.

CHAPTER TWENTY

GRADLE WOKE UP on Grandpa's chest to the sound of morning birds. They had fallen asleep in the swing, slept there all night wrapped up in each other's arms. The wire bird Grandpa constructed with a coathanger and her gold-cross earring nested in the crook of his elbow. She rose up, careful not to wake him, and stared at his face, his black caterpillar brows and silver boomerang mustasche. He looked different, reminded her more of a boy than an old man, and it made her wonder if what he told her last night had somehow made him young again, if keeping that inside for so long was what made him old in the first place.

A bird lit on the porch railing. Its twitchy eye inspected her and Grandpa for a while and flitted off. It dawned on her that Grandpa never said what happened to that little bird that flew in his house the night she was born.

She rose from the swing, went into her room, and sat down at the vanity mirror. She reached in her bra and took out the photograph of Grandpa and her mama standing barefooted on the banks of the Ohooppee River. She stared at her mother with a different view than all of the times she had stared at her before. All this time, she had tried to look like her, hoping she could make Grandpa happy, but now she knew that by looking like her, she had made him sad. It was clear now why he trembled in her presence, why he escaped inside his work, why he never looked at her.

She reached behind her back, unzipped the dress, and pushed the sleeves off her shoulders. She got up from the stool, and the dress fell into a green puddle around her feet. She looked at her unclothed self in the mirror and for once didn't try to mimic her mother's smile, for once she didn't see any resemblance at all.

She bundled the dress and smelled it one last time. Sweat, blood, Delvis's Old Spice, and the Holy dunking waters of Ceif and Sonny Joe's church. She pinned the photograph on the inside of the dress where her heart for so long had kept it warm. She spread the dress on her bed, folded it up with the photograph into a square, and placed them in the the box she'd unpacked her motel-life with, knowing that while she would covet them for the rest of her days, she would never wear them again.

She put on one of Grandpa's white undertanks and an old silk slip she found in the wardrobe, and she lay atop her bed.

Grandpa came in her room with his hair a nest and the wire bird swinging on his pinky. He climbed on her bed and shoved his glasses up his nose. "Where's your dress?" he asked, as he worked to attach the bird to her mobile.

"I put it back in a box," she said. "It was getting too small." She watched the muscle in his forearm as he hooked the bird onto the feet of another bird. "Grandpa?" she asked. "What happened to that little bird that flew in the house the night I was born?"

"It took a little shit on your precious little head and flew back out the window," he said. "There's an old wives' tale about that, too."

"What's that?" Gradle asked.

"It's a sign of good luck and riches," he said.

An urgent knock pounded on the front door. She and Grandpa left her room and saw Sheriff Hill chewing on a cigar. His gold badge shimmered like a Christmas ornament through the beveled glass.

Gradle opened the door, and the sheriff shifted his cigar to the other side of his mouth. He rattled the change in his pocket, nodded hello at Grandpa, and looked down the street away from her as if he couldn't face her gaze. "We've got a situation with your friend Delvis," he said, his eyes still parked on something down the street.

"Is he guarding the Piggly Wiggly pay phone again?" she asked.

The sheriff turned back her way and squinted his eyes through grey currents of cigar smoke. "It's more serious than that," he said, scratching the side of his face. "He's holding a boy hostage in his shack."

"Sonny Joe or Ceif?" she asked.

"Ceif," the sheriff said. "Sonny Joe reported it." He pulled his cigar from his mouth, spat on it, and the cherry sizzled to its death. "We need your help. We've been out there for a couple of hours. And we can't get him to come out of the house."

He fired his cigar back up and stared down at his mud-caked shoes. "I've known Delvis for a long time. You're the only person I've ever seen who halfway understands him. I was hoping you could help."

"What do you want me to do?" Gradle asked.

"I want you to talk him out of his shack," Sheriff Hill said, rattling the change in his pocket. "Y'all can ride out there with me."

Grandpa grabbed his gun propped by the door and pointed it at Sheriff Hill. "You can ride with us."

Gradle sat behind the wheel while Grandpa drove the sheriff into the backseat with his gun. Grandpa slammed the car door shut. Gradle cranked the Chrysler to life and burned rubber in reverse.

"Mind if I smoke?" Sheriff Hill asked, lighting his smoke.

Gradle rolled down her window and pushed the pedal down to the floor. The Chrysler barreled down the highway and the wind whipped Grandpa's silver-snaked hair. She turned down the dirt road leading to Delvis's house, and the canopy of green seemed to put everyone in the car at ease.

"The house is starting to come back how I remember it," the sheriff said with a puff of smoke. "You're a relentless man, Mr. Spivey."

Grandpa kept his gun trained on the sheriff's temple.

"It was sad what happened to Annalee," the sheriff said. He relit his cigar. "It'd kill me to have to let go of a child."

Gradle turned the Chrysler down Delvis's drive, and at the end of it were three police cars parked sideways in the yard. The uniformed men used their cars as shields to protect them from what lurked behind the bolted up door of Delvis's shack. An ambulance parked off in the distance next to Sonny Joe's Cheverolet.

Sonny Joe crouched beside his truck tire smoking a cigarette as if it was the only way he could get air.

Gravel popped under the Chrysler's tires as she slowed the car to a stop. She stared through the window at Delvis's shack and remembered the first time she came here. It had so much allure then and even now, even though she knew it like a home, there was still so much mystery left.

Gradle put the car in park and honked the horn three times. She waited for Delvis to come out, but the door didn't budge.

"He's threatened to shoot anybody who tries to break inside," Sherriff Hill said. "It's okay if you want to change your mind."

"He won't shoot me," Gradle said. "He's my friend."

"You can take that gun off me, Mr Spivey," the sheriff said. "I'm not gonna let anybody hurt him. But if I was you, I'd take it with me while you escort Gradle to the door," he said, and he got out of the car.

The atmosphere at Gradle's back grew deathly still, as if everyone in her wake had drawn their last breaths, except Grandpa, whose presence was strong like a giant. She climbed the front porch steps, ducked under the barbed wire, and knocked on the door three times.

"Step back you dirty outlaw!" Delvis yelled from the inside. "I done told you I'll shoot anybody who trespasses or tries to trespass through this door. I got a six-speed Ruger pistol, and I can draw and shoot in two seconds flat, ninety-seven percent accurate each and every time. You think you foolin' me with the three times honk and the three times knock? 'Cause you ain't. I done some studyin' on tricks and jokes, and I ain't gonna be taken to the advantage no more. Only real true friends know about the three horn honk code, and whoever you are, I know you ain't a real true friend!"

Gradle drew in a deep breath and let it out slowly. She turned back to Grandpa who stood at the top step with his shotgun aimed at the sheriff.

She put her trembling palm against the boarded door. "Delvis," she said. "It's Gradle."

The other side of the door went quiet.

"Can you let me in?" she asked.

The quiet stayed, but soon came the sound of shuffling feet. "You ain't gonna like what you see in here," Delvis answered.

"Why not?" Gradle asked.

"I done somethin' wrong. And you ain't gone be happy with me."

She pushed on the door, trying to find some give. "Can you tell me what happened?"

"I was the butt of a joke," he said. "And I ain't no good at understandin' jokes and make believes. I ain't a professional in that area."

"You can't be a professional at everything, Delvis."

"I should be at this, 'cause I'm the butt of a lot of jokes. And this one's gonna get me locked up, and they gonna put me to the electric chair."

"Don't worry, Delvis. I'll explain everything to them."

"Are they still out there waitin' for me to come out?"

"Yes," she said, and tried to turn the doorknob. "Is Ceif in there?"

"Yes, he's here," he said.

"Can I talk to him?"

"He can't talk."

An unease came to Gradle's stomach. She felt dizzy and light. "Why can't he talk?" she whispered.

She waited for Delvis to respond, but nothing came. "Delvis?" she called. "Delvis, let me in." She banged on the door three more times. "I won't let them hurt you. I'm your friend." She put her ear to the door and heard his breath. It was fast and scared.

She turned around and stared at the sheriff while Grandpa trained his gun on him. Cigar smoke snaked from his mouth. He removed the cigar and nodded at her. She should have been scared, but she felt at ease in a way she had never felt before.

She knocked on the door three more times and waited. One of the bolts turned and unlocked, and then another and another, and several more after that. "Delvis?" she whispered. She saw his eye, a painful and erupting blue, through the crack in the door.

"Slide in like a snake," Delvis said, cracking the door enough for her to squeeze in.

The room was dark, despite it being day, and a heavy, wet-metal scent hung in the air.

"I'm sorry," Delvis said, as he bolted the door back shut. His body began to shake. "I'm so sorry."

She cradled his head in her arms. "What are you sorry about?"

He embraced her with a clamping hug. "They gonna put me to the electric chair."

"What're you talking about?" she asked. She tried to pull away, but Delvis would not let her go.

"That boy said he wanted to challenge me to a duel and to meet me here. And he did. But it was the other boy who come. It was all a joke, and I done screwed it up. I'm so sorry. I'm guilty. I didn't mean to." His face burrowed in the crook of her neck.

Gradle relaxed with his weight and let him cry. Her collarbone grew hot and slick with his tears, and when Delvis's body shook, hers shook along with his.

He finally lifted his face, wiped his nose, and let her go. Wet blood stained the left side of his shirt.

"You're bleeding," she said.

"I done that to myself. I put the bullet I used on Ceif in me. I plucked it out of him and put it in me 'cause I should've took that bullet instead of him," he said. "It belongs in me."

"Where's Ceif?" she asked.

Delvis stepped to the side, allowing Gradle to see the bed where Ceif lay. The red tattered blanket was pulled up and neatly folded across his chest, as if he was a child tucked in for a good night's sleep.

She stood over the bed and nudged Ceif's shoulder. His body was cold, his flesh, graying. She lifted his hat sitting atop his navel and pulled the covers down. Her breath rushed down her throat at the sight of blood puddling in the sheets beneath Ceif's side.

She folded the covers back up. Her hand trembled as it fled to her mouth to catch the rising vomit.

She swallowed what had made it to her mouth. "What happened?"

"I shot him," he said. "Western duel style. I ain't braggin'. Just the facts."

"He's dead, Delvis," she said.

Delvis turned away from Gradle and bowed his head. "I'll be dead too," he said. "That's why they're all out there. They're waitin' for me to come out so they can put me to the electric chair."

"It's all a big mistake, Delvis. It was an accident. A misunderstanding."

"I been missed understandin' things all my life. And people been missed understandin' things about me." He paused long enough for his Adam's apple to slide up and down his throat. "I know I ain't easy to get. And I know I ain't considered average. Them people out there don't understand me like you."

"They're afraid," she said. "That's not your fault."

"I can't go out there like they been orderin' me to. With my hands up."

"You can't stay in here forever either," she said. "They'll get to you one way or another."

"Not if I turn into a flyin' diamond like the Tooth Fairy," he said.

"Delvis, the Tooth Fairy is make-believe. She's not real."

"Why'd you tell me she was real?"

"To make losing your tooth feel magical," she said.

"Ain't nothin' magical 'bout losing your teeth."

"I know."

Rain began to tap against the shack's tin roof, and soon it began to drum. As she listened to the drumming, she sensed an end was nearing, like the ending of the day's light outside. But unlike the light that would come again tomorrow the same as it had today, the end she sensed would never come back or be the same as it had before. She sat on the bed with Ceif's still body at her side and felt the twilight rapidly coming down.

Delvis picked up his tooth from his bedside table and held it between his thumb and index finger. "The Tooth Fairy ain't gonna never come for my tooth?" he asked, as he cradled his tooth in his hand.

"There's no such thing as the Tooth Fairy," she said.

Delvis shuffled his feet against the floor. "But I seen her with my own two eyes," he said. He nudged the tooth back in the vacant hole in his mouth. "They'll take everything from me in jail, but unless they got X-ray vision, they won't never know I got this. If anything, it'll remind me of you," he said. "And you're the most magic I ever seen in my life."

"Come out of the house, Delvis!" Sheriff Hill's voice vibrated through a loudspeaker outside, its sound blunted by the bolted up door. "We won't hurt you! We just need you to come out!"

Delvis stared at the door with his brows pitched up in triangles. He looked to her, his eyes a mixture of fear and resignation. "I ain't never been so scared in my whole entire life," he said.

She rose from the bed and gripped Delvis by his bicep. "Don't be afraid, Delvis. I'll go with you. I'll be with you the whole time."

She led him to the door and placed his hand on a lock. "Turn the bolt, Delvis," she said.

His hand shook on the bolt, but he would not turn it. She gently placed her hand atop Delvis's and helped him unlock the bolt. They jumped when it snapped unlocked, its sound like a gunshot in the silent, death-filled room.

He unlocked the bolts one by one, and as he unlocked each bolt, they gradually succumbed, as they were brought closer and closer to the reality of the world outside. After he unlocked the last bolt, he walked to the bed where Ceif lay and neatly folded down the blanket covering his body. He slid his hands under Ceif's knees and shoulder blades, and lifted him into his arms. Ceif's head fell back, limp like a sleeping child.

He carried Ceif to the door and waited for Gradle to turn the knob.

Gradle pushed the door open into the rainy night. A shine of lights blinded their faces, and the hot wet air grew tense with the click of gunmetal. Grandpa rose from the porch steps. His tall silhouette blocked them from the blinding lights as he led them forward with his shotgun drawn.

"Put your hands up!" a man yelled from behind a police car. "Freeze and put your hands up!"

Delvis ignored the commands and continued walking toward the light.

"Freeze or we'll shoot!" Sheriff Hill's voice blew through the speaker.

Delvis walked through the rain shimmering in the spotlights. He walked past the patrol cars and past four guns cocked and aimed at his chest. He walked toward Sonny Joe who leaned against his Chevy's hood smoking a cigarette.

Sonny Joe drew in a quick rip and threw the cigarette on the ground. He climbed into the cab, locked the doors, and cranked the engine. His headlights beamed against Delvis's chest, making Ceif light up like a star.

Delvis stopped in front of the truck's hood and stared at Sonny Joe, paying no mind to the men at his back who all had their fingers trained on slippery metal triggers. Time slowed. Seconds felt like hours, as Delvis and Sonny Joe communicated in silence.

Sonny Joe got out of the truck and walked toward Delvis. Their eyes held fast to each other. They were both wet and trembling. Sonny Joe held out his arms, and Delvis lay Ceif in them.

Delvis raised his arms high up over his head, and Sonny Joe bowed his head over Ceif's body and wept.

The men swarmed Delvis. There was a series of shouts and orders, a jag of chaos, but Delvis remained calm.

"It's not his fault!" Gradle yelled, as the men yanked Delvis's arms behind his back and cuffed his wrists. "Delvis!" she screamed, trying to cut through the men to get to Delvis. She kicked and scratched, but Grandpa's hand reached out and stilled her. "Delvis!" she yelled. Tears smeared her cheeks. "Don't be afraid!"

The men shoved Delvis toward the patrol car, and as they forced their hands on his head to push him into the seat, Gradle broke free from Grandpa's grip. She ran to Delvis, clawing at the men in order to see his face.

"Don't be afraid, Delvis," she told him. Her fingers found his cheek.

"I won't," he said, smiling. "She's holding my hand."

"Who's holding your hand?" Gradle asked.

"The Tooth Fairy," he said.

The door slammed. Blue lights spun. An officer tapped the roof, and Gradle, rain soaked and shaky, watched the car drive off with Delvis, wondering why she ever thought it was possible to bring any more magic into his already magical world.

CHAPTER TWENTY-ONE

GRADLE SAT ON the porch steps in the middle of a pink sunrise, staring at the portrait Delvis had drawn of her. She worried about him, wondered what they were doing to him, and if he was afraid, or if somehow his extraordinary mind had managed to convince himself to be brave through it all. She folded the portrait, put it inside her bra, and watched the sky grow bright.

A bicycle creaked a distance down the sidewalk, and from it a boy threw newspapers onto dew-sparkling lawns. He crossed the street before passing the old Spivey house, stopped on the other side of the median, and stared at her. She waited for him to warn her that Ms. Spivey was gonna scratch her back, but instead he raised his arm and waved.

She waved back, and he threw a paper that landed at her feet. She removed the green rubber band and unrolled the paper to the front-page news: LUNATIC MURDERS CRIPPLED BOY.

She stared at the photograph the editor had chosen, a mug shot of Delvis, his eyes captured in a perfect moment of wild fury that powerfully suggested truth to the headline. Twenty-four hours hadn't passed and already the town had produced a paper with the news, and even though there had been no judge, trial, or jury, they had already convicted him. She shoved the paper under her arm and ran down the sidewalk toward the north side of town.

She climbed the steps to the two-story jailhouse and banged on the front door. The glass panel rattled in its casing. She cupped her hands against the glass and peered inside the vacant foyer. Everything was still and asleep and had not yet risen to the newborn sun that lit her in a subtle rose. She banged on the door again and twisted the knob.

Down the dark hallway, Sheriff Hill's image came into view. He was half dressed in khaki pants, a white undershirt, and bedroom slippers. His eyes were sleep-swollen, his face was dark with a lather of morning stubble, and a cup of coffee steamed in his hand.

"Visiting hours aren't until two this afternoon," he said. He took a drink of coffee.

She shoved the newspaper into Sheriff Hill's chest. His coffee rocked out of his cup and spilled on the floor. "He's not a lunatic. And he's not a murderer."

Sheriff Hill snapped the paper open and read. The palm of his hand raked down the front of his face and settled over his chin. "I don't have any control what words the editor picks to put in his paper," he said.

"What words would you pick?" she asked.

"Writing headlines is not my business," he said.

"It's a big misunderstanding," she said. Her chin started to quiver. "Delvis is the victim."

Sheriff Hill's left brow peaked. "I'm afraid Ceif Walker is the victim in this crime."

"So is Delvis," she said.

"That's a reach for a man who confessed to killing a teen-aged boy with a .357 Ruger."

A woman stuck her head out of the kitchen with a skillet of bacon that fogged up the bottom floor with the smell of burnt salt and grease. The sheriff nodded at her and smiled. He turned back to Gradle. "Everybody in town knows Delvis. "Most won't find this surprising."

"Nobody in this town knows him." She paced the room and stopped at the foyer's window to watch a woman across the street pick up the newspaper from her porch and cover her mouth with her hand. "I can explain everything."

"Tell me what you know," Sheriff Hill said, leading her back to the kitchen.

They sat across from each other at a small breakfast table with nothing but a worn Bible on its top that reminded her of Ceif.

Sheriff Hill slapped the newspaper down and held his coffee mug between his hands as his wife filled his cup. Her eyes shifted from the front-page news splayed across the table to Gradle.

"Nance, this is Gradle Bird," Sheriff Hill said. "She moved into the old Spivey house not too long ago. She's a friend of Delvis's."

"I've always loved that old house," she said. "And I'm glad to know you're Delvis's friend." She picked up the newspaper from the table and tossed it in the trash. "How do you like your eggs cooked, Gradle?"

"I don't have a preference," she said, gulping down the fresh squeezed orange juice that seemed to appear in her hand like magic.

One by one, Nance took an egg from a basket, closed her eyes, and prayed a silent prayer over each one before she cracked it into a bowl, as if each egg encased something sacred. She hummed and sang while she beat the eggs with a fork.

Gradle tried not to stare at the woman, but she couldn't keep her eyes away. Her beauty alone pulled Gradle into a safe, calm orbit. She was both lady-like and man-like, was taller than the sheriff by a head. She had blue eyes and wore a bright red stain on her lips. Her black hair was pulled back into a slick neat bun and made her neck look a mile long. But her movements drew more gravity than her looks. It was as if everything she did had a higher purpose, that there was a deeper meaning in her lowering the gas on the burner, sectioning a grapefruit, running the water over her bleeding fingertip, which she made no fuss about when she sliced it with a knife.

"Tell me what you know," Sheriff Hill said. He smiled after Gradle startled and turned his way.

Gradle hugged her shoulders and acknowledged the sheriff. While she had met the man before, she felt as if she was meeting him for the very first time. In his kitchen at the table he was someone different than the man she thought he had been. He was no sheriff. He was a husband, a man, but one that she didn't think ordinary. She sensed Nance was on her and Delvis's side already. Perhaps the sheriff would get there, too.

"It started the day I went with Sonny Joe and Ceif to throw firecrackers at Delvis's house," she said. Tears gathered at the back of her throat. She wondered what else there was, what else had happened. So much had. She remembered that day and the days after. She remembered the day she wrote Delvis the letter and the day he wrote her back. She remembered the day she washed his feet, his guitar serenades, her running away to him when there was nowhere else she wanted to go. She remembered pulling his tooth and him cussing out the electricity meter. She remembered him cutting her hair, drawing her portrait, and helping her see who she was.

"His dog broke loose from its chain and attacked Ceif. And he shot and killed his dog to save Ceif's life." She stared at the steam rising from Nance's eggs and wondered where the hunger she felt just moments ago had gone. "I felt so bad about it, I went to his house to personally apologize for what I'd done. And we became friends," she said. "That's what happened."

"That's it?" Sheriff Hill asked. "An innocent boy is dead because Delvis Miles became your friend?"

"Yes, sir." She forked a bit of egg into her mouth. Her mouth watered, and she felt the food rise up her throat. "I should've never invited Sonny Joe and Ceif into Delvis's world." She pressed tears into her cheeks. "Because in his world everything is real."

Sheriff Hill cleared his throat. He put on a pair of reading glasses and reached for the Bible.

"Can I see him?" she asked.

"We usually eat our meals with our prisoners, but we couldn't get Delvis to come down this morning," Nance said. She stood behind her husband and placed her hands on his shoulders as he flipped through the Bible's pages. "Maybe you can get something on his stomach," she said, handing Gradle a plate.

The sheriff nudged his glasses up his nose and flipped slowly from Genesis to Revelations and back.

"First Corinthians," Nance said, combed his hair back with her fingers, and kissed the top of his head. "Chapter one verses twenty-seven through twenty-nine."

Sheriff Hill turned to First Corinthians and marked it with the Bible's satin ribbon. He tucked the book under his arm and grabbed a key hanging from a nail driven into the kitchen's doorframe. Where the key hung, a small sign warned: THOU SHALT NOT STEAL.

The sheriff led Gradle up a flight of stairs to the second floor of the jailhouse. The air felt considerably cooler there, perhaps from the cement floor and cement walls that covered everything in a thin sheet of grey ice. All of the cells were empty except for the last one where Delvis lay facing the wall, curled up like a dead worm.

"Delvis," Sheriff Hill said, "you have a visitor."

Delvis did not move. He remained as still as the metal cot that supported his curled body.

"She brought you breakfast," he said, opening the jail cell door.

Sheriff Hill took the plate from Gradle and placed it on a small desk. He stood over Delvis, opened the Bible to the place he had marked, and read, "But God hath chosen the foolish things of the world to confound the wise; and God hath chosen the weak things of the world to confound the things which are mighty. And base things of the world, and things which are despised, hath God chosen, yea, and things which are not, to bring to nought things that are. That no flesh should glory in his presence."

He knelt down at Delvis's bed, placed his hand upon Delvis's shoulder, and bowed his head. "Oh loving God, have mercy. Take away the stain of Delvis's transgression. Create in him a new, clean heart. Restore to him your salvation. In your name we pray. Amen."

As Sheriff Hill rose from his knees, the sound of someone playing the piano climbed its way up the stairs to the second floor. Gradle's ear bowed in its direction. The music was delicate and calm, the kind of music lyrics would ruin.

"That's Nance," Sheriff Hill said, as he closed the cell's door behind him. "She only plays when we have residents." He looked at Delvis who lay silent, facing the wall, unmoved by the music. "When you're ready, Gradle, you can tell me what really happened. I'll leave you two," he said. He walked down the stairs, the tap of his footsteps folding in with the music.

She held onto the cold bars and pushed her face between them. "Delvis? It's me, Gradle."

Neither her voice nor her presence seemed to make a difference, and this was something altogether new because in the past they had made all the difference to Delvis in the world. She slumped down to the floor in a heap. Her cheeks pressed into the cold metal bars, and she waited for Delvis to move, for his breath to lift his chest, for his pinky toe to twitch. He gave her nothing. Her hope grew dim and grey like the walls that surrounded her, and slowly she drifted off, holding hands with the music, into a demanding sleep.

At one point her eyes lifted when Nance brought her a pillow and at another point later when Sheriff Hill brought up lunch. But for the most part her eyes kept sealed in a chamber of darkness.

"Gradle, you should go home," Sheriff Hill said, nudging her shoulder with a plate of supper in his hand.

Gradle removed the pillow that had fallen behind her back and peeled her face from the bars. Delvis had not moved. His legs were still drawn up toward his belly as if he'd been punched in the gut.

"I can't leave him," she said.

"You've stayed here longer than the rules allow," the sheriff said, unlocking Delvis's cell. Sunset came through the barred window up high, a tender, disintegrating pink. "Here's your supper, Delvis." He removed the cold, untouched lunch plate from the table and replaced it with a supper plate. He knelt by Delvis's bed and prayed the same prayer Gradle had heard him pray at breakfast and now recalled hearing bits of it during lunch as she went in and out of sleep.

Sheriff Hill left Delvis's side and closed the cell's door behind him. "Go home, Gradle," he said. "There's nothing you can do."

"I'm not leaving," she said.

"Go home."

"No."

"Why?"

"Because I'm his real true friend."

"If you don't go home," the sheriff said, "I'll have to arrest you."

"Arrest me," she said. She held out her wrists for him to cuff.

Sheriff Hill cleared his throat and unlocked the cell next to Delvis's. He stepped aside as she led herself in. She grabbed the bars after the sheriff closed her in behind the heavy steel door. "Can't you help us?" she whispered to the sheriff.

He twirled the ring with the key around his finger once and bowed his head. It was enough to let her know he couldn't. His back turned, and her eyes followed him down the hall as far as they could track. He disappeared, but his footsteps echoed loud, as if there was nothing left behind them to absorb the sound, no metal bed, no mattress, no table, no chair, no prisoner, no soul.

She sat on the skinny bed, stared up at the tiny barred window, and watched the sunlight dissolve. Down below she heard dishes washing in the sink and them being put away into the cupboards. And soon after, she heard the piano stool scrape against the wooden floor and Nance play up to them a beautiful bedtime song.

Gradle removed the mattress from the cot and placed it on the floor against the divide separating her from Delvis. She wanted to be as close to him as she could. She lay down, facing the wall, and curled her body into a C. Her palm pressed against the cement, hoping to find warmth from Delvis's body. It was cold, but she kept her hand there, reaching out to him, hoping to touch him somehow, for him to feel her pulse through the cement wall, through the bits of rock, through the invisible pores. So badly, she wanted to make a connection, to make him believe everything would be okay, but a large part of her believed it wouldn't be, and she knew a larger part of him believed the same.

The lights in the cell clicked off, and she was left in a dark so dense it took extra muscle to move through. She drew her lips close to the wall.

"I forgive you," she whispered. In the silence and darkness, Delvis let out a breath that Gradle heard as a bellow, as if her words were the assurance he had been waiting for his entire life.

CHAPTER
TWENTY-TWO

ANNALEE FELT DELVIS'S limbs go limp and heard his breath even out and succumb to a deep, peaceful sleep. She let go of his hand for the first time since the men had pushed him into the patrol car. She ran her hand through his hair, around the side of his cheek, and cradled his face in her palm. The room was dark, except for the space near the high window, where light from the moon bled in. But even so, she could see him, every bit of him, down to the rise and fall of his heart.

She had been waiting for this time, for this perfect hour when everything was asleep and still. While she knew his situation, while she knew the score, there was no fear, no puzzle in her mind. Although she had never mothered him at all, she knew exactly what a mother should do.

She kissed his forehead and rose from the metal cot. She slid through the bars, and stopped at Gradle's cell to look in on her. She admired the girl's dedication. She admired the girl's heart.

Annalee walked down the hallway, down the stairs to the kitchen where the refrigerator hummed and cast out a warm light from its bottom. Her hand fondled the doorframe and found the nail where the key hung. She read the commandment on the sign: THOU SHALT NOT STEAL. She had heard thou shalts all of her life, and the words did not deter her from taking the key. She was already a criminal, had been guilty of worse crimes than theft, and was willing to risk the heat of hell if it meant setting her son free.

Her fingers gripped the key, and she moved back up the stairway and through the steel prison bars. She knelt at her son's bedside and inched her hand under his pillow. She found the tooth Delvis had secretly placed there and exchanged it for her portrait and the key. She cupped his tooth in her palm like a precious jewel. She brought it to her mouth and breathed upon it. He must have lost over twenty teeth, none of which she witnessed him teethe, none of which she wiggled and pulled, none of which brought her to his room in the middle of the night to take in exchange for a piece of magic. She had nothing to show, no collection of teeth in the far corners of her jewelry box, not even a memory. Delvis was sixty years old, she was seventy-five and dead, and until now she had never played his Tooth Fairy.

She covered Delvis with the sheet, lay by his side, and cradled his body against hers. For the remainder of the night, she listened to him sleep, his breath whisper in and out, his dreams wander through his head. She drew in his sweet carrot scent and held her breath for as long as she could in an effort to bottle his smell, for it to seep into her bones, for it to become their marrow, so that if she ever needed to feel the intimacy she felt now, all she would need to do was break her finger or break her arm. She nurtured every dark minute. She held fast to every second, for she knew this time would pass and never come again.

When dawn approached she could feel it at her back, creeping through the barred window, as if the early morning blue was not just a color, but also a touch. Delvis stirred under the sheets as if he had felt it, too. She tiptoed to a corner of the cell where she hid in the morning shadows.

Delvis rolled away from the wall. His eyes opened, and he sat up. His feet hit the cold slick floor. He stared at his prison pillow scooped in the middle from the weight of his head and ran his hand under it. He retrieved the portrait, unfolded its creases, and found the key. His fingers traced over the lines he had drawn so long ago. He brought the portrait to his nose, closed his eyes, and sniffed.

He opened his eyes and they hunted the cell. He searched under the bed, the table and chair, and inside his shoes. He looked in the corner and locked his eyes on Annalee.

"Mama?" he whispered.

Her hands fled to her mouth, and her eyes each pressed out a tear.

He moved her way and stopped at a distance uncomfortably, yet comfortably close. He wrapped his fingers around her diamond ring, brought her hand to his face, and placed it on his cheek. His head tilted into her palm. He closed his eyes and petted her diamond ring tenderly with the top tip of his finger.

"I knew you'd come back," he said. He removed her hand from his cheek.

He sat on the bed and picked up his shoe. He started to put it on, but stopped and placed it back on the floor. He pulled the sheet back, grabbed the blanket folded at the bottom of the bed, and formed it into the shape of his legs. He took his pillow and curled it into the shape of his torso, and once he was finished making his disguise, he covered it with the sheet and patted it gently with his hand. He put on his shoes, walked toward the heavy steel door, and pushed the key into the lock.

The lock clicked. The door opened, and Annalee felt the cold air trapped inside her bones release.

Delvis walked through the door and closed it behind him. He stared at her, this time, not at her ring, but deep into her eyes. He folded the portrait and hid it inside his clothes, beside his heart. "Fly away," he said, and he tiptoed down the hall.

Annalee brought Delvis's tooth to her mouth and positioned it in the warm pocket under her tongue, believing soon, very soon, she would.

CHAPTER
TWENTY-THREE

ANNALEE STARED OUT of the attic window at the change gathering about her house. She squinted into the new sun's light that pierced and broke apart the pall that had for so long loomed in its place. No longer could she smell the moonflower. No longer could she hear the flutter of the hawk moth's wings. The vine was turning yellow and dropping its leaves, and where the flowers once bloomed there were dried brown pods with seeds hardening inside. If Annalee listened hard, she could hear them rattling in the next season's breeze.

She looked down upon the drive and remembered the day they came. The two of them. The old man and the girl. She remembered wondering who they were and who they were some of, never in a million years believing they were some of her.

Annalee wondered what was next. She knew she was changing. Leonard said she was fading, and when she looked for her reflection in the window's glass, she was not there, no rotting corpse, no beauty queen. But still, the next season for her was not clear. She could not feel its temperature or see its sun, yet she could feel it was close.

From above, she watched Leonard race from the Chrysler and heard him pound up the porch steps, and run down the hall. He climbed through the flap. He seemed younger, his shoulders broader and stronger than she had ever seen them before.

"Annalee?" he whispered.

"I'm here," she said. "By the window."

"Where?" he asked, his eyes trying to locate her. His arms went out in front of him, and they felt the air for her. "I can't find you," he said.

"It's happening, Leonard," she said.

"What's happening?" he asked, but the panic in his eyes told her he already knew.

She bit her lip, trying to bridle the tears. When they unleashed, she didn't feel their weight or their warmth, but she saw them drop on the toe of Leonard's loafers.

He touched her tears with his fingers and looked up to see if there was a leak. He walked to the gramophone, cranked the handle, and positioned the needle in its groove.

"Come find me," he said. He held out his hand for her to take.

Annalee placed her hand in his, and he pulled her into his body. He raised her arm up high and led her into a waltz she would never forget, even if this new place, this new season didn't allow memories. They spun around the attic, and when she rested her cheek on Leonard's shoulder, she could feel its temperature; she could see its sun.

"'Til death," she whispered in Leonard's ear, and she walked into the light, leaving Leonard alone in the attic, dancing by himself.

CHAPTER
TWENTY-FOUR

GRADLE WOKE TO the smell of coffee and the sound of footsteps tapping down the hall. She wiped the sleep from her eyes, rose from the pallet she had made on the floor, and went to the cell's gate where she wrapped her fingers around the cold steel bars.

"You sleep well?" the sheriff asked, unlocking her cell.

"Pretty good for a prisoner," Gradle said.

"Mr. Miles," Sheriff Hill called out as he approached Delvis's cell. "You feel like coming down for breakfast?" he asked, stopping at the door. He waited for Delvis to answer, but Delvis didn't utter a word. "I'll bring you a plate when we're done," he said. He turned to Gradle. "Breakfast?"

Gradle nodded and followed Sheriff Hill's footsteps as he made his way down the hall. She stopped in front of Delvis's cell, hoping perhaps with a new morning she could somehow get him to stir.

"Delvis," she whispered, but he didn't move, nor did he whisper anything back. She watched him for a while, waiting to see some movement, some sign of life. As she watched him closer, she thought there was something odd about him, something strange about his shape. His legs were slight, his shoulders not near as broad, and nowhere could she find his head.

"You coming?" Sheriff Hill called from down the hall.

"I'll be down in a minute," she said. She looked back in the cell. "Delvis," she shouted in a whisper. She studied his shape again, and noticed his shoes were not under his bed. Her hand palmed her mouth, and a delighted smile spread past her fingers.

She raced down the hall, ran down the stairs, and stopped herself as she neared the kitchen. She stuck her head in the doorway and saw Sheriff Hill reading his Bible as Nance prayed over a clutch of eggs.

"I should go home," Gradle said. "My grandpa is probably worried."

"He knows where you are," Sheriff Hill said. "He's been waiting for you. Been parked outside for some time now." He marked his Bible and closed it shut. "I'll walk you to the door."

She tiptoed beside him. She was tense, worried that any minute he would discover Delvis's escape. Once they reached the foyer, she relaxed a bit, knowing she was that much closer to getting out without being caught.

"Thank you for your kindness," she said. She kissed the sheriff on the cheek.

"Don't worry about Delvis. We'll take good care of him."

She walked until she reached the sidewalk, and then she sprinted the rest of the way to Grandpa's car. Grandpa walked around the Chrysler and opened the passenger door. She climbed into the front seat and waited for Grandpa to sit behind the wheel.

"Delvis escaped," she whispered as if Sheriff Hill, who still stood on his porch, could somehow hear.

Grandpa turned the ignition, hit the gas, and threw her back. The Chrysler's wheels hissed on the asphalt, and he sped through the streets of town, passed the city limits, and turned down the dirt road leading to Delvis's house. As they passed his mailbox, Gradle noticed its red flag standing at attention.

"Stop, Grandpa!" she yelled. She got out of the car and opened the mailbox's lip. The padlock he used to keep his mail private and secluded to fans and real true friends only was gone. She reached inside and found an envelope sealed with duct tape and addressed to:

G-4
263 SouTH Spivey STREET
JaNesboro, GA 30431

She got back in the car, and they drove down the drive toward Delvis's shack. Grandpa rolled to a stop and put the car in park. The engine ticked under the hood.

Gradle took in the house and its yard and cocked her ear as if it could help her to better see. The barbed wire was gone, there were no locks on the windows and door, and the clapboards looked a paler shade of gray. The Opel Kadett was not in the yard, and the sunflowers in the garden had all gone to seed, their heavy heads bowed and weeping. The place looked like it had been abandoned many moons ago, even though there were fresh flowers atop Rain's grave and water dripped from the hanging baskets of coral geraniums, as if they had recently been tended.

"Delvis!" Gradle hollered, climbing the steps. A crow squawked from a scarecrow's shoulder, and the Coca-Cola can whirligig spun in the fall-like breeze.

She turned the knob and nudged the door open. Her eyes

examined the one-room shack, searching for some clue that would tell her if Delvis had been there, how long he had been there, and if he was coming back anytime soon. The bed was neatly made, and every piece of junk was in its own special spot. She had been there just two nights before, yet the place felt as if it hadn't been visited in years. The air smelled stale, like it had never been stirred, never been walked through, and all of the decorations looked faded and aged, the pink of the plastic flamingos, paler, the fur on the stuffed animals tacked to the wall, graying, the artificial flowers sitting on the windowsills, wilting.

She scanned the room several times again, sensing something other than Delvis was missing, something important. She paused to concentrate, but she couldn't grab it. She closed her eyes and imagined the place with Delvis in it, and when she did she saw bright colors and heard music. She opened her eyes and searched the room for his guitar and found it missing.

She walked outside and sat on the top porch step beside Grandpa who was waiting there, staring out solidly at the horizon.

"He's not here," she said. She turned the envelope over in her hand and tore through the duct tape. Inside the envelope was a portrait and a letter. The portrait was of the sad young woman who would never tell him her name. Its title read, **PORTRAIT of ThE TOOtH FaIRY.** She unfolded the letter and read it out loud.

"**Dear GRaDle,**" she said. She swatted a horsefly from her knee.

> **If yOu are geTTIng this I'm In the PLACE called Long GoNe with a capital L aNd G. YOU doN't NEED to worry ABOUT me. Just PRAY for me In JESUS NAME always. I AIN'T PROUd of WHAT I done AND I AIN'T NevER goNna be able to get**

it out of mY heart. Thank YOU for fORGIVINg me. GRaDLe the Tooth Fairy FINALLY CAME AND GOT MY TOOTH. I figureD OUt I kNOwn her all my LIfe. She cAme for my TOOTH LAST niGht aND LEFt a key UNDER MY PILLOW that looKEd like this:

Gradle's finger traced the key Delvis had drawn in the letter. It was identical to the key Gradle remembered hanging by the jail kitchen's doorframe. Her brows pitched, and she continued reading the letter.

After MY esCAPe I put the KEY bACK iN WHere it beloNged so the ToOTH FaiRY WOUldN't get into TROUBLE FOR stealiNg. TheM Nashville MUSIC MeN kNocked on MY DOOR just about aN HOUR AGO. They WAs passing through towN aNd said they hEARd MY music up at the Piggly Wiggly. THEY told ME There WAS A BOY up therE with BLoNde hair aNd a tattoo was PreachiNg with a Bible out of the back of his truck. They SAid he hELd a cross made out of a caNe AND HAD My music playiNg in the backgrouNd. They described my souNd as humble and USED ANother WORD I hAD TO LOOK up spelLed B-E-G-U-I-L-E. They said my sound was

HUMBLE and beguiles this cURrent day aNd age. I quote them on that. ThEY SAID THEY waNt to sign ME UP FOR A millioN DOLLAR music coNtract. ANd I ain't eveN mentioNed my ART yet. ENclosed is the TOOTH FAIRY's PORTRAIT for you to give to your graNdpa for keepsake. I thought he'd LIKE TO HAVE IT. It's A REPLIcA of THE ORIGINAL. This portrait is the only oNe I left behind cause I got THE FEELING they goNe waNt to see my PIctures aNd purchASE THEm for very lARGe SuMs. I aiN't bRAGGINg. JUST the FACTS. But by No means WILL I let thEM PURChase the replica portrait I drawN of you. It's too Precious for moNey to buy. It WILL ALWAYs BE MY KEEPSAKE. I also took WITH me YOUR poNytail I cut off for you. I'll MAKE SURE TO wear it eVEry chaNce I'm ON stage. It will enhaNce MY SIGNature style.

Gradle paused and handed the portrait of the Tooth Fairy to Grandpa. "This is for you," she said. He took the portrait and studied it, ran his fingers over the Tooth Fairy's face, and stared back out at the horizon.

Gradle read on.

I'm GONNA need to take out a NeW CODE name. I'm a profESSIONAL at code Names. IT will no daubt be soMEthing the GBI and FBI won't be able TO Track or break. No dog BLOODHoUND won't be able to SNIFf it out BECAUse I'LL make sure it DON'T have no Smell. I'm thINKINg it mighT STArt WITH a G. But SHHHHH. DON'T TELL NOBODY.

GRaDle, I was AFRAId for a WhiLE I might be dumb, but I done figured it out AND I reckon you done FIGUREd it out too that we is SOME KIND of kiN. It's my preDICTiON GraNdpa IS GONNA TELL YOU a WHOLE lot ABOut me ANd the TooTH JAIRY if he hadn't alREADy told you. TELL him I loVE HIM and I ain't got no hard feelings.

She stopped for a moment and looked at Grandpa, but he was deep in thought with the horizon. She continued to read the rest of the letter out loud.

GRaDle, what I got to tell you next is very important. After you read THIS letTER You Need to GET RID OF IT. If pEOPle tried to tamPER with it they will be THROWN iN jail. TampeRING With mAIL IS A FEDeral offeNse. I learNed THAT in my uNDERCOVER AGeNt sTUDiEs. SET it TO FIRE OR TEAR it up iNto little plEces and BUry them or seNd them off down THE RIVER wHAT

have **you**. *CauSE* **THEY** *goNe be* **LOOKINg** for me.
I know I **CAN** trust *YOU* **CAUSE** yOU are **the**
best REaL TRue frieNd I ever had. I **GOT** so much
to **TELL YOU AND WRITE** BUT I *got to get* **ON**
THE lICKety splIt. THEM music MeN **ARE** OutsIde
waIting on me. It wIll **TAKE** eight hours **TO** get
up to NasHVILLE **AND** when I get there I'LL be A
REAL LIVE MUSIC staR. So listeN OUT for me ON
THe radIO WaVes.

ALwaYS a **REAL TRUe frieND**

Yours TRULy,
D-S DelvIs **MiLes** The LoNe SiNger

Gradle read the letter to herself twice through and memorized every bit of it, every capital letter, every artistic curl, the expression of every realistic eye he had drawn to dot his *i*'s. She tore the letter into tiny pieces, placed each piece on her tongue, and chewed them up one by one. She stared off with Grandpa into the horizon and wondered what their tomorrow would bring. It was something she could not answer, something she could not see, and yet it didn't make her afraid. The crow on the scarecrow cawed, and they watched it lift from the straw-veined shoulder and fly through the sky, a shimmer of black against the purest and most perfect blue.

She thought about her dreams, how she always wanted to drive an eighteen-wheeler out to California and stop in the Petrified

Forest along the way. That part of her life seemed so distant and so long ago. They say some dreams never come true, but these were no longer her dreams. As she watched the crow soar through the air, she found peace and a new perspective. Dreams change, and the ones that don't, always come true.

"Where you reckon he is?" Grandpa asked.

"He's on his way to becoming a real live country music star."

Grandpa wrapped his arm around her shoulder and pulled her close. His lips turned up into his half-dimpled smile, and he looked her in the eye. And for the first time in a long time, he did not look through her or see into the past.

ACKNOWLEDGMENTS

Bren McClain, godmother, mentor, soul sister, and spiritual guide. My writing life would not be possible without you in it. It is a privilege to bear this beautiful cross with you by my side. Thank you for your discipleship.

Shannon "Shay-Dawg" House Keegan, water creature and pen pal extraordinaire, thank you for urging me to take a writing class in the first place. Now, look what you started. You should be ashamed of yourself!

My teachers. Larry Carlson, who forced me to cut my teeth on playwriting and taught me the only three words required in this venture: MAKE ME CARE. JJ Flowers, my earliest adopter and most devoted supporter. Thank you for bringing me into your house and taking me under your safe and magical wing. And the late Jack Wolf, the first to ever ask for my autograph. Breakfast is not the same without you.

Readers and fellow writers who offered critical feedback and constant encouragement. Allison Gregory, Frances Pearce, Lee Cox, Rey Rivera, Billy Bliss, and Jacqueline Gum. Thank you for rooting me on.

Jeff Kleinman, thank your generous investment, recognizing early promise, and urging me to dig deeper. I am a better writer because of you.

Shari "The Shark" Stauch, marketing Einstein, and epitome of cool. While you don't consider yourself a literary agent, I consider you mine. Thank you for finding this book a home and acting on my behalf. Thank you for kicking my ass into shape and believing in my work as much as I do. The hanging baskets of coral geraniums are dedicated to you. Any aspiring writer should subscribe to this workhorse of a woman at www.writerswin.com. She is a genuine author activist.

The cast and crew at Köehler Books. John Köehler, my devout, painfully handsome and wicked-smart publisher, who recognized an early flaw, which resulted in a life-giving rewrite. Thank you for your patience, taking the chance, and reinforcing to me the definition of faith. Joe Coccaro, my banjo-picking editor. Thank you for your tender hand and finding the notes that didn't ring true. Kellie Emery, thank you for inciting the visual narrative in the creepy-cool cover design and adding all of the special touches in the layout. You win the award for nailing the 'something's not quite right' look. It is all so beautiful.

Randi Sachs, my copy editor. Thank you for your discerning eye, pointing out my bad habits, and teaching this ignorant Southerner a thing or ten about grammar.

My hometown of Metter, Georgia, and all of the colorful characters rooted there. You are my gold. I may never write of another place.

My brother, the Prince of Darkness, Hec Cromartie, who swears my work is the most original he's ever read. Thank you for reliving our childhood with me. Skeet Trapnell, a.k.a. Dad G., thank you for being a cheerleader and finding the perfect titles. My Mema, Rubye Trapnell Becker, and Daddy, Hugh Esten Cromartie Jr., the best storytellers in all of the South. Thank you for the gift.

T.C. and Robert Esten Sasser, my two little critters and most creative endeavors, thank you for finding me in the attic and showing me daily the power of imagination.

Thomas Choe Sasser, my husband, collaborator in life, and harshest critic, who staged an exodus of Siamese fighting fish at the local Wal-Mart to aid in research. Thank you for your endurance, driving me toward the essence, and giving me the perfect end. You are poetry.

Discussion Guide

J.C. Sasser invites you to use these questions as a guide to discussions in your book discussion groups and book clubs. Should you wish to connect with the author for a personal or Skype appearance with your club, email jana@jcsasserbooks.com or visit www.JCSasserBooks.com.

1. Gradle is old enough to run away from her life and strike out on her own. Why do you think she chooses to stay with her grandfather Leonard?

2. In what ways does Gradle compensate for the lack of love from her grandfather? Why is male attention so important in a teenage girl's life? How would you describe Gradle's father complex? How is this complex positive or negative and what are the consequences of each?

3. Why do you think Gradle is so drawn to Delvis Miles?

4. In what ways is Gradle naïve? In what ways is she wise? In what ways is Delvis naïve? In what way is he wise?

5. How do you think Gradle changed over the course of the novel? Which character do you think played the most important role in her self-discovery?

6. Did your opinions about Delvis change over the course of the story? If not, why? If one were to attempt to clinically diagnose Delvis, what would his diagnosis be?

7. How does the setting compliment the themes of the novel?

8. What role does Christianity play in Gradle Bird?

9. Guilt and forgiveness are prevalent themes; how do each of the main characters deal with guilt? How has their handling of guilt impacted their lives and those around them?

10. How do each of the characters attempt to forgive themselves? Are any of these attempts successful? Which is more powerful and why: forgiving yourself or having others forgive you?

11. All of the main characters in Gradle Bird are tragic. Which character do you think is the most tragic and why?

12. Do you believe Annalee is real or a figment of both Leonard's and Delvis's imagination? Why are they the only two characters who see her?

13. Gradle Bird explores facets of human cruelty. How would you explain human cruelty? Why do you think Delvis Miles is a target? Why do you think Sonny Joe is an aggressor of cruelty? Why do you think Ceif entertains these cruel acts alongside Sonny Joe? In the beginning, why do you think Gradle entertains these cruel acts?

14. Why in the beginning do you think Gradle is attracted to Sonny Joe? What makes him both attractive and unattractive? Young girls are often attracted to bad boys: is the attraction biological or psychological, or a combination of both?

15. Three of the characters in Gradle Bird have committed unspeakable crimes. Do you consider them criminals?

16. Do you think Delvis should be prosecuted for his crime? If so, why? If not, why? Do you consider Delvis's act an accident or crime?

17. Do you believe Sonny Joe was an accessory to Delvis's crime? If so, why? If not, why? If so, do you think Sonny Joe should be punished? If so, why? If not, why?

18. What do you think Sonny Joe's future holds? Do you believe Ceif's hopes for Sonny Joe's salvation come to fruition?

19. What do you think happens to Delvis?

20. What do you think Gradle's and Leonard's future holds?

For upcoming book events with J.C. Sasser,
visit www.JCSasserBooks.com!

CPSIA information can be obtained
at www.ICGtesting.com
Printed in the USA
LVHW01s2324030118
561741LV00002B/294/P